THE SEEN AND THE UNSEEN

Also Available from Valancourt Books

RENSHAW FANNING'S QUEST
Bertram Mitford
Edited by Gerald Monsman

THE MAGIC GOBLET
Emilie Flygare-Carlén
Edited by Amy H. Sturgis

THE WEIRD OF DEADLY HOLLOW
Bertram Mitford
Edited by Gerald Monsman

THE JOSS: A REVERSION
Richard Marsh
Reprint of the 1901 edition

Forthcoming Titles

LADY OF THE SHROUD
Bram Stoker
Edited by Sarah Maier

THE SORROWS OF SATAN
Marie Corelli
Edited by Julia Kuehn

ROUND THE RED LAMP
A. Conan Doyle
Edited by Robert Darby

THE MANXMAN
Hall Caine
Edited by David MacWilliams

THE SEEN AND THE UNSEEN

BY

RICHARD MARSH

AUTHOR OF "THE BEETLE: A MYSTERY", "THE JOSS: A REVERSION", "THE DATCHET DIAMONDS", "THE GODDESS: A DEMON", "MARVELS AND MYSTERIES", "A SECOND COMING", &C. &C.

Chicago:
VALANCOURT BOOKS
2007

The Seen and the Unseen by Richard Marsh
First published by Methuen in 1900
First Valancourt Books edition, June 2007

Library of Congress Cataloguing-in-Publication Data

Marsh, Richard, d. 1915.
  The seen and the unseen / by Richard Marsh. — 1st Valancourt
Books ed.
     p. cm.
  ISBN 978-1-934555-00-2
  I. Title.
  PR6025.A645J67 2007
  823'.912—dc22

                          2007015477

Composition by James D. Jenkins
Published by Valancourt Books
Chicago, Illinois
http://www.valancourtbooks.com

CONTENTS

THE SEEN AND THE UNSEEN

I.

A PSYCHOLOGICAL EXPERIMENT

THE conversation had been of murders and of suicides. It had almost seemed as if each speaker had felt constrained to cap the preceding speaker's tale of horror. As the talk went on, Mr. Howitt had drawn farther and farther into a corner of the room, as if the subject were little to his liking. Now that all the speakers but one had quitted the smoking-room, he came forward from his corner, in the hope, possibly, that with this last remaining individual, who, like himself, had been a silent listener, he might find himself in more congenial society.

"Dreadful stuff those fellows have been talking!"

Mr. Howitt was thin and he was tall. He seemed shorter than he really was, owing to what might be described as a persistent cringe rather than a stoop. He had a deferential, almost frightened air. His pallid face was lighted by a smile which one felt might, in a moment, change into a stare of terror. He rubbed his hands together softly, as if suffering from a chronic attack of nerves; he kept giving furtive glances round the room.

In reply to Mr. Howitt's observation the stranger nodded his head. There was something in the gesture, and indeed in the man's whole appearance, which caused Mr. Howitt to regard him more attentively. The stranger's size was monstrous. By him on the table was a curious-looking box, about eighteen inches square, painted in hideously alternating stripes of blue and green and yellow; and although it was spring, and the smoking-room was warm, he wore his overcoat and a soft felt hat. So far as one could judge from his appearance, seated, he was at least six feet in height. As to girth, his dimensions were bewildering. One could only guess wildly at his weight. To add to the peculiarity of his appearance, he wore a huge black beard, which not only hung over his chest, but grew so high up his cheeks as almost to conceal his eyes.

Mr. Howitt took the chair which was in front of the stranger. His eyes were never for a moment still, resting, as they passed, upon the bearded giant in front of him, then flashing quickly hither and thither about the room.

"Do you stay in Jersey long?"

"No."

The reply was monosyllabic, but, though it was heard so briefly, at the sound of the stranger's voice Mr. Howitt half rose, grasped the arm of his chair, and gasped. The stranger seemed surprised.

"What's the matter?"

Mr. Howitt dropped back on to his seat. He took out his handkerchief to wipe his forehead. His smile, which had changed into a stare of terror on its reappearance, assumed a sickly hue.

"Nothing. Only a curious similarity."

"Similarity? What do you mean?"

Whatever Mr. Howitt might mean, every time the stranger opened his mouth it seemed to give him another shock. It was a moment or two before he regained sufficient control over himself to enable him to answer.

"Your voice reminds me of one which I used to hear. It's a mere fugitive resemblance."

"Whose voice does mine remind you of?"

"A friend's."

"What was his name?"

"His name was—Cookson."

Mr. Howitt spoke with a perceptible stammer.

"Cookson? I see."

There was silence. For some cause, Mr. Howitt seemed on a sudden to have gone all limp. He sat in a sort of heap on his chair. He smoothed his hands together, as if with unconscious volition. His sickly smile had degenerated into a fatuous grin. His shifty eyes kept recurring to the stranger's face in front of him. It was the stranger who was the next to speak.

"Did you hear what those men were talking about?"

"Yes."

"They were talking of murders."

"Yes."

"I heard rather a curious story of a murder as I came down to Weymouth in the train."

"It's a sort of talk I do not care for."

"No. Perhaps not; but this was rather a singular tale. It was about a murder which took place the other day at Exeter."

Mr. Howitt started.

"At Exeter?"

"Yes; at Exeter."

The stranger stood up. As he did so, one realised how grotesquely unwieldy was his bulk. It seemed to be as much as he could do to move. The three pockets in the front of his overcoat were protected by buttoned flaps. He undid the buttons. As he did so the flaps began to move. Something peeped out. Then hideous things began to creep from his pockets—efts, newts, lizards, various crawling creatures. Mr. Howitt's eyes ceased to stray. They were fastened on the crawling creatures. The hideous things wriggled and writhed in all directions over the stranger. The huge man gave himself a shake. They all fell from him to the floor. They lay for a second as if stupefied by the fall. Then they began to move to all four quarters of the room. Mr. Howitt drew his legs under his chair.

"Pretty creatures, aren't they?" said the stranger. "I like to carry them about with me wherever I go. Don't let them touch you. Some of them are nasty if they bite."

Mr. Howitt tucked his long legs still further under his chair. He regarded the creatures which were wriggling on the floor with a degree of aversion which was painful to witness. The stranger went on.

"About this murder at Exeter, which I was speaking of. It was a case of two solicitors who occupied offices together on Fore Street Hill."

Mr. Howitt glanced up at the stranger, then back again at the writhing newts. He rather gasped than spoke.

"Fore Street Hill?"

"Yes—they were partners. The name of one of them was Rolt—Andrew Rolt. By the way, I like to know with whom I am talking. May I inquire what your name is?"

This time Mr. Howitt was staring at the stranger with wide-open eyes, momentarily forgetful even of the creatures which were actually crawling beneath his chair. He stammered and he stuttered.

"My name's—Howitt. You'll see it in the hotel register."

"Howitt?—I see—I'm glad I have met you, Mr. Howitt. It seems that this man, Andrew Rolt, murdered his partner, a man named Douglas Colston."

Mr. Howitt was altogether oblivious of the things upon the floor. He clutched at the arms of his chair. His voice was shrill.

"Murdered! How do they know he murdered him?"

"It seems they have some shrewd ideas upon the point, from this."

The stranger took from an inner pocket of his overcoat what proved, when he had unfolded it, to be a double-crown poster. He held it up in front of Mr. Howitt. It was headed in large letters, "MURDER! £100 REWARD."

"You see, they are offering £100 reward for the apprehension of this man, Andrew Rolt. That looks as if someone had suspicions. Here is his description: Tall, thin, stoops; has sandy hair, thin on top, parted in the middle; restless grey eyes; wide mouth, bad teeth, thin lips; white face; speaks in a low, soft voice; has a nervous trick of rubbing his hands together." The stranger ceased reading from the placard to look at Mr. Howitt. "Are you aware, sir, that this description is very much like you?"

Mr. Howitt's eyes were riveted on the placard. They had followed the stranger as he read. His manner was feverishly strained.

"It's not. Nothing of the sort. It's your imagination. It's not in the least like me."

"Pardon me, but the more I look at you the more clearly I

perceive how strong is the resemblance. It is you to the life. As a detective"—he paused, Mr. Howitt held his breath—"I mean supposing I were a detective, which I am not"—he paused again, Mr. Howitt gave a gasp of relief—"I should feel almost justified in arresting you and claiming the reward. You are so made in the likeness of Andrew Rolt."

"I'm not. I deny it! It's a lie!"

Mr. Howitt stood up. His voice rose to a shriek. A fit of trembling came over him. It constrained him to sit down again. The stranger seemed amused.

"My dear sir! I entreat you to be calm. I was not suggesting for one moment that you had any actual connection with the miscreant Rolt. The resemblance must be accidental. Did you not tell me your name was Howitt?"

"Yes; that's my name, Howitt—William Howitt."

"Any relation to the poet?"

"Poet?" Mr. Howitt seemed mystified; then, to make a dash at it, "Yes; my great-uncle."

"I congratulate you, Mr. Howitt, on your relationship. I have always been a great admirer of your great-uncle's works. Perhaps I had better put this poster away. It may be useful for future reference."

The stranger, folding up the placard, replaced it in his pocket. With a quick movement of his fingers he did something which detached what had seemed to be the inner lining of his overcoat from the coat itself—splitting the garment, as it were, and making it into two. As he did so, there fell from all sides of him another horde of crawling creatures. They dropped like lumps of jelly on to the floor, and remained for some seconds, a wriggling mass. Then, like their forerunners, they began to make incursions towards all the points of the compass. Mr. Howitt, already in a condition of considerable agitation, stared at these ungainly forms in a state of mind which seemed to approach to stupefaction.

"More of my pretty things, you perceive. I'm very fond of reptiles. I always have been. Don't allow any of them to touch you. They might do you an injury. Reptiles sometimes do." He turned a little away from Mr. Howitt. "I heard some particulars of this affair at Exeter. It seems that these two men, Rolt and Colston, were not only partners in the profession of the law, they were also partners in the profession of swindling. Thorough-paced rogues, both of them. Unfortunately, there is not a doubt of it. But it appears that the man Rolt was not only false to the world at large, he was false even to his partner. Don't you think, Mr. Howitt, that it is odd that a man should be false to his partner?"

The inquiry was unheeded. Mr. Howitt was gazing at the crawling creatures which seemed to be clustering about his chair.

"Ring the bell!" he gasped. "Ring the bell! Have them taken away!"

"Have what taken away? My pretty playthings? My dear sir, to touch them would be dangerous. If you are very careful not to move from your seat, I think I may guarantee that you will be safe. You did not notice my question. Don't you think it odd that a man should be false to his partner?"

"Eh?—Oh!—Yes; very."

The stranger eyed the other intently. There was something in Mr. Howitt's demeanour which, to say the least of it, was singular.

"I thought you would think it was odd. It appears that one night the two men agreed that they would divide spoils. They proceeded to do so then and there. Colston, wholly unsuspicious of evil, was seated at a table, making up a partnership account. Rolt, stealing up behind him, stupefied him with chloroform."

"It wasn't chloroform."

"Not chloroform? May I ask how you know?"

"I—I guessed it."

"For a stranger, rather a curious subject on which to hazard a guess, don't you think so? However, allowing your guess, we will say it was not chloroform. Whatever it was it stupefied Colston. Rolt, when he perceived Colston was senseless, produced a knife—like this."

The stranger flourished in the air a big steel blade, which was shaped like a hunting-knife. As he did so, throwing his overcoat from him on to the floor, he turned right round towards Mr. Howitt. Mr. Howitt stared at him voiceless. It was not so much at the sufficiently ugly weapon he was holding in his hand at which he stared, as at the man himself. The stranger, indeed, presented an extraordinary spectacle. The upper portion of his body was enveloped in some sort of oilskin—such as sailors wear in dirty weather. The oilskin was inflated to such an extent that the upper half of him resembled nothing so much as a huge ill-shaped bladder. That it was inflated was evident, with something, too, that was conspicuously alive. The oilskin writhed and twisted, surged and heaved, in a fashion that was anything but pleasant to behold.

"You look at me! See here!"

The stranger dashed the knife he held into his own breast, or he seemed to. He cut the oilskin open from top to bottom. And there gushed forth, not his heart's blood, but an amazing mass of hissing, struggling, twisting serpents. They fell, all sorts and sizes, in a confused, furious, frenzied heap, upon the floor. In a moment the room seemed to be alive with snakes. They dashed hither and thither, in and out, round and round, in search either of refuge or revenge. And, as the snakes came on, the efts, the newts, the lizards, and the other creeping things, in their desire to escape them, crawled up the curtains, and the doors, and the walls.

Mr. Howitt gave utterance to a sort of strangled exclamation. He retained sufficient presence of mind to spring upon the seat of his chair, and to sit upon the back of it. The stranger remained standing, apparently wholly unmoved, in the midst of the seeming pandemonium of creepy things.

"Do you not like snakes, Mr. Howitt? I do! They appeal to me strongly. This is part of my collection. I rather pride myself on the ingenuity of the contrivance which enables me to carry my pets about with me wherever I may go. At the same time you are wise in removing your feet from the floor. Not all of them are poisonous. Possibly the more poisonous ones may not be able to reach you where you are. You see this knife?" The stranger extended it towards Mr. Howitt. "This is the knife with which, when he had stupefied him, Andrew Rolt slashed Douglas Colston about the head and face and throat like this!"

The removal of his overcoat, and, still more, the vomiting forth of the nest of serpents, had decreased the stranger's bulk by more than one-half. Disembarrassing himself of the remnants of his oilskins, he removed his soft felt hat, and, tearing off his huge black beard, stood revealed as a tall, upstanding, muscularly-built man, whose head and face and neck were almost entirely concealed by strips of plaster, which crossed and recrossed each other in all possible and impossible directions.

There was silence. The two men stared at each other. With a gasp Mr. Howitt found his voice.

"Douglas!"

"Andrew!"

"I thought you were dead."

"I am risen from the grave."

"I am glad you are not dead."

"Why?"

Mr. Howitt paused as if to moisten his parched lips.

"I never meant to kill you."

"In that case, Andrew, your meaning was unfortunate. I do mean to kill you—now."

"Don't kill me, Douglas."

"A reason, Andrew?"

"If you knew what I have suffered since I thought I had killed you, you would not wish to take upon yourself the burden which I have had to bear."

"My nerves, Andrew, are stronger than yours. What would crush you to the ground would not weigh on me at all. Surely you knew that before." Mr. Howitt fidgeted on the back of his chair. "It was not that you did not mean to kill me. You lacked the courage. You gashed me like some frenzied cur. Then, afraid of your own handiwork, you ran to save your skin. You dared not wait to see if what you had meant to do was done. Why, Andrew, as soon as the effects of your drug had gone, I sat up. I heard you running down the stairs, I saw your knife lying at my side, all stained with my own blood—see, Andrew, the stains are on it still! I even picked up this scrap of paper which had fallen from your pocket on to the floor."

He held out a piece of paper towards Mr. Howitt.

"It is the advertisement of an hotel—Hotel de la Couronne d'Or, St. Holier's, Jersey. I said to myself, I wonder if that is where Andrew is gone. I will go and see. And if I find him I will kill him. I have found you, and behold, your heart has so melted within you that already you feel something of the pangs of death." Mr. Howitt did seem to be more dead than alive. His face was bloodless. He was shivering as if with cold.

"These melodramatic and, indeed, slightly absurd details"—the stranger waved his hand towards the efts, and newts, and snakes, and lizards—"were planned for your especial benefit. I was aware what a horror you had of creeping things. I take it, it is constitutional. I knew I had but to spring on you half a bushel or so of reptiles, and all the little courage you ever had would vanish. As it has done."

The stranger stopped. He looked, with evident enjoyment of his misery, at the miserable creature squatted on the back of the chair in front of him. Mr. Howitt tried to speak. Two or three times he opened his mouth, but there came forth no sound. At last he said, in curiously husky tones—

"Douglas?"

"Andrew?"

"If you do it they are sure to have you. It is not easy to get away from Jersey."

"How kind of you, Andrew, and how thoughtful! But you might have spared yourself your thought. I have arranged all that. There is a cattle-boat leaves for St. Malo in half an hour on the tide. You will be dead in less than half an hour—so I go in that."

Again there were movements of Mr. Howitt's lips. But no words were audible. The stranger continued.

"The question which I have had to ask myself has been, how shall I kill you? I might kill you with the knife with which you endeavoured to kill me." As he spoke, he tested the keenness of the blade with his fingers. "With it I might slit your throat from ear to ear, or I might use it in half a hundred different ways. Or I might shoot you like a dog." Producing a revolver, he pointed it at Mr. Howitt's head. "Sit quite still, Andrew, or I may be tempted to flatten your nose with a bullet. You know I can shoot straight. Or I might avail myself of this."

Still keeping the revolver pointed at Mr. Howitt's head, he took from his waistcoat pocket a small syringe.

"This, Andrew, is a hypodermic syringe. I have but to take firm hold of you, thrust the point into one of the blood-vessels of your neck, and inject the contents; you will at once endure exquisite tortures which, after two or three minutes, which will seem to you like centuries, will result in death. But I have resolved to do myself, and you, this service, with neither of the three."

Again the stranger stopped. This time Mr. Howitt made no attempt to speak. He was not a pleasant object to contemplate. As the other had said, to judge from his appearance he already seemed to be suffering some of the pangs of death. All the manhood had gone from him. Only the shell of what was meant to be a man remained. The exhibition of his pitiful cowardice afforded his whilom partner unqualified pleasure.

"Have you ever heard of an author named De Quincey? He wrote on murder considered as a fine art. It is as a fine art I have had to consider it. In that connection I have had to consider three things: 1. That you must be killed. 2. That you must be killed in such a manner that you shall suffer the greatest possible amount of pain. 3—and not the least essential—That you must be killed in such a manner that under no circumstances can I be found guilty of having caused your death. I have given these three points my careful consideration, and I think that I have been able to find something which will satisfy all the requirements. That something is in this box."

The stranger went to the box which was on the table—the square box which had, as ornamentation, the hideously alternating stripes of blue and green and yellow. He rapped on it with his knuckles. As he did so, from within it there came a peculiar sound like a sullen murmur.

"You hear? It is death calling to you from the box. It awaits its prey. It bids you come."

He struck the box a little bit harder. There proceeded from it, as if responsive to his touch, what seemed to be a series of sharp and angry screeches.

"Again! It loses patience. It grows angry. It bids you hasten. Ah!"

He brought his hand down heavily upon the top of the box. Immediately the room was filled with a discord of sounds, cries, yelpings, screams, snarls, the tumult dying away in what seemed to be an intermittent, sullen roaring. The noise served to rouse the snakes, and efts, and lizards to renewed activity. The room seemed again to be alive with them. As he listened, Mr. Howitt became livid. He was, apparently, becoming imbecile with terror.

His aforetime partner, turning to him, pointed to the box with outstretched hand.

"What a row it makes! What a rage it's in! Your death screams out to you, with a ravening longing—the most awful death that a man can die. Andrew—to die! And such a death as this!"

Again he struck the box. Again there came from it that dreadful discord.

"Stand up!"

Mr. Howitt looked at him, as a drivelling idiot might look at a keeper whom he fears. It seemed as if he made an effort to frame his lips for the utterance of speech. But he had lost the control of his muscles. With every fibre of his being he seemed to make a dumb appeal for mercy to the man in front of him. The appeal was made in vain. The command was repeated.

"Get off your chair, and stand upon the floor."

Like some trembling automaton Mr. Howitt did as he was told. He stood there like some lunatic deaf mute. It seemed as if he could not move, save at the bidding of his master. That master was careful not to loosen, by so much as a hair's-breadth, the hold he had of him.

"I now proceed to put into execution the most exquisite part of my whole scheme. Were I to unfasten the box and let death loose upon you, some time or other it might come out—these things do come out at times—and it might then appear that the deed had, after all, been mine. I would avoid such risks. So you shall be your own slayer, Andrew. You shall yourself unloose the box, and you shall yourself give death its freedom, so that it may work on you its will. The most awful death that a man can die! Come to me, here!"

And the man went to him, moving with a curious, stiff gait, such as one might expect from an automaton. The creatures writhing on the floor went unheeded, even though he trod on them.

"Stand still in front of the box." The man stood still. "Kneel down."

The man did hesitate. There did seem to come to him some consciousness that he should himself be the originator of his own volition. There did come on to his distorted visage an agony of supplication which it was terrible to witness.

The only result was an emphasised renewal of the command.

"Kneel down upon the floor."

And the man knelt down. His face was within a few inches of the painted box. As he knelt the stranger struck the box once more with the knuckles of his hand. And again there came from it that strange tumult of discordant sounds.

"Quick, Andrew, quick, quick! Press your finger on the spring! Unfasten the box!"

The man did as he was bid. And, in an instant, like a conjurer's trick, the box fell all to pieces, and there sprang from it, right into Mr. Howitt's face, with a dreadful noise, some dreadful thing which enfolded his head in its hideous embraces.

There was a silence.

Then the stranger laughed. He called softly—

"Andrew!" All was still. "Andrew!" Again there was none that answered. The laughter was renewed.

"I do believe he's dead. I had always supposed that the stories about being able to frighten a man to death were all apocryphal. But that a man could be frightened to death by a thing like this—a toy!"

He touched the creature which concealed Mr. Howitt's head

and face. As he said, it was a toy. A development of the old-fashioned jack-in-the-box. A dreadful development, and a dreadful toy. Made in the image of some creature of the squid class, painted in livid hues, provided with a dozen long, quivering tentacles, each actuated by a spring of its own. It was these tentacles which had enfolded Mr. Howitt's head in their embraces.

As the stranger put them from him, Mr. Howitt's head fell, face foremost, on to the table. His partner, lifting it up, gazed down at him.

Had the creature actually been what it was intended to represent it could not have worked more summary execution. The look which was on the dead man's face as his partner turned it upwards was terrible to see.

II.

THE PHOTOGRAPHS

CHAPTER I

THE governor glanced up as Mr. Dodsworth entered.

"Anything the matter, Mr. Dodsworth?"

"Rather a curious thing in connection with the photograph of the man George Solly. If you could spare me a moment I should like to show it you."

Mr. Dodsworth produced a pocket-book. From the pocket-book he took a photograph. It was the photograph of a man who was attired in prison costume. He was seated on a chair, and he held in front of him a slate on which was written in large letters, "George Solly." Mr. Dodsworth handed this photograph to the governor.

"Well, Mr. Dodsworth, what is there peculiar about this?"

"There is something about it which is very peculiar indeed, sir, to my eye. If you will look at the photograph closely, you will see that there is something behind the man."

Mr. Paley brought the photograph nearer to his spectacled eyes.

"I see—a sort of shadow. Well?"

"You will notice that that shadow looks very much like a veiled figure—as though a veiled figure was standing at the back of the man Solly."

"Exactly! It does bear some resemblance to a veiled figure. What then?"

"This, sir: that no one was standing behind Solly. No one, and nothing."

"I don't quite see what you are aiming at, Mr. Dodsworth."

"I am aiming at obtaining your permission to take another negative of the man."

"Another negative! Why? Isn't this a sufficiently good likeness?"

"The likeness is not exactly a bad one, though it is not a very good one, either. But will you allow me to explain, sir? The day on which I took that plate was, for photographic purposes, a very fair day. Solly sat, where the men generally do sit, about fourteen or fifteen feet from the wall. There was nothing between the wall and him. I ought to have had nothing on the plate but Solly. What I want to know is, how came that veiled figure there?"

"Veiled figure! You call the shadow a veiled figure? Don't you think that the resemblance is somewhat fanciful?"

"No, sir, I don't. The focus is not quite right, so that it comes out a little dim; but I have not the slightest doubt that a veiled figure has been introduced into my plate, as standing behind George Solly's chair. I should very much like to take the man again."

"In fact, you are a little curious, eh? I am not sure that I should be justified in allowing you to make experiments at prisoners' expense. I don't know why they want this man Solly's likeness at Scotland Yard. It is his first offence, he is a good-conduct man, and I don't know that I am entitled to allow you to put him to unnecessary inconvenience."

"But, to put it on no other grounds, the likeness might be very easily improved."

Dr. Livermore had just come in from his rounds. He stretched out his hand to the governor.

"Let me look at it," he said.

Mr. Paley handed him the photograph. The doctor examined it.

"Do you mean to tell me, Mr. Dodsworth, that there was nothing behind the man when you exposed this plate?"

"I do. Ask Mr. Murray; he was present at the time."

Chief Warder Murray, standing by, corroborated Mr. Dodsworth's word.

"Then what have you done to the plate since you exposed it? You know, Mr. Dodsworth, this looks to me very much like one of those so-called spirit photographs—you know what I mean—printed from two exposures, and that kind of thing."

"I know what you mean. But I assure you, doctor, that that is a print from an ordinary development of the plate which I exposed in Mr. Murray's presence. It seems to me to be rather a curious thing. How did that veiled figure get upon that plate?"

"Quite so! If what you say is correct, it is a curious thing. Mr. Paley, I think you might allow Mr. Dodsworth to make another trial. No harm will be done."

The governor gave his permission. Some days afterwards Mr. Dodsworth came into the office just as Mr. Paley had concluded his matutinal interviews with such of the prisoners as were "reported," and such others as desired "to see the governor." Dr. Livermore had also just entered the office to sign the report after making his rounds.

"Well, Mr. Dodsworth," inquired the governor, "and what is the result this time?"

"Before showing you the result, sir, I should like to ask a question or two." Mr. Dodsworth turned to Chief Warder Murray, who had been present, in his official capacity, during the governor's recent interviewing. "You were present, Mr. Murray, when I photographed the man George Solly?"

"I was."

"And you also, Slater?" Mr. Dodsworth turned to Warder Slater, who had entered with him. Warder Slater allowed that he was.

"Mr. Murray, where was Solly sitting when I photographed him?"

"He was sitting where the men always do sit—perhaps twenty feet from the wall."

"Was there anything behind him—I mean, any person, or any object of any kind?"

"There was nothing."

"Could there have been anything behind him without your having been aware of the fact?"

"Certainly not. It was a sunny day, half-past two in the afternoon, and I myself stood within a dozen feet of Solly, to the left of him."

"Slater, is what Mr. Murray says correct?" Warder Slater allowed that it was. Mr. Dodsworth turned to the governor. "I have asked these questions in your presence, Mr. Paley, because the results of my second attempt at photographing the man Solly have been so curious. I availed myself to the full of your permission. I made up my mind that there should be no doubt about the thing this time. So I exposed three separate plates. This is the result of the first exposure, Mr. Paley."

Mr. Dodsworth handed the governor a photograph.

"I don't understand you, Mr. Dodsworth. Is this a photograph of Solly? Who is the woman standing at the back of his chair?"

"Just so—that is what I should like to know. Who is the woman standing at the back of his chair?"

Mr. Paley glanced up in surprise. "What do you mean, Mr. Dodsworth?"

"I mean, sir, what I say—that I should like to know who the woman is who is standing at the back of his chair. Did you see a woman standing at the back of his chair, Mr. Murray?"

"There was no woman."

"Mr. Murray says that there was no woman; the camera seems to suggest that there was."

"Let me look at the thing."

The doctor took the photograph out of the governor's hand. It was the photograph of a man, in prison dress, who was sitting holding out a slate in front of him, on which was written, in characters which were only too legible, his name, "George Solly." Behind the chair on which he was sitting stood a woman. Her pose was curiously natural—not at all the rather-death-than-move pose which is dear to the average photographer. She rested one hand lightly on the man's shoulder, and she was stooping a little forward as if she was curious to see what was written upon the slate which he was holding. Her features were not quite clear, and the whole photograph, so far as she was concerned, was rather dim—but there could be no possible doubt of the fact that she was there.

"Dodsworth," said the doctor, "do you mean to tell me that you have not been trying some little novelty of your own in the way of spirit photographs?"

"Upon my honour, doctor, no. I looked at that negative directly I got home, and when I saw that woman standing there, well—I declare to you that I felt queer. I have brought that negative here, and the other two negatives. Anybody who knows anything about photography will be able to see at a glance that they have not been tampered with since their original exposure. The print which the doctor has is the result of the first, and this, Mr. Paley, is the result of the second exposure."

Mr. Dodsworth handed Mr. Paley a second photograph. It was a repetition of the first, only, in this case, instead of standing at the back of the man's chair, the woman was kneeling on the ground at his side, and was stretching out her hand and arm in such a manner that they screened the words which were written on the slate.

"You see," commented Mr. Dodsworth, "she has concealed the prisoner's name."

"Do you mean to tell me seriously, Mr. Dodsworth, that you wish me to take this as a bona fide portrait of the man Solly?"

"Here is Mr. Murray, and here is Mr. Slater: they were present at the time—ask them! I took the negatives straight home; they are now lying before you on the table. What you are holding in your hand was printed, in the usual manner and in the ordinary course, from the second plate which I exposed."

"Then do you wish me to infer that about the matter there is something supernatural, Mr. Dodsworth?"

Mr. Dodsworth shrugged his shoulders.

"It is not for me to draw inferences. I am a photographer. It is my duty to lay before you the results of the camera. That is a print from the third exposure, Mr. Paley."

Mr. Dodsworth laid the third photograph before the governor.

"Really, Mr. Dodsworth, this is too much! Do you expect me to take this as a portrait of the man George Solly? Why, there's nothing of the man to be seen!"

"Quite so—the woman has stepped in front of him, and conceals him wholly."

"Do you wish me to infer that the man is behind the woman then? They will require the magnifying glasses which Sam Weller alluded to, if that portrait is to be of much service to them at Scotland Yard."

"I repeat, Mr. Paley, that I wish you to infer nothing. That is the portrait of a woman, which was not taken under ordinary conditions, because, when it was taken, there was no woman there. No woman, that is, who was visible to my eyes, or to Mr. Murray's or to Mr. Slater's, and it was broad daylight. We saw George Solly, and George Solly only; but it seems that the camera saw something else, and I believe it is a well-authenticated fact that the camera cannot lie."

"That does not look like an ordinary photograph, Mr. Dodsworth."

"It is an extraordinary photograph, Mr. Paley."

"It looks so dim."

"Perhaps it is because the woman was only dimly visible to the exquisitely sensitised plate that she was invisible to our less sensitive eyes."

"You are, in fact, suggesting a ghost story, Mr. Dodsworth."

"I am suggesting a possible explanation, Mr. Paley."

"And I will suggest another." The doctor was holding the photograph in his hand. He was eyeing it askance. "I suggest that I bring my camera to bear. Let me try my hand at photographing this remarkable Mr. Solly. Have I your permission, Mr. Paley?"

The governor leaned back in his chair. He drummed with his finger-ends upon the table. His manner became official.

"I don't know, doctor, that we are entitled to make experiments upon this man."

"We are entitled to endeavour to get a good portrait of him if we can, without adjuncts. I suppose that you hardly intend to send either of these negatives up to Scotland Yard. You will have inquiries made into the matter if you do. I don't wish to suggest anything in the least unkind, but I am inclined to think that, although a mere amateur, I shall be able to obtain more satisfactory results than Mr. Dodsworth, the professional. Perhaps when I try the spooks will be sleeping."

"So far as I am concerned I very earnestly hope that the governor will allow you to make the experiment, doctor."

The governor delivered his decision.

"The circumstances are peculiar. Ordinarily, doctor, I should feel myself bound to decline to accede to your request. The prisoners are not here for us to experiment upon. But—I have received instructions from headquarters to forward to Scotland Yard a negative of the man George Solly. None of Mr. Dodsworth's negatives are suited to the required purpose. It becomes, therefore, my duty to procure one more suitable. It is in the hope that you will be able to provide me with a more suitable negative that, Dr. Livermore, I accede to your request."

CHAPTER II

"Well, I've done it!"

There were in the office when Dr. Livermore made this remark—the governor, Mr. Dodsworth, the chief warder, and the doctor.

"You were all of you present when I made my little trial, so as to the conditions under which that trial was made I presume that we are all agreed. What I photographed was the man George Solly. There was no one else there to photograph. Upon that point there can be no doubt whatever—is that not so, Mr. Paley?"

"Certainly, no one else was there—that is, within the range of your camera."

"Just so; I mean within the range of my camera, so that there can be no reason why the results should not have been satisfactory."

"No reason with which I am acquainted—none whatever. Are the results not satisfactory?"

"Wait one moment and you shall judge for yourself. As you are aware, I went one better than Mr. Dodsworth—I exposed four plates. As each plate was exposed I sealed it up in your presence, without even glancing at it myself. Directly I reached home I forwarded the sealed plates to a firm in town to be developed.

I mentioned to no one that I intended to do so. I have mentioned the fact of having done so to no one since. I simply instructed that firm to develop the plates in the ordinary way, to print six impressions from each, and to return both prints and plates to me. The results have only reached me this morning. Here they are. There cannot be the slightest doubt that these are my plates, that they have not in any way been tampered with, that they have simply been developed by ordinary processes, and that these prints are merely reproductions from the plates. Yet, when I saw these prints, I did what I think you will do—I stared. Mr. Paley, here is the result of the first exposure."

The doctor handed Mr. Paley a photograph. The governor directly he saw it gave utterance to an exclamation.

"Doctor! You are dreaming."

"I assure you I am not. Mr. Dodsworth, allow me to hand you a print from the first exposure. Mr. Murray, allow me to hand you one. Mr. Dodsworth, you perceive that the laugh is now upon your side."

The photograph which the doctor had handed round was not the photograph of a man at all, but of a woman. She was costumed in ordinary feminine attire. She wore no covering on her head. She was seated squarely on the chair on which prisoners were wont to sit when enjoying the luxury of having their likenesses taken at their country's expense. She was looking straight at the camera. And in the eyes there was a certain defiance, and upon her face a look of stern, resolute determination, which is not in general to be noted upon the countenances of those triumphs of the photographer's art with which we adorn our albums.

"Honestly, doctor," inquired the governor, "aren't you having a little joke at our expense? Or perhaps you have made a slight mistake in giving us one print for another. Are you aware that the portrait you have given us is not the portrait of a man at all, but of a woman?"

"I am aware of it, and of a woman who, to my eye, has the light of a great purpose in her face. There can be no doubt that that woman was sitting in George Solly's chair."

"And where is George Solly then?"

"That I cannot tell you. But, as Mr. Dodsworth remarked the other day—and I shall have to make my apologies to Mr. Dodsworth—it is a well-authenticated fact that the camera cannot lie. On this occasion it has seen something which was concealed from our less sensitive vision."

Mr. Paley laid down the photograph with that acid yet courteous smile for which the governor was famous.

"And where is the result of the second exposure? Is the woman still sitting in George Solly's seat!"

"No, she has left it, and this time, as you see, we have at least George Solly's face. Here is the result of the second exposure."

The doctor handed round another photograph. In this the man Solly was seated in the usual attitude, holding out the slate, and the woman was kneeling before him. Her profile was towards the camera, and she had just rubbed out the name upon the slate. At any rate, the slate was blank.

"Isn't that a remarkable photograph?" asked the doctor. "I mean a remarkable photograph from any and every point of view? Just look at the expression on the woman's face, and at the suggestion of complete unconsciousness on the face of the man. She looks as though she could, and would, do anything. He seems to be wholly innocent, even of the knowledge of her presence there."

"This photograph is, in some respects, not unlike one of Mr. Dodsworth's."

"Which makes the thing the more remarkable. But I want you particularly to observe that the slate which Solly holds is blank. Now, I ask all of you, whether at any moment during the time I was exposing the plates that slate was blank."

"Certainly not," declared Chief Warder Murray.

The others, by their silence, acquiesced in Mr. Murray's declaration.

"If I could trust my eyes, during the whole time I was exposing the plates, the words 'George Solly' were there, ostentatiously there, upon that slate. You see that in that print the slate is blank. Now look at this—this is the result of the third exposure!"

In the fresh photograph which the doctor produced a curious

change had taken place. The blank upon the slate was occupied; a name was written on it from corner to corner. It seemed that it had just been written by the woman, because the handwriting was feminine; and with her face towards the camera, still kneeling on the ground before the man George Solly, she pointed at it with a sort of defiant rage, as though she gloried in the fact of having written it, and dared them to deny the suggestion it conveyed.

"Now, what do you think of that?" cried Dr. Livermore. "You will remember that these exposures followed each other at intervals of perhaps a couple of minutes. Just now the slate was blank, now the blank is filled. The name 'George Solly' remained upon the slate throughout the several exposures, so far as we could see. But 'George Solly' is not the name with which the woman, during the couple of minutes which intervened between the two exposures, has filled the blank."

Mr. Paley was peering through his spectacles at the name which, in the photograph, appeared upon the slate.

"It is certainly not 'George Solly.' It looks like 'Evan'— 'Evan——'"

"It's 'Evan Bradell.' The thing's as clear as day."

"Evan Bradell—so it is. Really, doctor, this is, in its way, remarkable."

"But I venture to say that the most remarkable part is still to follow. We had, first of all, the woman sitting on the chair, on which, if we can trust the evidence of our senses throughout, no one but George Solly sat. Then we had the woman, having rubbed out the name upon the slate, George Solly now upon the chair. Then we had the woman, having substituted the one name for the other, George Solly still upon the chair. And now, in this fourth exposure, you will see that not only has the woman gone, but George Solly has vanished too, and in George Solly's chair is seated—another man! Here it is, look for yourselves."

It was as the doctor said. In the fourth photograph the woman had disappeared. There was the familiar chair, but the individual who was seated on it bore not the least resemblance to Solly. To begin with, this individual, with the exception of the hat—he was hatless—was clad in commonplace civilian costume, decorous frock-coat, and the rest of it. But it was not only a question of difference of clothing; he was altogether a bigger and an older man than Solly. And he dandled on his knee, with an air of curious discomfiture, the slate on which was inscribed, in a clear, feminine hand, the name "Evan Bradell."

While his hearers continued to examine the result of the fourth exposure the doctor delivered himself of a few observations.

"While I do not wish to suggest that we are in the presence of a manifestation from the supernatural, I do insist that we are, at any rate so far, in the presence of a mystery. I doubt if any photographer ever before discovered that, while he supposed himself to having been photographing Mr. Brown, he had, in reality, been photographing Miss Smith. I want you to note one or two points which strike me about the affair, and which may lead to a possible solution. First of all, there is the presence of the woman. In Mr. Dodsworth's original plate it requires no strong effort of the imagination to suppose that the veiled figure at the back of the chair is that of a woman. In Mr. Dodsworth's subsequent three plates the woman is certain. In my first three plates she is, if possible, more certain still. And just observe that Mr. Dodsworth's woman and my woman are identical; she has changed her dress, but the woman is the same. Possibly, Mr. Paley, you will be able to offer us an explanation of how it is that Mr. Dodsworth and I should both of us have been photographing a woman whom neither of us have ever seen."

Mr. Paley leaned back in his chair. He looked up at the ceiling. He pressed the tips of his fingers together. And he preserved that silence which is golden.

"It is to be noted that the attitude of the woman is, throughout, one of protection to the man and defiance to us—of defiance, that is, to the manipulator of the camera. She first of all, in Mr. Dodsworth's plate, tries to hide the name upon the slate. Then she actually, with her own person, conceals the man. In my first plate she confronts me boldly, as if to give me to understand that it is with her I have to reckon. Then she rubs out the name upon the slate, she writes another in its place. And, having substituted one name for the other, she seems, by a mere effort of will, to have effected an exchange of men: George Solly is gone, Evan Bradell occupies his place. She appears as Solly's guardian angel, resolute, at all hazards, to prove that she is on his side; and she seems to be making frantic efforts to express her unwavering faith in Solly's innocence, even going so far as to point out the man on whose shoulders the guilt should properly be laid."

The doctor paused, and the governor spoke.

"With regard to Dr. Livermore's fanciful explanation of the somewhat peculiar circumstances connected with these photographs—and the doctor will excuse me if I say that I did not think that he was capable of such flights of imagination——"

"Laugh away, Mr. Paley! 'He laughs longest who laughs last.'"

"Quite so, doctor, quite so! With regard to your guardian angel theory, about a woman watching over Solly, and so on, I may mention that a letter has been received in the prison, addressed to the man Solly, which comes from a woman—from a woman who is, apparently, his wife. Whoever she is, she is, if one may judge from the evidence of the letter itself, certainly a remarkable woman. And I am bound to allow that, in view of recent events, and of what we have heard from Doctor Livermore, this letter is, in a sense, a coincidence. In pursuance of the powers which are invested in me to make such use of convicted prisoners' letters as may appear to me to be justified by circumstances, I will read to you this letter which has been sent to the prison, addressed to Solly."

The governor read aloud the following letter. It sounded strange in his cool, clear, slightly acid tones. One fancied that it had been written in a different spirit to that in which it was read.

"'MY OWN, DEAR, NOBLE HUSBAND,

"'God bless you, sweetheart! I hope you realise, my dear, that I am with you in Canterstone Jail. Not only in spirit, but actually, and in fact. I am with you in the morning when the bell rings, and you rise from your plank bed. I am with you on the treadwheel, love, and I am proud to keep step at your side. And I am with you when, in the evening, you lie down again upon your plank, I lie down on the plank beside you, and I creep into your arms as I used to do when I had you at home, and as I will do when, soon, I have you home again, my love. Do not think that I speak figuratively. I have been with you all the time that you have been in jail; I have been ever at your side, I have seen all that you have done, although I do not think, sweetheart, that you have been conscious of my presence. I have kissed you many times upon the lips, although I do not think that you have felt my kisses there. But, now that you know that I am with you, always and ever, and that I often kiss you, watch for me, dear husband. Something, I am sure, will reveal to you my presence, and you will feel my kisses.

"'But do not think, because I am ever with you in the jail, that I am not outside as well—because indeed I am. There has come to me, during this our time of sorrow, I know not from whence or how, a dual personality. I am with you there; I shall be with you, sweetheart, when you read this letter; watch for me. I shall be leaning over your shoulder as your eyes light upon these words—and I am here, watching and working to establish the truth. And the truth is coming out. I know whose is the guilt. It is his whom we both of us suspected from the first. And soon it shall be proved: by his own conscience and by me. So the time is drawing very near when your innocence shall be made known to all the world—I would not say so if I was not sure.

"'God bless you, sweetheart; and God permit me to continue with you in your cell. It will not be for long. And God has been so good to us in spite of sorrows, that I have a full assurance that He will not withhold from us this further boon.

"'My own, dear, noble husband, I am the happiest and the proudest woman in the world, because I am able to write myself

'YOUR WIFE.'"

"Queer letter!" observed Mr. Murray, when the governor had finished reading.

"I should say, off-hand," remarked Mr. Dodsworth, "that that woman must be wrong in the head."

The doctor smoothed his shaven chin with his open palm before he spoke. "I am not so sure of that. But of one thing I am sure. I am sure I know who is the original of the woman in the photographs."

The governor glanced up from the letter which he still held in his hand.

"Who is it?"

"The woman who wrote that letter—George Solly's wife."

The governor appeared to consider the matter for a moment.

"That is a point that can be very easily decided. Murray, go and fetch George Solly here."

The chief warder departed. When, in the course of a few minutes, he returned with the object of his quest, it was seen that George Solly was a young man, of perhaps six- or seven-and-twenty years of age. The prison costume which he wore was not a thing of beauty, but its ugliness was not sufficient to conceal the fact that he was a man of gentle breeding, and not only of gentle breeding, but of modest bearing. He was fair, with clear brown eyes, and well-shaped mouth and chin, not by any means the criminal type of man, and he was a man of quiet fortitude. Despite that ghastly uniform, there was about the man a certain dignity.

Directly he had taken up the regulation stand-at-attention attitude in front of the governor's table, Mr. Paley held out to him a photograph.

"Solly, whose portrait is that?"

As soon as Solly's glance fell upon the portrait, which he took from Mr. Paley, his eyes moistened and his lips twitched.

"Has she sent it to me? May I have it, sir?"

"Whose portrait is it, Solly?"

But the man appeared unconscious of the governor's inquiry. He continued to gaze steadfastly upon the portrait. And he said, as if he had forgotten that anyone was present beside the portrait and himself, in a tone of voice whose tenderness, to a toneless pen, is indescribable—

"How came she to be sitting on that chair? And what a strange look she has upon her face! My darling!"

In the presence of those iron-bound officials he kissed the face which was imaged in the photograph.

"I don't think you can have heard my question, Solly. Whose portrait is that?"

"Whose? My wife's. Are you not aware of that? Has it not come from her for me?"

"No." The governor held out his hand. "Give it to me." Solly shrank back a little. He seemed to hold the portrait with an intenser grasp. Then he gave it back to Mr. Paley. "That portrait is the property of the prison. I merely wished to know if you recognised the subject. Here is another portrait, Solly. Can you tell me who is the original of this?"

Solly stared, as though he could not quite make out the purport of the proceedings. He held out his hand, rather doubtfully, for the fresh photograph which the governor passed to him by way of the chief warder. But when his glance fell upon the photograph he started and he stared, and he stared and he started, as though he could not believe the evidence of his own eyes.

"It—it can't be! At last! oh, my God, at last!"

The man's emotion was intense. But the governor paid no heed to that whatever. He repeated his inquiry in his cool, clear, acid voice.

"Are you acquainted with the original of that photograph?"

"Am I? Aren't I? Oh, Mr. Paley, have they found it out—have they discovered it was he? Am I to have my freedom? Is it known at last that I was innocent?"

"Be so good as to answer my question, Solly. Are you acquainted with the original of that photograph?"

"Certainly I am. Here is his name, written on the slate. It is Evan Bradell. From the first I suspected him. I even suspected that it was his deliberate intention to lay the onus of his guilt on me! God knows why; I never did him harm. Is he in custody upon another charge? Or how comes it, if he is in custody for the crime of which they found me guilty—guilty! me!—that I have heard nothing of it, and that I am not set free?"

The man's tones were hot and eager. The governor's, as ever, were cool, and clear, and acid.

"Solly, give me back that photograph. That also is the property of the prison. As in the case of the other, I merely wished to know if you were acquainted with the original. I would advise you, Solly, not to buoy yourself up with any hopes that the verdict which has been pronounced against you will be revised, or that the term of imprisonment which was allotted you will be diminished. I have heard nothing which would lead me to suppose anything of the kind. Indeed, I have heard nothing about your case, either one way or the other, since you were tried. I merely sent for you here to put to you certain formal questions—that is all."

As the words were uttered in the governor's judicial, monotonous tones the man shrank back as though he had received a blow.

"There is another matter, Solly, which I wish to mention to you. A letter has been received in the prison addressed to you. It infringes one of the prison rules, which requires that every communication intended for a prisoner should be signed in full, with Christian and proper names. Moreover, the letter is couched in language which I cannot, in some respects, call proper, nor calculated to increase your peace of mind while you are here. However, I am informed that your conduct has, so far, been satisfactory, and I am therefore disposed to waive these matters upon this occasion. But you must distinctly understand that, upon another occasion, I shall not do so. Mr. Murray, see that this man has, in the dinner-hour, the letter which has been addressed to him."

And the governor handed the chief warder George Solly's letter.

CHAPTER III.

They sent up a report to the Commissioners. It was rather a compound document. It was drawn up by the governor, the doctor, and Mr. Dodsworth in concert, with here and there a word or two from Mr. Murray, while in a sort of postscript Warder Slater was brought in. It narrated at some length, and with a considerable amount of circumlocution—in accordance with official traditions—the story of the photographs. The negatives went with the report. They were submitted to the impartial judgment of the Commissioners, to take or leave just as they pleased.

Mr. Paley was particularly anxious that in the report there should not only be no suggestion of the supernatural, but that there should be a distinct disclaimer of any suggestion of the kind. On this point there was a slight difference of opinion. The doctor insisted that the things which had occurred could not have occurred without the interposition of something out of the natural. He wished to insert, in his portion of the report, a gentle hint to the effect that they might have hit—which hit would tend to the advancement of photographic science—upon a novel force. Mr. Dodsworth had, or declared that he had, no theories either one way or the other. He would have liked the report to have contained nothing but a bald statement of facts. While Mr. Murray—however, no one paid the slightest attention on this point to Mr. Murray, because, while he had the smallest possible belief in human nature, he had the strongest belief in ghosts. As for Warder Slater—what was Warder Slater's state of mind upon the matter may be better judged from a report which he made to the governor, upon his own account, a couple of days after "the report" had been sent.

The "reports" on that particular morning numbered only one: that one was Warder Slater, and the man "reported" was George Solly. Warder and prisoner took up their positions before the cord which was drawn across the room, and on the other side of which sat the governor at his table. The warder, if small in height, was large in girth—a prodigy of stoutness. The prisoner was tall and slender. As regards physical proportions, they presented a pleasing contrast. The officer seemed, for some cause or other, to be not altogether at his ease. The governor opened the inquiry.

"Well, Slater, what is it?"

"Man talking in his night-cell, sir."

"To himself? Or to whom?"

The officer fidgeted—with Batavian grace.

"It's my belief, sir, he had someone in his night-cell along with him."

"Someone with him in his night-cell?"

"Yes, sir; and it's my belief it was a woman."

"A woman?"

The governor looked at the culprit—probably becoming for the first time fully conscious that that culprit was George Solly. Just then Dr. Livermore entered the office at the back. He stood and listened. The officer explained.

"I was on night-duty last night, sir, and I was going my rounds about half-past one, when, as I entered Ward C, I heard sounds of someone talking. I found that someone was talking inside of 13 C."

George Solly's prison number was 13 C, the number being that of the cell he occupied.

"I listened outside of 13 C, and I heard two voices."

"Two voices?"

"Yes, sir, two voices—and one of them a woman's."

"A woman's?"

"Yes, sir, a woman's—I heard it most distinct. I could hear what they were saying. They were regularly carrying on. I heard Solly say, 'My own true love!' I heard the woman say, 'Sweetheart!' and a lot more like that."

As if suspecting the presence, somewhere, of a smile, Warder Slater all at once became emphatic.

"I'm willing to take my Bible oath I heard it!"

The governor regarded the slightly excited officer through his spectacles with that calm, passionless, official look which he was famous for. He turned to the culprit.

"Solly, what have you to say?"

Solly's reply was somewhat unexpected.

"What Mr. Slater says is true."

"You were talking in your night-cell to a woman?"

"I was. I was talking to my wife."

"Don't trifle, my man, with me. I suppose you mean that you were engaged in some little ventriloquial performance?"

Solly hesitated. It was noticed when he spoke that in his manner there was a certain exultation—a suggestion of suppressed excitement.

"You will remember that, some days ago, I received a letter from my wife. In that letter she told me that she was always with me in the jail, and that I was to watch for her." Solly paused. The governor made a slight gesture as of interruption; but then seemed to change his mind, and the man continued. "I did watch. It seemed to me that sometimes I felt her touch, that I heard the rustle of her garments, that I even heard her voice. But the consciousness of these things was such a faint one that I supposed, my attention being so acutely strained, that I had allowed myself to be deceived by my imagination. Until last night." Solly paused again. This time the governor made no attempt at interruption. "Last night I could not sleep. I lay, dreaming, wide awake. I was wondering where my wife was, and what she was doing, and whether she was thinking of me, as I was thinking then of her, when—I felt a touch upon my lips, and found that my wife was in my arms. I don't think that I was startled, because I had half expected that she would come to me in some such way as that. But I was very glad. We sat together on the side of the bed, and she talked to me and I to her—as Mr. Slater says, we carried on—until Mr. Slater entered."

"Yes," said Warder Slater, "when I had had enough of listening, and wondering whoever could be carrying on with Solly, I opened the door soft like, so that I might catch 'em at it, whoever it was, and I saw Solly sitting on the side of the bed, and someone—I couldn't quite make out who, because I don't mind owning that I felt a bit flurried, because how anybody, let alone a woman, could have got in to Solly was more than I could understand—but I saw it was a woman was sitting by his side, and she had her arms about his neck, and he had his arms about her waist."

"Well?"

The monosyllable came from the governor. Warder Slater had paused.

"Well, sir, I just caught a glimpse of her, and she was gone—gone like a thing of air, before I had a chance to open my mouth. I don't mind owning that I didn't quite like it, at that time of night, and all; but I says to Solly, 'Who's that you had in here along with you?' And he says, 'It was my wife.' 'I shall report you,' I says, and I went outside."

"Did you hear any more talking?"

"No, sir, I did not, although I stopped outside some time and listened. And I came back half a dozen times, and each time I listened, but I never heard a sound."

The prisoner took up the tale.

"She came back once and kissed me, and whispered just one word. And after that I fell asleep, and slept until the morning."

The governor leant back in his chair. He seemed to be considering. He regarded the prisoner intently, the prisoner meeting his glance with perfect self-possession. At last he said—

"That will do. Take the man away." And Warder Slater and the prisoner departed.

As they went out Dr. Livermore came forward. The governor turned to him.

"Is that you, doctor? Have you heard that edifying little story? What do you think of it? Murray, you can go."

On that hint the chief warder also went. The governor and the doctor were alone. When they were alone the two officials dropped to a perceptible degree their official manner.

"Frankly, Paley, I don't know what to think."

"You don't mean to say that you believe in the genuineness of that story as it was told to us?"

"I repeat, I don't know what to think. You see, there are not only those photographs and the woman's letter, but there is something else besides. Paley, I've been breaking the rules."

"How?"

"I've been carrying a detective camera about with me, and I've been taking a snap-shot at that man Solly whenever I got the chance."

"You have, have you? It's just as well you didn't tell me, or I should have been down on you, my friend. Well, and what was the idea?"

"Never mind what the idea was, I'll tell you what the result is. The result is nineteen photographs, and in each of them, with the exception of two, there's the woman."

"You don't mean it!"

"I do mean it. Those photographs are my own property. I've half a mind to lay them before the Society for Psychical Research. I flatter myself that they would constitute as neat a case for inquiry as that august society has yet encountered."

"Livermore! None of that! There'll be trouble if you do!"

"I'm only jesting. I'm not likely to give myself away. But I mean to keep those photographs; I mean to write their history, and I mean to leave them to my—heirs, and a ghost story to the ages. Seriously, Paley! It's nonsense to suppose that I could have photographed a woman—seventeen times—if she hadn't been there to photograph. She must have been visible to the camera if she was invisible to me. And from being visible to the camera, to being visible, and even audible and tangible, to Solly, and even Slater, it's but one step further. And that's why I say, referring to the story which Solly and Slater have just now told, that I don't know what to think; and candidly, I tell you again, I don't."

"I tell you what I mean to do; I mean to have that man transferred."

"That's one way out of it, certainly—transfer the solution of the ghost story on to someone else's shoulders. Have you heard anything about the report—our report I mean?"

"Yes. This morning. Hardinge's coming down to-morrow."

"Hardinge! Nice sort of man to whom to entrust a case like that! Might as well expect an elephant to dance lightly upon eggshell china! Blundering bull!"

Major Hardinge, the gentleman thus disrespectfully alluded to, was no less a personage than one of the inspectors of Her Majesty's prisons. As such he was a personage who, as is well known, ought to have been regarded by all properly constituted official minds with awe and respect—to speak of nothing else. On the morrow he appeared. Having scampered round the prison in his usual twenty-mile-an-hour fashion, he attacked the subject in hand in that tumultuous, hearty way he had.

"Paley, what's all this stuff and nonsense about those photographs? I'm surprised at you; 'pon my word, I am."

"May I inquire, Major Hardinge, why?"

The governor was the official to the finger-tips again.

"Send up a cock-and-bull story like that to headquarters! What do you think that we're likely to make out of it? A ghost story! There can't be the slightest doubt in the world, Paley, that somebody's been playing tricks with you—that's the general opinion at the office."

"May I ask, Major Hardinge, if I am supposed to be the person who has been playing tricks on Mr. Paley?"

The inquiry came from Dr. Livermore.

"I'm not here to inquire who is, or who isn't. In fact, I'm not here to make any inquiry at all—the case, upon the face of it, is too trivial for inquiry. We've decided to squash it. But since I am here I may as well see this man—eh—what's his name? Solly!—just so! It appears that there are some peculiar circumstances in the case of this man—eh?—Solly. I shouldn't be surprised if you've got the wrong man here after all."

"The wrong man, major! How do you mean?"

"Those wise heads at the Quarter Sessions have made a mistake—one more example of the immaculate perfection of the system of trial by jury. Mind, I don't say that this is so. I say that it seems possible that it is so. The circumstances, as they exist at present—and which are not to be disclosed to the man Solly"—the major glared, first at the governor, then at the doctor; these three were closeted together—"are as follows. The other day a man walked into the Yard and gave himself up for embezzlement—the day before yesterday it was. When they began to inquire into the matter, it turned out that the thing of which he accused himself had taken place down here—at Bedingfield, over the way there—and was the very thing for which the man Solly had been tried, found guilty, and sentenced to two years' hard labour."

"What is the name of the man who gave himself up?"

The major scratched his head.

"A nasty name. I know it struck me directly I heard it as being a nasty name. The sort of name you'd rather be hung than have. Let me see—I've got it here." The major took out a bulky pocket-book, and out of the pocket-book a paper. "Here it is—

Evan Bradell—that's the fellow's name. I've known men commit suicide for less things than having to own to a name like that."

The doctor took something from his pocket. It was a photograph.

"Do you see the name which is written upon the slate which that man holds?"

"Eh?"

"Do you see, major, the name which is on that slate?"

The major took up the photograph. He peered closely at it.

"Evan—Evan Bradell, isn't it? Is this the man?"

"That, major, you should know better than I. You may have seen him, I haven't. But that appears to be his name—of which fact I was unaware until you mentioned it. If that is a likeness of the man Bradell, I think, major, that even you will allow that the thing is curious, because that happens to be a print from one of the negatives which we sent to the Commissioners, and which was taken from the man George Solly."

The major glared.

"You're at that cock-and-bull story again; in this age of enlightenment, and you a medical man, sir, I'm surprised at you, I really am! I don't want to discuss the matter; the Office is willing to consider the incident as closed, and I may say that I'm instructed not to discuss the matter. A pretty thing it would be if it got about in the papers! 'Ghost at Canterstone Jail!' Upon my word! There'd be a scandal! I shouldn't be surprised if the Commissioners felt themselves impelled to institute changes; changes, sir! To—to—to return to this man Solly, and the man, eh, what's his name? Bradell! It—it appears that this man Bradell tells a cock-and-bull story——"

"Another cock-and-bull story, major?"

"Yes, sir, another cock-and-bull story; there are always plenty of them in the air, as you will learn for yourself when you reach my age. As I was saying when I was interrupted, it appears that this man Bradell tells a cock-and-bull story about being haunted, and even persecuted by this man Solly's wife, in dreams, and that sort of rubbish, until she has driven him to remorse, and that kind of thing. In fact, there seems every probability that the man will be found to be a lunatic."

"I should like to bet two to one he isn't."

The major glowered at the doctor as though he could scarcely believe his ears.

"Bet, sir! bet, sir! Do I understand you to say that you offer to bet, sir? You appear to have extraordinary notions of the proper method of conducting an official inquiry, sir! In spite of your sporting offer, sir, perhaps you will allow me to repeat—although I have no desire to bet, sir—that I have a strong reason to believe that the man will be found to be a lunatic; and I base that statement to a great extent upon the grounds that, in my opinion, every man who tells a cock-and-bull story, and persists in it in spite of common sense, is, upon the face of it, a lunatic."

The doctor, deeming discretion to be the better part of valour, contented himself with bowing. So the major was free to air himself in another direction.

"But although, as I say, it is my opinion that the man will be found to be a lunatic, and the whole affair fall through, still, as I am here, I may as well see this man Solly, and put to him a question or two."

Solly was seen by the major. The major asked him if his name was Solly, what his age was, if he was married, if he had any children, what he had been charged with, where he had been charged, and such-like questions, and finally he asked him if he had any complaint to make of the treatment he had received in the jail. Solly replied that he had none. Then the major drew himself up in a manner which seemed intended to impress the beholders with the fact of what a very remarkable man he was. He threw his frock-coat open, and he thrust his thumbs into the armholes of his waistcoat.

"There is another question which I wish to ask you, Solly. Have you ever been photographed?"

"Do you mean in prison?"

"No—I am aware that you have been photographed in prison." The major glinted at the doctor out of the corner of his eyes. "I mean outside—before you came to prison?"

"Certainly—several times."

"You will understand, Solly, that you are in no way bound to answer the questions which I am putting to you now. I am only asking them for my own private satisfaction. But have you any objection to tell me whether any difficulty has been experienced in taking your photograph?"

"Difficulty? In what way?"

"In any way. Have the photographs which have been taken of you been satisfactory?"

Solly smiled, a little faintly.

"Perfectly; indeed, I have understood that I am rather a good subject than otherwise. May I ask why you inquire?"

"I ask because the photographs which have been taken of you in the prison have not been satisfactory. That will do; you can take the man away. I am glad that he has no complaint to make."

When Solly had departed the major turned to the doctor.

"I believe, Dr. Livermore, that you are an amateur photographer; of course, the fact of your being a medical man explains that you are."

"I am. But my being an amateur has nothing to do with these particular photographs. I have no hesitation in saying that, regarded merely as photographs, they are first-rate."

"In your opinion, doubtless." The major's tone was dry. He rose. "I mean nothing offensive to Dr. Livermore, but the Commissioners object to experiments being made in Her Majesty's prisons. In future you will please, Paley, not to allow them. The treatment to which that man Solly has been subjected can scarcely be justified. Who is the man Dodsworth, who is responsible for some of the photographs? Have you employed him before?"

"Mr. Dodsworth is a highly respectable photographer in the town. He has been frequently employed in the prison, and has always given satisfaction."

"Don't employ him again. Employ somebody else next time. If you can't find anyone the Commissioners will send you a man from town. I'm going, Paley. I think that's all I have to say."

And Major Hardinge shook the dust of Canterstone Jail from off his feet.

That night in Canterstone Jail something rather curious occurred. It was very late. Not only had the prisoners retired—they retired at eight, as they should have done in the days when they were young!—but the warders had retired too—they retired at ten—and even the governor, who, of course, retired when he pleased, but who observed virtuous hours as a rule, had sought his pillows with the rest. It was the rule at Canterstone, when the prisoners withdrew to their plank couches, for the day-warders to withdraw from the actual precincts of the jail; they occupied a row of cottages on the other side of the wall. The night-warders came on duty. In list slippers they promenaded, with more or less frequency, the wards, in the silent watches of the night.

At the absolutely sepulchral hour of two a.m., on the occasion which has been referred to, a figure might have been observed stealing along the path which ran outside one of the wards in the direction of the governor's house. The figure was not that of an escaped felon—not at all. The figure was the figure of a warder. He appeared to be in considerable haste, for he had not stayed to remove the list slippers from his feet, and he moved along as fast as he possibly could—he was great in girth—with his lantern in his hand. The governor's house was in the very centre of the prison. When this warder reached it he rang the bell; and he not only rang it, but he gave it a mighty tug. The bell, like a surgeon's, was a night bell. It was hung in the apartment which was occupied, not only by Mr. Paley, but by Mrs. Paley too. So that when the bell was tugged like that the lady could scarcely fail to hear it, if the gentleman deemed it wiser to sleep on. Warder Slater—for the warder was Warder Slater—had no necessity to give a second tug. In a remarkably short space of time a window was opened overhead and a head came out. The head was the governor's.

"Who's there?"

"Warder Slater, sir."

"What's the matter?"

"There's a ghost in Ward C, sir."

"A ghost?"

"Yes, sir—there's that woman in Solly's cell again, sir."

It is no slight thing for the warder of a prison to rouse the governor in the middle of the night, or what is the same thing, at so early an hour as two a.m. It is well understood that there are occasions on which the governor must be roused. But the Commissioners have not distinctly stated whether the occasion of the presence of a ghost is one of them. Perhaps the omission has occurred because a ghost is so rare a visitor—even in a prison, which sees strange visitors—that the thing seemed scarcely worth providing against. Whatever may have been the governor's private opinion on the matter, he contented himself with saying, before he closed the window—

"Wait!—I'm coming!"

And he did come, slipping into some of his clothes with a degree of despatch which would have done credit to the schoolboy who delays his rising from bed until he hears the breakfast bell.

"Some more nonsense, Slater?"

That was the governor's drily-uttered observation as he joined the warder.

"Well, sir, you will see for yourself, sir, when we get there!"

Governor and warder started off together towards Ward C. As they moved over the pebbly path the warder, whose state of mind did not seem to be a state of perfect ease, endeavoured to explain.

"I've been in that ward a dozen times to-night, sir. I thought more than once that I heard the sound of someone whispering, but I wasn't quite sure until I went in just now, sir. Directly I went in this last time I knew that there was something up. I stood outside of Number Thirteen's door, and sure enough I heard that woman talking to Solly, and carrying on with him, just as she was the other night, sir. I didn't hardly know what to do, sir, because, I says to myself, if I report the man the governor won't believe me. Then I makes up my mind to come and tell you, sir, so that you could come and see for yourself. I don't know if we shall find her there now, sir: she may have gone. But that she was there a couple of minutes ago, when I came to fetch you, I'll take my Bible oath!"

"That'll do. We shall see if she's there when we get there."

The governor's tone was not reassuring—but then it seldom was. His official tone was not reassuring. Warder Slater heartily hoped that she would be there. He began to be conscious that it was quite within the range of possibility that the governor might be disposed to make an example of a warder who routed him out of bed in the middle of the night to see a ghost which was neither to be seen nor heard.

They entered the prison, which was itself a ghostly place to enter. They went in by the round-house, and there it was not so bad; but when they began to mount the cold, worn, stone steps which wound up between the massive whitewashed walls, the darkness rendered still more visible by the lantern in the warder's hand, one began to realise that, after all, there might be "visions about."

Canterstone Jail was an old-fashioned jail, built in the good old-fashioned days when stone walls, six feet thick, were considered a *sine quâ non* in jails. In the broad noonday glare the wards in which the night-cells were were dimly lighted. Entering them at two a.m. one received an object-lesson in "Egyptian darkness." One had but to stretch out one's arms to more than span the flag-stoned passage. And when one realised that on one side there was a six-foot wall, and on the other—surrounded, it is true, by other six-foot walls, but none the further off for that—lay the representatives of every shade of crime, one did not need to have an abnormal imagination to begin to comprehend that it is not always the part of wisdom to laugh at the tales which are told of churchyards yawning, and of the graves which yield their dead.

At Canterstone there were, in each ward, four floors: the ground floor, the first floor, the second floor, and the third floor. Solly's sleeping-place was on the third floor, that farthest from the ground and nearest to the sky. The governor and Warder Slater entered the ward at one end, Solly's cell being at the other. Directly they reached the landing the warder laid his hand on Mr. Paley's arm. "Do you hear, sir? She's with him still!"

There was a note of exultation in the officer's voice which seemed, all things considered, to be a little out of place. The gov-

ernor made no reply. He stood and listened. The general stillness
rendered any sound there might be still more audible. That there
was a sound there could be no doubt. The governor listened, so as
to be quite clear in his own mind as to what the sound was. It was
the sound of voices. Unless his sense of hearing played him false
the speakers were two.

"Which is Solly's cell?"

The governor put the question in a whisper. In a whisper the
officer replied—

"Number thirteen—right the other end, sir. That's where
they're talking—he and the woman. Come along with me, sir,
and we shall catch them at it."

The governor checked the impulsive Slater.

"Darken your lantern. You have your keys? When we reach
the door keep perfectly still until I give you the order. Then un-
lock the door and throw the light of your lantern into Solly's
cell."

Warder Slater darkened his lantern. In the pitchy blackness
the governor and the warder stole along the corridor. They were
guided by the sense of sound. Guided by that sense, they paused
at the spot where the talking seemed to be most audible.

"Is this the cell?"

The governor's voice seemed scarcely to penetrate the darkness. The warder's "Yes" was but an echo. The silence was pro-
found, except on the other side the door on the outer side of which
they two were standing.

There was someone talking in the cell. The speakers seemed
to be two. An attentive ear could catch the words which were being spoken.

"I could not rest unless you knew, and so I came to tell you, so
that there might be an end to your suspense, and that you might
not need to wait until the morning for the news."

The speaker was a woman—of a surety, the speaker was a
woman!

"My darling!" This time the speaker unmistakably was
Solly.

Then there ensued what Warder Slater had described as "carryings-on." The governor's sensations must have been of a somewhat speckled variety as he played the part of eavesdropper to proceedings such as those, because there could be not the slightest possible shadow of doubt that within that cell there were "carryings-on." There came to them who listened the sound of a woman's voice, uttering, in tones so tender they fell like sweet music on the ear, "loves," and "sweethearts," and "my own, own darlings!" and such-like vanities. And to her replied a man, in tones as tender if not as musical, who did his best to give the woman a fair exchange for her conversational sweetmeats of affection. But when it came to kissing, audible, in its prolonged ecstasy, on the outer side of that thick oaken door, the governor seemed to think that it was time that something should be done.

"Now!" he whispered.

And, almost simultaneously, the key was turned in the well-oiled lock. The door was thrown wide open, and Warder Slater's lantern gleamed into the cell. Then there was silence, both in the cell and out of it; and the governor stood within the open doorway, with the warder just in front of him, a little to one side, so as not to obstruct the governor's view, and the lantern in his hand. And both of these officials stared—stared hard! For in front of them stood Solly in considerable undress, and at his side——

It is probably owing to the governor's proverbial official caution that he could never be induced to say what was at Solly's side—to say positively, that is. It seemed to him it was a woman. Not such a woman as we meet in daily life, but, as it were, the shadow of a woman. It seemed to the governor that she was attired in *robe de nuit*. Solly held her by the hand. The governor thought he saw so much, but before he had a chance of seeing more she fled, or vanished into air. His eyes never ceased to gaze at Solly's side, and there was nothing there.

When there could be no doubt that the tangible presence of the something which had been standing there had gone, the governor's voice rang out sharp and clear—

"Solly, who was that you were talking to?"

"It was my wife."

"Your wife?" The governor stared. There was a peculiar ring

in his voice, which probably no prisoner had ever heard in it before. "I will have you punished in the morning."

The prisoner smiled. In his voice there was also a ring, but it was a ring of a different kind.

"No, Mr. Paley, you will not, because in the morning I shall be free." Solly paused, as if to give the governor an opportunity of speaking; but the opportunity was not taken. So he went on, "My wife has come to bring me good news." He turned; he held out his arms as if to take someone within them, but they could see no one there to take. And he said, "Good-bye until the morning, wife!" He advanced his face as if to kiss someone, and there was the sound of a kiss, but they could see no one who could have kissed him. Then he turned again to Mr. Paley, crying, in a voice which was half tears, half laughter, "It's all come out at last! Bradell's confessed! The Home Secretary has procured a free pardon! You will have it in the morning. My wife has been to tell me so."

It is certain that the governor could not have had much sleep that night. Warder Slater roused him at two a.m.; and if, when he returned to bed again, he was inclined to slumber, he had not much opportunity for the indulgence of his inclination. At an unusually early hour he was roused again. A special messenger had arrived from town, bringing with him a communication from the Home Secretary for the governor of Canterstone Jail. The communication took the form of that bitter wrong of which the system of English jurisprudence still is guilty. The Home Secretary informed the governor of Canterstone Jail that Her Majesty the Queen had been graciously pleased to grant a free pardon to the prisoner George Solly for what he had never done.

III.

A PACK OF CARDS

PART I.

"You see these? They belong to Francis Farmer; Colonel Farmer he called himself; the Colonel he was known as among his pals. Did you ever hear of him?"

I could not say that I ever had.

"He was a card himself, the Colonel was. An American. He had had something to do with the army, once upon a time, I fancy; but he had had more to do with the police. He was one of the greatest swindlers of modern times—an artist the Colonel was."

"And these are some of the implements of his profession?"

I was paying a visit to the Rogues' Museum at Scotland Yard, that queer establishment in which they preserve mementoes of criminals who, at various periods, have, in some way or other, had dealings with the police. The constable who was acting as my cicerone was holding in his hand a pack of cards. I took them into mine. They were a pack of what are commonly called "squeezers." They had rounded corners, and in the corner of each card was a statement of its value. Such a pack, indeed, as is generally used by properly constituted persons for the game of poker. There was nothing about the cards in any way remarkable, so far as I could see, except that on their backs was painted a large, bluish-red rose, as it seemed to me, by hand. But according to the constable they had a history.

"The Colonel won thousands with those cards."

"By the exercise of his skill?"

"It's as you choose to call it. They're hand-painted" (I thought they were), "and excellently painted too. If you look at them closely you'll see that the rose is not placed in exactly the same position on the back of each of them. There's just a shade of difference."

I did look at them closely. It was as the constable said. But it needed good eyes to observe the fact, the difference in position was so slight.

"He used to travel up and down the line to Brighton."

"That's odd. I'm going down to Brighton myself by the 2.30 this afternoon. I live there."

"Ah! He was well known upon that road. They used to think he was a big pot in the City who liked his hand at cards. City gentlemen often have a game as they come up to town. It's a regular thing. It was a well-known pack, the Colonel's. He won his fare, and a bit over, many a time."

"And where is this enterprising person now?"

"He's dead, that's where he is. Francis Farmer was sentenced for the term of his natural life for attempted murder. Perhaps you remember the case. It was on the Brighton line. They spotted him at last—he was a little too fond of winning, the Colonel was. He drew a revolver and put a bullet into the man who spotted him. For that he was sent to Portland. He tried to escape, and when they nabbed him he committed suicide in his cell."

"Then there is quite a curious interest connected with this pack of cards?"

"You may say so. There are some very queer tales told about them—very queer. They say they're haunted. I don't know much about that sort of thing myself, but some of our chaps do say that wherever those cards are the Colonel isn't very far away." I smiled. The constable seemed a little huffed. "I only know that I shouldn't care to carry them about with me myself."

As we were going out a gentleman entered. The constable seemed to know him, for he allowed him to pass without challenge. I went to Simpson's to lunch. I was thinking, as I ate, about what I had seen, memorials of hideous murders, a unique collection of burglars' tools, coiners' moulds, forgers' presses, ingenious implements for every sort of swindling—a perfect arsenal of crime! I am free to confess that that pack of cards was present to my mind. What a relic for a man to possess—a haunted pack

of swindler's cards! I ought to have looked at them more closely: perhaps some of the victim's blood was on the back of one of
them. *De gustibus non disputandum.* Some men would give a good
round sum for such a curio!

After luncheon I strolled along the Embankment to Victoria.
I caught the 2.30 to Brighton. As I was standing at the door of
the carriage two other persons entered in front of me, brushing
past me as they went. When I had taken my seat a third person
entered just as the train was starting. I was seated with my back
to the engine, at the end which was farthest from the platform.
The newcomer sat facing the engine at the other end of the carriage. He was a tall, slight, military-looking individual, with a
slight moustache, and, as I could see under the brim of his top-
hat, crisp, curly black hair. The two persons who had entered previously were seated in front of me at my end of the carriage.

I had some papers with me, but felt disinclined to read. I had
had a heavy lunch, and the result was to make me drowsy. I fancy
that I was all but dropping off, when someone spoke to me.

"Haven't we met before?"

I glanced up. The man speaking was the man in front of me,
who sat nearest to the door. When I eyed him closely I remembered him. He had sat next to me at a dinner which had been
given, a few days previously, to Lord Labington, whose political
exertions, as everyone is aware who is of the right way of thinking, have saved the country! An amusing neighbour I had found
him. He had struck me as a fellow of lively wit and of infinite jest.
I was glad to meet him again. I told him so.

"Awfully slow this kind of thing." I suppose he meant going
down by rail to Brighton. He did! "This train is a dreadful slow-
coach; takes no end of a time."

"It's a pity," I said, thinking of the Colonel's exploits upon that
very line, "that we haven't such a thing as a pack of cards!"

While I was speaking I thrust my right hand into the pocket
of the light summer overcoat which I was wearing. It lighted upon
something whose presence in my pocket I had not been conscious
of before. There were several articles, in fact. Supposing that I had
put some things there and forgotten all about them, I drew one

of them out to see what it could be. It was a playing-card. I drew more of them out. They were more playing-cards. There was an entire pack. And—could I be dreaming?—it was the pack of cards which had belonged to "Colonel" Francis Farmer!

It was entirely out of the question to suppose that I was mistaken. I had seen them too recently, observed them too attentively, and bore them too well in mind for that. They were altogether unmistakable, with the hand-painted red roses on their backs. But how came they in my pocket? To describe my feelings when I realised that they really were that "haunted" pack is altogether beyond my power. I remembered returning them to a constable; I remembered his replacing them in a glass case; I remembered his turning the key in the lock; and yet——

I suppose that there was something in the expression of my countenance which to an onlooker was comical, for I was all at once conscious of the sound of laughter.

"Hallo!" exclaimed my opposite neighbour. "Why—you do appear to have a pack of cards!"

"I—I do appear to have a pack of cards; but—but how I have them is more than I can say."

"You didn't steal them, I suppose?"

"Not—not consciously."

My opposite neighbour and his friend began to laugh again. The man at the other end of the carriage sat quietly cold. How I knew I cannot say, but I did know that his eyes were fixed upon me all the time.

"Never mind how you got them, you have got them; that is the point. Supposing we have a hand at Nap. What do you say, Armitage?" He turned to his friend. Then to me: "I don't know if you're aware of it—I don't think we got so far as exchanging cards the other night—but my name's Burchell."

"And my name's Ranken."

"Very well, Mr. Ranken, supposing after this general naming of names we set to work. Hand me over the cards."

He stretched out his hand. I hesitated before I gave him these. To put it gently, they were not mine. And—should I tell him their history or should I not? He did not give me time for reflection.

"Come along! Are you afraid I'm going to steal them?"

He took them out of my grasp. I was so bewildered by the discovery of their presence that I had really not recovered sufficient presence of mind to say him either yea or nay.

"What points? Suppose we say pounds?"

Pounds! I started. Pound points at Nap! Not if I knew it. Pennies were more in my line. I was pleased to observe that his friend, Mr. Armitage, did not second his suggestion.

"Don't you think pound points are a trifle stiff?"

"Well, make it half-sovereigns then, and a pound in the pool."

"I don't mind half-sovereigns."

But I did most emphatically. Why, with a pound in the pool, I might lose fifty pounds and more before I reached the other end. I have played penny Nap, and risen poorer by half a sovereign. I had been up to draw my dividends; I wondered what Mrs. Ranken would say if I returned to her minus fifty pounds!

"I—I'm no player. I—I couldn't think of playing for half-sovereigns."

"Make it dollars then. We must have something on the game."

Something on the game! If we had five-shilling points we should have a good deal more than I cared to have upon the game. But without waiting for my refusal Mr. Burchell commenced to deal the cards—the "Colonel's" cards!

I never had such luck before. It really was surprising. From the very first I won. Not spasmodically, but persistently—hand after hand, with a regularity which, in its way, was quite phenomenal.

"It's a pity," said Mr. Burchell, when I had made Nap for the third time within a quarter of an hour, "that we didn't make it pounds. I don't think anything could stand against your cards."

"I have had some decent hands," I agreed. "It's rather odd too, because generally I do no good at Nap."

"No? I should imagine, by the way in which you're going it, that you're like that third player in *Punch*, who held thirteen trumps at whist."

I laughed. Curiously enough, my luck continued. It was quite a record in its way. I never lost; I always had three trumps.

"Do you know," observed Mr. Armitage, when I again took Nap, "that I'm nearly thirty sovereigns to the bad? I think it's quite as well we didn't make it pounds."

"I'm about that much nearer the workhouse since I left Victoria," chimed in his friend.

I was amazed.

"You don't mean that I've won sixty pounds?"

"It looks uncommonly like it."

It was incredible. And yet my luck continued. I went three tricks that round, and made them. Then another three, then four, and then another Nap. Reckon that up, and you'll find that, with the points and the dealer's ten shilling contribution to the pool, I had made thirteen pounds in considerably less than half that number of minutes.

"You will excuse my asking you," said Mr. Burchell, as he was settling for the Nap, "if that pack of cards is bewitched?"

"I think it possible," I answered, half in jest and half in earnest. "There is a curious history attached to them, at any rate."

"There will be another curious history attached to them if this goes on much longer."

It did go on. In the very next hand I signalled four, and made them. My antagonists began to look blank; no wonder!

"We ought to send this to the *Field*. It ought to have a niche among curious games," said Mr. Armitage.

Mr. Burchell shuffled, Mr. Armitage cut, and I dealt the hand. Burchell went three, Armitage four, and I went Nap! I had ace, king, queen, and four of clubs, and king of diamonds. Not a bad Nap hand when three are playing.

"What, Nap again!" cried Burchell. "Great Scott!"

"Never mind," said Mr. Armitage, "I'm prepared for anything."

I was about to lead the ace of clubs when the stranger, who was seated at the other end of the carriage, left his end and advanced towards ours.

"Excuse me, gentlemen!"—he addressed himself to my antagonists—"you are being robbed. This gentleman is too clever a player for you. I should say that he was a professional swindler!"

"What the dickens do you mean?" asked Mr. Armitage. "And who are you?"

"I'm an old traveller. I've seen this kind of thing before. But I've never seen quite such beautiful simplicity as yours. I do believe you'd let him get Napoleon in continuous succession, right from here to Brighton, and still think it all serene—just a little accident worth sending to the *Field!*"

There was silence. Armitage and Burchell both looked at me. I felt that suspicion was in their glances. As for myself, I was so startled by the enormity of the charge that I momentarily was stricken dumb. I could not realise that the fellow was actually accusing me of theft.

"Do you—do you mean to suggest," I gasped, when I had sufficient breath to gasp, "that I—I've been cheating?"

"That is what I do mean. You have hit it on the head. It is inconvenient for you, no doubt. But I'm going to make it more inconvenient still. I'm going to prove it before the sitting's ended."

"You—you infernal scoundrel!"

I sprang up, as if to strike the fellow to the ground. But he remained entirely unmoved. His calmness, or assurance, rather reacted on me, and I refrained.

"Suppose we leave the adjectives till a little later on? Then, it is just possible that each man will have a few of his own to scatter round."

He turned to my antagonists.

"It's funny, gentlemen, very—but directly I saw those cards I thought I'd seen that pack before. I have a good eye for a card. The more I saw of them the more I felt that we had met before. And now I'll swear we have. A pack of cards very like that pack once belonged to a very famous personage; more famous, perhaps, than worthy. His name was Francis Farmer."

My surprise at hearing this name from the stranger's lips must have betrayed itself in my countenance. He immediately turned to me.

"I fancy that is a name which this gentleman has heard before. Is that not so?"

"I—I have heard it before," I stammered.

"I thought you had. Yes, gentlemen, there is the own brother to this pack of cards at this moment in the museum at Scotland Yard. Perhaps this gentleman's knowledge of the profession which he adorns so well will enable him to corroborate that fact."

"This—this is the pack."

"Do tell! That's candid, now. What, the Colonel's own! It's beautiful: for, gentlemen, Francis Farmer was a swindler, a card-sharper, a thief. He had all the talents. Permit me, sir, to exploit his favourite pack of cards."

The stranger took the cards which Mr. Armitage was holding in his hand.

"If you observe the beautiful rose which adorns their rears, you will observe that there is a slight variation in its position on the back of every card."

"I don't deny it for a moment."

I regained my presence of mind when I perceived that the fellow was not a mere impudent vagabond who wished to make himself objectionable, but that, in appearance, he really had something on which to base his assumptions.

"That is very good of you; more especially as we have eyes of our own which would enable us to perceive it for ourselves even if you didn't."

"If you will allow me I will explain how I became possessed of this pack of cards, which I believe really were the property of the infamous individual of whom this gentleman speaks. You will remember that I was surprised when I found them in my pocket?"

I addressed myself to Armitage.

"I remember that you appeared to be."

I did not like his tone at all.

"I not only appeared to be, I was. But before I explain, I suppose, Mr. Burchell, that you do not require an explanation. The place in which I met you is sufficient proof of the absurdity of what this person alleges."

"How so? I sat next to you at a public dinner. Anyone could go who chose to buy a ticket. It does not require a great effort of the imagination to suppose it possible that one might light upon a doubtful character at such a function."

I liked Mr. Burchell's tone even less than his friend's.

"You scarcely state the case correctly. It was not by any means open to anyone to buy a ticket. However, I will pass on to my explanation."

"We are waiting," murmured the stranger.

"I was this morning at Scotland Yard."

"And they let you out again? I always said the English police were fools."

"Where I saw this pack of cards."

"And pinched it? Under the constable's nose. The man's a genius."

"No, sir; I did not, as you phrase it, pinch it, under the constable's nose."

"Did he give it you?"

"No, sir, he didn't give it me."

"Did he sell it you?"

"He did not."

"How, then, does it come here?"

The stranger, thrusting his hands into his pockets, tilted his hat over his eyes.

"That, unfortunately, is exactly what I am myself unable to understand."

"Hark at that! And that is what you call your explanation? Well, sir, you are the most promising disciple of the late Francis Farmer's I have had the pleasure of meeting. You have what made him the man he was—his impudence."

"I pay no attention at this moment to this person's insinuations. After what has passed I insist on returning the moneys I have won."

"That would be advisable. It will save us trouble afterwards."

"Please to understand that I shall remain with you in this carriage until we reach Brighton. I shall then require you to accompany me to my residence. There I shall place before you ample proof that this person is an impudent traducer, and a barefaced liar."

"Softly at that. Let us wait for the adjectives still a little longer. There are one or two little points which you have forgotten in the excellent and copious explanation with which you have seen fit to favour us. Perhaps you will allow me to glance at the cards which you are holding in your hand?"

I gave him them.

"Here we have the ace, king, queen, four of clubs, and king of diamonds. A nice little hand. Perhaps you will be so kind as to tell me how many cards there are in the remainder of that pack?"

Mr. Armitage, being thus appealed to, took up the pack of cards which was lying on the seat at my side, and having added his own hand and Mr. Burchell's, proceeded to count them. He announced the result.

"There are forty-two cards here."

"And five I hold make forty-seven. It is perhaps my ignorance, but I have always supposed that fifty-two constitute a pack of cards. Perhaps you will be able to tell us what has become of the other five?"

The inquiry was addressed to me.

"How should I know?"

"You have not got them, by the merest chance, in either of your pockets."

"If you are not careful you will go too far!"

"That would be a pity. I should think that, for you, I've gone far enough already. Perhaps it would not be too much trouble to feel, say, in the left-hand pocket of that elegant summer overcoat which you have on."

"You impudent——"

I stopped short. Thrusting my hand into my left pocket, to my unutterable amazement, it lighted upon what unmistakably were cards. I drew them out. The stranger snatched them from me. He held them up in the air.

"Hey, presto—the missing five! I thought there might have been an accident. Now let us see what cards they are. Ace, king, queen, and four of hearts,' the ace of clubs—another pretty little hand! Perhaps, gentlemen, you commence to see how it is done?"

"I think I do," said Mr. Armitage.

"I am sure I do," said Mr. Burchell.

"If—if you think that I put those cards in my pocket," I began to stammer. Mr. Burchell interrupted me—

"Pray do not trouble to offer any wholly unnecessary explanations. Perhaps you will be so good as to return the money which you have won."

He laid a wholly unmistakable accent upon "won."

"It is I who insist on that, sir, not you."

"Pray do not let us quarrel as to phrases," said Mr. Burchell with a smile—a smile for which I could have strangled him. I counted out the moneys. Just as I had completed the act of restitution—restitution! To think that an honest man should have had to endure such humiliation!—the train drew up at Red Hill Junction—it was scarcely more than three-quarters of an hour since we left Victoria. Mr. Burchell rose.

"I wish you good-day, Mr. Ranken."

"A wish in which I join." And Mr. Armitage rose too.

"You are not going?" I cried.

"But indeed we are."

"Then I say that you shall do nothing of the kind. Do you think that I am going to allow you to place on me such a stigma without offering me an opportunity to prove my innocence?"

"If you dare to touch me, Mr. Ranken"—in my excitement I had grasped Mr. Burchell by the arm—"I shall summon an officer. As I am unwilling to appear as your accuser in a police-court, if you take my advice, you will let me go."

PART II.

A police-court! In my amazement at being threatened with a policeman I let them go. I sank back upon the seat, feeling as though I had been stunned. The train started. I still sat there. My faculties were so disorganised as to render me unable to realise my situation. To have had contemptuous compassion dealt out to me as though I were a swindler and a thief!

It was only when Red Hill had been left behind that I became conscious of the fact that I had not been left alone in the carriage. My accuser remained. He himself drew my attention to his presence.

"Well, how do you feel?"

I looked up. He had placed himself on the opposite seat, right in front of me. I glared at him. He smiled. Had I obeyed the impulse of the moment I should have caught him by the throat and crushed the life right out of him. But I restrained my indignation.

"You—you villain!" He laughed—a curious, mirthless laugh. It was like adding fuel to the flame. "Do you know what you have done? You have endeavoured to put a brand of shame upon a man who never, consciously, was guilty of a dishonourable action in his life."

"Well, and how do you feel?"

"Feel! God forgive me, but I feel as though I should like to kill you."

He put up his hand and stroked his beardless chin.

"Yes, that is how I used to feel at first."

"What do you mean?"

He leaned forward and looked me keenly in the face.

"Do you not know me?"

I paused before I answered. So far as my recollection went his face was strange to me. Still, my memory might err.

"Is it possible that we have met before? Can I have given you any, even the slightest, cause to do this thing?"

"You are right in your inference. I did it all. It was I who put the cards in your pocket."

"You—you devil!"

This time my indignation did get the better of me. I sprang forward to seize him by the throat, but, with a dexterous movement, he eluded me. Missing my aim, I fell on my knees on the floor. Rising to his feet he looked down at me, and smiled.

"Do you not know me now?"

"Know you? No!"

"I am Francis Farmer."

"Francis Farmer!"

"I am the guardian of the cards. Did not the constable tell you that where they were I was always close at hand?"

"But—Farmer's dead!"

"That is so. He's dead."

Scrambling to my feet I caught hold, for support, of the railing which was intended for light luggage. What did he mean? Was the fellow, after all, some wandering lunatic who should not have been suffered to be at large? He was standing at the other end of the carriage regarding me with his curiously mirthless smile. He did not look a lunatic; on the contrary, he appeared to be a person of even unusual intelligence. He was very tall. He was dressed from head to foot in black, after the undertaker fashion, which is so common in the United States. His cheeks were colourless, his eyes almost unnaturally bright. With those two exceptions there was nothing about him which was in any way uncommon, and even pale cheeks and flashing eyes are not phenomenal.

"Still, I am Francis Farmer."

His voice was not at all American; it was soft and gentle. Stooping, he picked up the pack of cards. He began, as it were, to fondle them with his hands.

"My cards! My own old cards! The tools which have so often won for me both bread and cheese! Is it strange that I should regard them almost as my own children, sir? That I should be careful where they are—to be always close at hand? I fashioned them with my own fingers. And so fine was the art I used that skilled eyes have beheld them many and many a time, yet never perceived a flaw."

"Do I understand you to say deliberately that you are Francis Farmer?"

"Indeed I am."

"Then at the next station at which we stop I will give information to the police. So notorious a rogue cannot be allowed to be at large."

"But Francis Farmer's dead."

"He was supposed to be. You are not the first rogue who has feigned to be dead."

"But, in truth, he's dead. They sat upon his corpse. They brought it in that he'd been guilty of felo-de-se. And, since no one came to claim his body, they buried him at Portland, among his brother rogues; and there he lies, within hearing of the sea. Permit me to show you the place where the rope was about his neck, and where he thrust the knife into his breast."

Tearing his waistcoat open he advanced towards me, as if to show me the hall-marks of the suicide. I waved him back again.

"Do not think to fool me with such tricks!"

He paused, and eyed me—always with his curious smile.

"You are a shrewd man. I perceived it when I saw you at Scotland Yard."

"You saw me at Scotland Yard!"

"Where else? I was with you in the Museum, when you were seeing all the sights. And when the constable took out the cards— my cards!—I perceived that you were a man after my own heart. So when the superstitious fellow—you remember, he was a little superstitious, was he not?—put them back into their place, I took the liberty to borrow them—why not? They were my own, the works of my own hand!—and I went with you down the stairs."

"You went with me down the stairs!"

"And along the Strand, to Simpson's. I sat beside you as you lunched—you did not see me. It was not strange. Permit me but one word—you are too fond of beef! It was a meat which, in my hungriest days, I never loved. When you had lunched, I slipped my arm through yours——"

"You slipped your arm through mine!"

"But indeed I did, and at the same moment I slipped my cards into the pocket of your overcoat. For I liked you, although for your beef I had a constitutional disrelish."

I had a constitutional disrelish for the style of conversation which he appeared to favour. As I listened to him talking in that cold-blooded way, of what, to say the least of it, were absolute impossibilities, I began to be conscious of a fit of shivering, as though I had plunged, unawares, into a bath of ice-cold water.

"You—you don't expect me to believe these fairy tales?"

"I went with you to the station; then, when the train was starting, I thought it time I should appear. So I appeared. I resolved that you should win, say, sixty pounds, and then—I would expose you."

"Expose me! Good heavens! man or demon—why?"

"Because I hoped to find in you a worthy successor to my fame."

I stared at him aghast. What could he mean?

"Do you—do you mean that you hoped to find in me the making of a thief?"

"Such words are hard. I hoped to find in you an artist, my dear sir."

"You consummate scoundrel! Man or demon, I shall be very much tempted, in half a minute, to throw you through the carriage window."

"Try it." The fellow stood upright, his arms to his sides. There was no appearance of bravado in his tone. He seemed completely at his ease. "Touch me! Grasp me, if you can!"

I took up his challenge on the instant. But scarcely had I advanced a step than I was seized with a sickening faintness, so that I was compelled to take refuge on the seat. He stood and watched me for a moment. Then he came and touched me. His touch was real enough, but I shrank from it with a sense of loathing which I am powerless to put into words.

"See, I am quite real." Strangely enough it was then that, for the first time, I doubted it. "It is only when I wish it that I am a thing of air." Bending over, he fixed his bright eyes upon my face. His glance had on me that paralysing effect which is popularly supposed to be an attitude of certain members of the serpent tribe. "Let me teach you the secret of my cards."

He held the pack in front of me—I knew he held it, although for the life of me I could not have removed my eyes from off his face. So we remained in silence for some moments. Then he went on, his tone seeming to steal like some stupefying poison into my veins.

"This is a great day for me. It is a day I have looked forward to ever since I—died. It was not an heroic death—to stab oneself with a common warder's common knife, to hang oneself with a prison sheet from the bar of a broken window. One would not choose a death like that. And yet, if die one must, what matters it how one dies? And time has its revenges! All things come to those who wait—at last! at last! After many days I've found a friend."

I tried to breathe. I could not. Something seemed to choke me. I was overcome by a great weight of horror and disgust. It seemed to stifle me.

"Do you know where we are sitting, you and I? This carriage is an old familiar friend. It was here I shot John Osborn."

"What!"

The sense of loathing, even the sense of fear, with which I heard him make, so callously, this hideous confession, gave me strength to snap the spell with which he had seemed to bind me to the seat. I sprang from him with a cry. He was not in the least disturbed.

"Yes, it was in this very carriage. Some strange fate has led us hither. See, he was seated there." He pointed to the corner of the carriage which was behind my back. Turning, I glanced over my shoulder with an irrepressible shudder. "I almost think I see him now. Ah, John Osborn, where's your ghost? Would it not be a strange encounter were we ghosts to meet? He was seated there. I was seated just in front of him, behind you on the other side. There were four other men with us in the carriage. I think I see them. Would that all we ghosts were met again, so that we might react the scene before your eyes! I had won—ah! what a sum I'd won. John Osborn's temper was a little warped. He had said a nasty thing or two. He did not like to lose. I made an awkward pass with an ace of clubs. He caught me by the wrist, crying, 'Got you, you thief!' I looked round the carriage. I saw that the others were on his side. They all had lost, you see. I replied, 'Release my wrist.' 'Not,' he said, 'till you show me that card!' 'Take it!' I cried, and flung it in his face. I have not so sweet a temper as you, my friend. As I flung the card into his face, with my other hand I drew a revolver, which it was my custom to carry, so that any little difficulties which might arise might be settled without any unnecessary delay. I fired at John Osborn. Someone struck up my wrist. I missed. I fired again. That time the shot went home. It burst his eye. I flattered myself that it had entered into what he called his brain. He gave just one gasp, and dropped. I fancy that I hear him gasping now. It seemed as though the passage of his throat was choked with blood. There was a fight. They all went for me. I emptied my revolver. And then—then I was done."

He paused and smiled. I was cowering at the other end of the carriage—close to the spot on which, according to his account, this hideous tragedy had happened. And the chief actor was standing there in front of me, bringing back the scene, so that it all seemed to be happening before my very eyes. A wild desire flashed across my mind that an accident would happen, that the train would go off the line, so that in some way I might escape this man.

"See here." He was holding the pack of cards. He advanced towards me with them in his hand. I would have opened the door of the carriage and got out upon the footboard, if I had dared to turn. "As I fired a few drops spurted from John Osborn's eye and fell upon a card. See, here they stand as a record unto this day."

He held out to me a card with this horrid memorial upon its back. I tried to close my eyes, but the lids rebelled. I was compelled to look.

"I have often wondered where that first bullet went with which I missed. I was seated there. My wrist was struck up—so! I never heard that it was found. It was not produced against me at the trial. It must have gone in this direction. Let us see."

He began at a particular place to prod the cushioned back of the seat with the fingers of his right hand. I watched, as a man might be supposed to watch with his mental eye, the horrors of a nightmare. At last he gave an exclamation. "Oh! What have we here?"

Actually, with his finger-nails, he commenced to pick a hole in the cushion. What an officer of the railway company would have thought of the proceedings is more than I can say. I could but look on. With diabolical dexterity he tore a hole in the cushion, and into this hole he inserted his finger and thumb. With these he groped about inside. When he withdrew them he held them up.

"You see, my friend, that it is found. The missing bullet! It is a little shapeless, but I know it well." He pressed it to his lips. He advanced to me. "The first shot which I fired at John Osborn. Take it and keep it, my friend, in memory of me."

It was a nice keepsake to offer to a friend. Conceive a notorious murderer returning to these shades and offering you as a token of his regard and continuing esteem the hatchet, say, with which the deed was done.

"No," I gasped; "not I."

"Let me entreat you, my dear friend."

He pressed it on me, as though it were a gift of priceless worth.

"I won't."

"Consider the interest which attaches to this thing. It is not much to look at, but a little lump of shapeless lead, but consider the scene on which it figured. Oh, my friend, it might have burst John Osborn's eye—I almost think it grazed his head."

The train was slackening. Thank the powers! I thrust my arm through the window of the carriage, intending to grasp the handle of the door. Was I to have this reeking relic forced on me by a ghost! He misunderstood my meaning.

"Is it suicide you seek?"

"It—it's escape from you!"

"Then let us go together."

"How are we to go together, if I am to get away from you?"

"Ah, my friend, but that you cannot do."

"Cannot! I at least can try."

"Remove your grasp from the handle of that door, or I swear that I will not leave you, never for an instant, night or day, till you, like me, are dead."

He did not raise his tones, but his eyes were strangely light. Thank heaven, the train was slackening fast. In a few moments we should reach a station. Then—then we should see! He read my thoughts.

"You think to escape me when we reach the station. Bah, my friend, I shall disappear, but to return again!"

Still—we should see!

The train stopped. The platform was on the opposite side. I made a movement towards the other door. He stood in the way. Unmistakably then he was flesh and blood enough. I could not pass unless I forced him to one side. In my rage I grappled him. For an instant a struggle would have undoubtedly ensued, but in the very nick of time the opposite door was opened. Other passengers came in.

"Thank God!" I cried. "Someone has come at last."

I turned to see who the new-comers were. They were Messrs. Burchell and Armitage. In my surprise I lost my presence of mind again. The stranger stood like a figure of Mephistopheles, and smiled at me. He addressed himself to my late antagonists.

"Well, gentlemen, have you decided to make it a case for the police? I think, if you will take the advice of an unprejudiced on-looker, you would be wise if you did."

This insolence was more than I could stand.

"Gentlemen," I cried, "this—this demon has confessed to me that it was he who did it all."

I looked at Mr. Burchell and his friend. They met my troubled glances with what seemed, in my confusion, to be a meaningless stare. The stranger still continued to regard me with his careless smile.

"I am afraid," he murmured, "that you're an old, old hand."

What was I to say? How was I to refute his calumnies?

"Gentlemen, you will understand what sort of character this person is when I tell you that he informs me he's a ghost."

"A ghost!"

The exclamation came from Burchell, I was sure.

"Yes, a ghost. He tells me that he is Francis Farmer."

"Not Francis Farmer." The stranger touched me on the arm.

"You said that you were Francis Farmer."

"But Francis Farmer's ghost. The difference is essential. You will do me the favour to admit that I stated that I was Francis Farmer's ghost. I was prepared to show you where the rope was passed about my throat and the exact spot where the knife was thrust into my breast."

Was he in jest? His manner was all the time so calm that it was difficult to tell if he was in jest or earnest.

"If you're not a ghost then you're a raving lunatic."

"If I'm not a ghost."

He stood close in front of me, wagging his forefinger in my face. There was silence. For my part, I knew neither what to do nor say. At last, taking out my handkerchief, with it I wiped the perspiration from my brow.

"I think I'm going mad."

As I uttered these words in a tone which, I do not doubt, sufficiently suggested the confusion which was paralysing my mental faculties, there came a sound very like a titter from the other end of the carriage. I turned. Mr. Armitage was laughing. At first it seemed that he was endeavouring to restrain his mirth, but, as I continued to stare, it gathered force until it became a veritable roar. His example was contagious. Suddenly Mr. Burchell burst into peals of merriment. And directly he began the Mephistophelian stranger, bending double, sank back upon the seat and indulged in laughter to such an immoderate extent that I really thought that there was imminent danger that he would crack his sides. As I gazed at this amazing spectacle I daresay that, from one point of view, which was not mine, the expression of my face was comical enough. Was I going off my head? Or had fate destined me to journey down to Brighton in the society of lunatics?

"Oh, man!" gasped Mr. Burchell between his bursts of laughter, "don't look like that, or I shall die!"

I endeavoured, doubtless quite ineffectually, to assume an imposing attitude.

"Perhaps, gentlemen, when you have quite finished, you will condescend to favour me with an explanation of this extraordinary scene."

"If I'm not a ghost!" screamed the Mephistophelian stranger.

And off they all went again.

"There may be something comical in the present situation, and perhaps it is owing to some constitutional defect that I altogether fail to see it—but I don't!"

"Oh, man!" Mr. Burchell gasped again, "don't talk like that or you will kill me." All at once he rose and clapped me on the shoulder. "Why, don't you see it's all a joke?"

"A joke!"

I stared at him. Could he be joking?

"Yes, a practical joke, my boy."

"A practical joke!" I fancy that I was the colour of a boiled beetroot. "Perhaps, Mr. Burchell, you will explain what you mean by a practical joke."

"Why, we three were outside the door when the bobby was showing you the things at the Yard, and we heard him pitch the yarn about Francis Farmer and his cards, and how they were haunted, and all the rest of it, so we thought we'd have a game with you."

"A game with me? Still I fail to understand."

"I'm a clerk at the Yard, you know."

"Excuse me, but I do not know that you're a clerk at the Yard."

"Well, I am—in the Criminal Investigation Department. Of course they know me, and directly you went out I walked in as bold as brass and collared the cards." I remembered that someone had gone in as we came out. "I arranged that Bateman—this is Bateman"—he jerked his thumb towards the Mephistophelian stranger; that individual raised his hat, possibly to acknowledge the introduction—"should shadow you. He was to play the ghost. We had heard you tell the bobby that you were going down to Brighton by the 2.30 from Victoria, so we agreed that we would all go down together—this happening to be an afternoon on which the exigencies of the public service were not too pressing. We found you at the station, standing outside the carriage door. As I brushed past you on one side I slipped forty-seven cards into one pocket of your overcoat, and as Armitage brushed past you on the other side he slipped five cards into the other. I am a bit of a conjurer, and Armitage is a dab at all that kind of thing; so between us we manipulated the cards so that you were forced to win. And you won!—sixty pounds!—until the exposure came off in style. I say, old man, how did the ghost go off?"

The venerable Mr. Burchell turned to Mr. Bateman. For my part, not for the first time on that occasion, I felt too bewildered to speak. The modest Mr. Bateman smoothed his chin.

"I am afraid that for details of the ghost I must refer you to Mr. Ranken. But I may mention that I discovered that this was the actual carriage in which the tragedy took place, and that there was a memorial of the victim's fate on the back of one of the cards. I also alighted on the identical bullet which almost did the deed. What the railway company will say about the damage to their cushion is more than I can guess. It may turn out to be a couple of pounds."

"Mr. Burchell," I spluttered—I was reduced to such a condition that spluttering was all I was fit for—"I have only one thing to say to you, since your idea of what constitutes a joke seems to be so radically different to mine, and that is to remind you that you have been guilty of this extraordinary behaviour towards an entire stranger."

"Not an entire stranger!"

"Yes, sir, an entire stranger!"

"But henceforth one whom I hope to be allowed to call a friend."

He had the assurance to offer me, with an insinuating smile, his hand. I put my hands behind my back.

"There is one other point, Mr. Burchell. I won from you and your friend nearly sixty pounds. I returned it to you on an imputation being made of cheating. I presume that imputation is now withdrawn!"

"Of course. It was only a joke."

"In that case I must request you to repay me the amount I won!"

The fellow looked a little blank.

"Isn't it rather a curious case?"

"It is exactly on that account that I insist on your refunding what you obtained from me by means of what looks very like a subterfuge. I intend to present the amount, as a memorial of what you very rightly call a curious case, to the Home for Lost Dogs."

"A joke may be made a little expensive," murmured Mr. Burchell, as he counted out the coin.

"And the laugh, after all, be on the other side," said Mr. Armitage.

"The laugh," I answered, as I received my winnings, "is with the curs."

IV.

THE VIOLIN

I.

I am unable to say exactly why I bought it. I suspect that the purchase had a certain connection with the price. Three-and-sixpence for a "Full-sized violin, splendid instrument; rich tone; in perfect condition; best bow" did not strike me as extravagant. In fact, it tickled me. The shop looked liked a marine-store dealer's. There were old books, old boots, old bottles and jampots, cheek by jowl with that "fine violin." Had it—that "splendid instrument"!—been the last resource of a street musician, I wondered.

The proprietor of the shop appeared to be a lady. She was very dirty and very fat. I asked to see the fiddle. Taking it from the window, without a word she placed it in my hands. I am not a judge of violins. I should not know an Amati if I saw one. As to Stradivarius, Ernest told me the other day that violins—posthumous violins—of his manufacture are being turned out by the dozen, cheap, at a little town in Germany. I know very little more about Stradivarius than that. But Ernest does; he is a musician. And I thought it would amuse him if I made him a present of a "fine violin" and "best bow," which together cost me three-and-sixpence.

"How much for the case?"

The fiddle had been reclining on the lid of an ordinary baize-lined wooden case.

"Shilling," said the lady.

It did not occur to me that this was dear. The lady, however, seemed to suppose that my temporary silence conveyed a hint that it was. Because, presently, she observed—

"I won't charge you anything for the case."

"You will let me have the violin, the bow, and the case for three-and-sixpence?"

"Yes," said the lady.

I struck the bargain. As I bore away the prize it crossed my mind that there was something perhaps a little remarkable about that violin. A suspicion, say, of a receiver and a thief. One must purchase violins, bows, and cases at a very low price to be enabled to sell them at a profit for three-and-sixpence. My morality may have been lax, but I told myself that that was the lady's affair, not mine.

Ernest came to dinner that night.

"I have been buying you a present," I remarked as he came in.

He looked at me and laughed. I don't know if he imagined that my words contained a joke.

"A present? What sort of present?"

"A violin."

He glanced at the case upon the table.

"A violin! I say, uncle, I hope you haven't——"

"Been making a fool of yourself," he was on the point of saying, but he wisely stopped in time.

"Just look at that violin, and tell me what you think of it."

He opened the case. He glanced at the violin as it lay within; then he took it out. He handled it reverently. I have noticed that a genuine musician always does handle a fiddle—even a common fiddle—with a sort of reverence. He turned it over and over; he rapped its back softly with his knuckles; he peeped into its belly; he smelt it; he tucked it under his chin; then, putting it down, he fixed his eyes on me, with a light in them as of a smile.

"It's odd, but, do you know, I seem to have seen this violin somewhere before."

"Where have you seen it?"

"I fancy you know better than I. You have a little secret, uncle; come, what is it?"

"Is it a good violin?"

He drew the bow across it, tightening the strings. Then he

played a little exercise and a snatch of some quaint melody. Then he lowered it and looked at it with glistening eyes.

"It is a good violin."

"How much is it worth?"

"It depends upon the man who buys it, and upon the length of his purse. I hope you did not give a fancy price."

"Is it dear at three-and-sixpence?"

"Three-and-sixpence? You are joking."

"That is what I gave for it—fiddle, bow, case, and all."

He was turning it over and over.

"Where did you get it?"

"In a dirty shop, in a dirty street, off Lisson Grove."

"I feel sure I have seen it before."

"Do you recognise it by any mark?"

"I recognise it by every mark, and"—he touched it with the bow—"I recognise it by its voice."

The idea struck me as fanciful. In an orchestra of violins, all playing the same music, if one among them could be recognised by its voice, it seems to me that that violin would not be popular. But he *is* fanciful, is Ernest.

We went down to dinner. During the meal he told me about a young man in whom he was much interested. The name of this young man was Philip Coursault, and he, too, was a musician. According to Ernest, he was a strange and wild young man. Poor and proud. Impracticable, too. He relied upon his art for bread. And his art had failed him. Nor was it strange, from all that Ernest said. He had composed oratorios, and grand operas, and elaborate symphonies—all the heavy artillery of music. Ernest declared that genius had inspired them all—that unmistakable genius which rings clear and true. But an unknown young man cannot go into the market with a grand opera in his hand, and have it produced and paid for on the spot, especially when that young man is a crotchety young man, who has ideas of his own as to the way in which he wishes his work produced.

So Mr. Coursault found. Pupils he scorned. Ernest, for instance, had found him one or two. But his treatment of them was so extraordinary, that, as a matter of course, he lost them. He was never punctual. He kept them waiting hours. Sometimes he never came at all. And when he did appear he spent his breath, and exhausted a considerable vocabulary, in reviling them for their musical incompetence and crass-headed ignorance. Young lady pupils, too, and in the presence of their mothers! Mrs. Jones told him that he need not call again, which was not strange of Mrs. Jones, who did not pay to have the pleasure of hearing her daughter rated as being lower than the beasts that grovel.

As I have said, my nephew was telling me about that friend of his as we were eating our dinner. My dining-room is under the drawing-room, and in the drawing-room we had left that three-and-sixpenny fiddle. While the fish was being removed we distinctly heard, above our heads, the sound of a violin. It was Ernest who heard it first.

"You have a musician in the house."

"A musician? What do you mean?" For the change of themes was sudden. He was in the very middle of the story of his friend.

"Someone in the drawing-room is favouring us with a solo on the violin."

I listened. It was as he said. The sound was unmistakable. Someone was fiddling while we dined.

"Which of your maids is a mistress of harmony?"

"I was not aware that I had such a paragon. It is the first I have heard of it." Just then Rouse came in with the entree. "Rouse, who is in the drawing-room?"

The question appeared to surprise him.

"I am not aware, sir, that anyone is."

"There is someone. Go up, and see who it is."

Rouse went. Almost immediately the sound of playing ceased.

"Rouse has stopped the concert."

The man returned.

"Well, who was it?"

"No one, sir, is in the drawing-room."

"No one is, or no one was?"

"No one was, sir."

He smiled. I glanced at Ernest, and Ernest glanced at me. He seemed to be a trifle incredulous.

"Then who was that playing the violin?"

"I fancy, sir, that it must have been someone in the street."

If it was someone in the street then my ears had played me a curious trick. I thought it possible that Rouse was screening one of the maids. I chose to let it pass. I recurred to the subject of our conversation.

"Well, and about your friend?"

"He has disappeared."

"Disappeared?"

"Into thin air, like that performer on the violin." There was a suggestive twitching about the corners of Ernest's lips. I am afraid he thought that Rouse had been guilty of what may be politely termed a subterfuge. "More than a week ago he left his lodgings, with his violin-case in his hand, and he has not been heard of since. Ha! there is the performer back again."

There was. This time it sounded as though someone upstairs was tuning the violin.

"Rouse, who is upstairs?"

The man stood listening.

"I will go and see, sir. There was certainly no one there just now."

As before, the sound ceased almost directly he had left the room.

"Rouse has stopped the concert for the second time. Just as the fair musician was tuning up too!"

Ernest seemed to take it for granted that it was a maid. When Rouse reappeared in the room his bearing was a trifle disturbed.

"There was no one upstairs, sir. It must have been in the street."

I kicked at this.

"Come, Rouse, that won't do. Did it sound to you as though it were in the street?"

"It didn't, sir. But it must have been. There's no one upstairs, and the maids are all below. Besides, sir, there's no one in the house as plays the fiddle."

Ernest interposed. A smile was twinkling in his eyes.

"Where was the violin?"

"There's a violin-case upon the table, sir. I don't know if a violin is in it. The case is closed."

"I *left* it closed."

Ernest's tone was dry. I could see he had his doubts as to the man's veracity. Rouse has been in my service nearly thirty years, and I do not remember having once detected him in a lie. If he was screening anyone, I would have it out with him when my visitor had gone. I did not intend to humiliate a tried and faithful servant in the presence of my young gentleman. I returned to the erratic Mr. Coursault.

"I suppose when your friend disappeared he left a little bill behind."

"You little know Coursault! He had the most astonishing notions about money matters. Some time ago, when I knew he was in a tight place, I ventured to offer him a loan. I never ventured to repeat the offer."

"That sort of thing sounds very well, my boy, among boys! But *did* he leave a little bill?"

"Not a ghost of one. He paid up his week's lodging the very day he left. His landlady says that she believes he expended his last penny in doing so. She says, too, that she believes that he has been starving himself for weeks. I myself have noticed that he has become worn almost to a shadow. But, with such a man as that, what could you do? The more he needed help the farther he would shrink from it. In his uttermost extremity he would owe nothing, even to his dearest friend."

"Do you know his haunts?"

"I ought to—none better! But he has been seen nowhere, and by no one. As is the case with our friend upstairs, he has vanished into air."

I did not like the allusion myself. As for Rouse I saw he winced.

"Did this remarkable friend of yours burden himself with any portion of his baggage?"

"He took nothing but his violin."

"Was that his instrument?"

"All instruments were his. But it was his first love, and his last! He used to say of his violin that to him it was mother, father, wife, and friend."

As I was hesitating whether to smile at the folly of these young men Ernest half rose from his seat. He pointed upwards with his hand.

"Back again!"

As he put it the sound of the violin was back again.

"Listen! Don't trouble yourself, Rouse, to go upstairs and stop the concert, but stand a bit and listen. Let us hear of what metal the performer's made."

We listened the while Ernest held up his hand, as if commanding silence.

"Is that in the street?"

It did not *sound* as though it were. Ernest moved a little from the table.

"Come! let us go upstairs and surprise this fair musician. Possibly this is the case of a light which hitherto has shone unseen."

He went to the door. He opened it softly, so as to make no noise. With the handle in his hand he stood and listened.

"Hark! Let us hear what it is she, or he, is playing."

We all were silent, listening to the music, which came floating through the open door.

"Uncle!" Ernest turned to me. A startled look was on his face. "Surely—surely I know that air!"

It was strange to me. Quaint and sweet and mournful, like the refrain of an old-world song. I would I were a musician. I would write it here.

"It is a thing of Coursault's!"

Suddenly Ernest threw the door wide open. He went into the hall.

I went with him, amused at his eagerness. We stood at the foot of the stairs and listened.

"Do you mean that it is a composition of the friend of whom you have been telling me?"

"I do. I'll swear to it! I've heard him playing it!"

"Then, possibly, he has attained to greater fame than he imagines."

"But it's unpublished. Uncle, Coursault is upstairs!"

He grasped my arm with a degree of force which was a little disconcerting.

"Nonsense! Your friend would scarcely carry his eccentricity so far as to enter, uninvited and unannounced, the house of a perfect stranger—that is, unless he is burglariously inclined."

"I know his touch. Do you think that anyone but a master could play like that?"

It was fine playing. Very soft and delicate, but instinct with a strength, and a force, and a passion, which was perceptible even at our post of disadvantage at the foot of the stairs. A street musician would scarcely play like that—and a parlour-maid!

"It is one of his freaks. He has heard that I was here, and thought he would surprise me. The presence of the violin upon the table was a temptation beyond his strength—it is the man all over! Uncle, let's turn the tables—we'll surprise him!"

He began gingerly to ascend the stairs. I followed a step or two behind. About half-way up he stopped.

"I call that playing!"

So did I. As we mounted higher the sound was clearer. The voice of the violin was sweeter than any human voice I ever heard. Unwilling as I was to be disturbed at dinner—the food spoiling on the table!—I could not but acknowledge that, as Ernest said, it was the hand of a master which held that bow. A moment, listening, we paused; then again ascended. Sweeter and sweeter grew the music, until, just as we reached the uppermost stair, all at once it ceased.

"He has heard us! But, never mind, he can't escape us."

Ernest rushed forward. He threw the door wide open. He entered the room.

"Coursault! Philip! Hallo! Why—there's no one there!"

There did not seem to be. I followed pretty close upon my enthusiastic nephew's heels. The room was empty.

"He's in hiding. Come, you rogue, where are you? We know

you're here, Philip. Do you think I don't know your touch, and that queer song of yours? Come out, you beggar! Why, wherever can he be?"

Yes, where? My drawing-room contains no screen, no cupboard. Not an article of furniture behind which even a child could hide. Ernest, in his impetuous way, scoured round the room. It was empty. I confess that I was puzzled. We both of us stared round and round the room as though staring would resolve the mystery. Rouse was standing in the doorway. He, apparently, had taken French leave, and followed us upstairs. He spoke.

"There wasn't no one in the room when I came up just now. It was the same with me. I heard the fiddling most distinct as I was coming up the stairs; when I reached the landing it stopped. I made sure that whoever it was had heard me, and I should find him in the room; but when I opened the door there wasn't no one there. You see, sir, although it didn't sound as though it was, it must have been in the street."

"In the street, you idiot! Do you think I'm deaf?"

I mildly interposed—

"But, my dear fellow, there is the violin in its case upon the table. It doesn't look to me as if the case had even been opened."

Ernest made a dash at it. He opened the lid. He took out the fiddle. As he did so he gave a start which was quite dramatic. He stared at it as though he had never seen such a thing as a fiddle before.

"It's Coursault's violin!"

His exclamation startled me. Coursault's violin! It reminded me of Mr. Box's remark to Mr. Cox, "Have you a strawberry mark on your left arm?" "No." "Then you are—*you are* my long-lost brother." The recognition was too opportune.

"Come, Ernest! Ernest! don't strain the thing too far. You recognise it, I presume, by the catgut and the bridge."

Ernest paid no heed to my admittedly feeble attempt at chaff. I am no great hand at badinage. He continued to hold the fiddle in front of him with both his hands, glaring at it as if it were a ghost.

"It's Coursault's violin. I thought I knew it when I saw it first. I know it now. It's Philip's!"

"How do you know it's Philip's?"

He did not directly answer me. Placing the fiddle very carefully upon the table, he stood for a moment in apparent agitation.

"Uncle, there is some mystery. Don't laugh at me!" I daresay I was smiling. "Something has happened to Coursault."

"From the character you have given the man the thing is very possible, and *still* there may be no mystery."

"Some time ago Coursault wrote the words of a little song, which he set to music. The thing was in commemoration of certain pleasant days which he and I had spent together. I am nearly certain that no one ever heard of its existence except we two. He called it 'Where the Willows cast their Shade.' It is that which we have just heard played."

"'Where the Willows cast their Shade'—rather a curious title for a song; but, even in titles, curiosities seem to be the mode. Are you sure it was the same?"

"Am I sure! It was the quaintest thing—like all he wrote, even the merest trifles, peculiarly characteristic. Is it not strange that I should hear Coursault's song, whose very existence was known only to him and to me, played on Coursault's violin?"

I stared.

"Do you mean to say that the man has been in this room, and at our approach, to use your own phrase, vanished into air?"

Ernest became preternaturally grave; he is the funniest lad.

"Uncle, strange things have happened."

"They have. As witness my being disturbed in the middle of my dinner. How on earth do you know that that three-and-six-penny affair *is* Coursault's violin?"

"That is easily solved. We will go to the shop at which you bought it, and ascertain from whom they got it."

We went, there and then, with the dinner not half-eaten. Rouse must have had doubts about my sanity. I have declared, not once, but a hundred times, that not for the Queen of England would I be disturbed at dinner. Yet, before we had even eaten the entree, that young man—whom I had invited to dinner—dragged me from my own house on a dirty night, and put me into a hansom, and drove me through the slums of London in search of a rag-shop. As the vehicle rattled over the stones I reflected upon what could be brought about by the expenditure of such a sum as three-and-sixpence—the rule of a lifetime shattered at a blow! The cabman could not find the street. I did not know its name; how I originally chanced on it is more than I can say. I am not in the *habit* of wandering in the purlieus of Lisson Grove. We went poking out of one hole and into another. I should think we must have penetrated at least half a dozen when, just as I really believe the cabman was on the point of insulting us, we lighted, not only on the street, but on the shop as well.

The lady was in—the *same* lady. A little dirtier, perhaps, but still the same. My nephew conducted the negotiations.

"We have called about a violin which this gentleman purchased here this afternoon."

The lady stared at us with a watery, a gin-and-watery, eye.

"Could you tell me from whom you got it?"

The lady's response was oracular.

"Perhaps I could, and perhaps I couldn't."

"The fact is that I have reason to believe that it belonged to a friend of mine, whose whereabouts I am very anxious to discover."

"That don't make no odds to me."

"But it makes considerable odds to me. Such odds that I am willing to give half a sovereign if you will tell me from whom you got it. If, for instance, he was a stranger to you, could you describe his appearance?"

"Well, I could, and that's sacred truth. Good reason I have to remember him."

"Indeed?"

Ernest's tone was sympathetic.

"'Cause I gave more for that there fiddle than what I sold it for."

"I should think that you are hardly in the habit of doing that, are you?"

Perhaps this time there was the suspicion of a sarcastic intonation.

"I ain't. I shouldn't make much of a living if I was, should I? I
don't mind saying it now I've sold the thing, but that there fiddle
ain't all there."

"Do you mean that part of it is missing?"

"No, I don't. I don't believe in ghostesses, nor none of them
there rubbishes, but if there ain't a ghost about that there fiddle, I
never heard of one."

I glanced at Ernest; Ernest glanced at me. The lady continued.

"It's got a trick of playing tunes all by itself, when there ain't
no one there to play 'em."

"No one there to play them! Of course, you're joking."

"I ain't joking. I ain't a joking sort." (To do her justice, I am
bound to own that she didn't look as though she were.) "The very
first night it played a tune, and it's played the same tune every
blessed night since it's been in the shop."

"The same tune—always the same? Would you know it if
you heard it?"

"I ought to. I've heard it often enough, Lord knows; and I
ain't over and above anxious to hear it again."

"Is this it?"

Ernest whistled a little air. It was the same which we had
heard being played as we were ascending the stairs. Quite an uncomfortable change took place in the lady's bearing. Hardly had
Ernest whistled a couple of notes than, with a sort of groan, she
shrank back against the wall.

"That's it! Stop it! It gives me creeps and crawlers!"

"Now, tell me, from what sort of person did you purchase the
violin?"

"A little chap, about up to your shoulder—the queerest-look-
ing little chap ever I see. He had long black hair, and big eyes—
ah, as big as bull's-eye lanterns!—and that there wild, they made
him look stark mad. He was that there thin—anybody could see
he hadn't had a square meal for a month of Sundays. He says,
'What'll you give me for my fiddle?' I wondered if it was a swap

that he was after. 'Do you mean how much money?' I says. 'Yes,' he says; 'how much money?' 'I'll give you five bob,' I says. 'Five bob!—for my fiddle!' He gives a kind of laugh, though it wasn't the sort of laugh what did you good to hear, not by no manner of means. 'I'll take it,' he says. So, after all, she hadn't given so much more for the thing than she had sold it for. "I was took back. Course I see it was worth more than five bob. But it wasn't my business to tell him so—'ardly! I hands him the pieces. 'Let me play a last tune upon my fiddle,' he says. He picks it up, and he plays that same tune which you've just now whistled. He could play, he could! Then he kisses the fiddle and he goes away."

The lady paused; we stood silent.

"I puts the fiddle on that shelf just where you're standing. That night I woke up sudden. I couldn't make out what it was had woke me. Then I heard a noise. First I thought it was cats. But it wasn't no cats; it was someone fiddling, right in the shop! 'Well,' I says, 'blame their impudence, if someone ain't busted in.' So I comes downstairs without my shoes and stockings on, and I stands outside the door what leads into the shop, and I listens. If it wasn't the same tune the little chap had played! 'If this ain't good,' I says to myself. 'Blow me if he ain't come back after his fiddle! I'll fiddle him!' I has the lamp in my hand, and I opens the door sudden, and I goes in."

The lady paused.

"You may believe me or you mayn't, but there wasn't no one there—ne'er a one. I couldn't make it out, I tell you that. As I was going forward I all but steps upon the fiddle and the bow what's a lying on the floor. 'Now then,' I says; 'where's the party as put you there?' Believe me, or believe me not, there wasn't a creature in the place. It ain't a large shop, you see, and I routs in every corner. I looks at the window and the door. The shutters was up, and the door was locked and bolted just as I left it. I thought it queer; but I thought it queerer when the same thing comes the next night, and the next, and the next. It preys upon my mind so, not being used to nor yet partial to ghostesses and such-like rubbishes, that I says to myself, I'll get rid of the thing, even if I does it at a loss."

As we were going away I said to Ernest—

"Rather a curious story that of the lady's."

Ernest was sitting back in the cab. He seemed to be lost in reflection.

"Very." There was a momentary silence. "I told you it was Coursault's violin. That was Philip, the queer little man with the long black hair and the great big eyes. I used to half fear sometimes that in those big eyes genius was struggling with insanity; he was at times so strange. 'Starved for a month of Sundays'— Philip! What a wrench to have parted with his violin—how bitterly he must have been amused by her offer of five shillings. He played his last tune and kissed it—Philip!"

We dismissed the cabman at the corner of the square. The night had become fine. We walked together towards my house. We were distant from it, perhaps, twenty yards, when Ernest, pausing, laid his hand upon my arm.

"Listen!" There is little traffic in the square at night. All was still. "He is playing!"

For a second or two I did not grasp my nephew's meaning. But, as I strained my ears to catch the slightest sound, I understood it better, for I caught the sound of a fiddle. It was very faint, so faint as to be scarcely audible. But it was unmistakable.

"Come," said Ernest; "let us go nearer."

We approached the house. In front of it we paused. Beyond doubt the music came from within, and from an upper room; the same quaint melody which we had heard before, played by a master's hand.

"I wonder why he always plays that tune?"

I was unable to supply the information. Frankly, I was becoming a little bewildered. With the lady at the rag-shop, I had no faith in "ghostesses and such-like rubbishes," but the thing was getting curious.

I opened the front door with my latchkey. An unusual spectacle greeted us as we entered the hall. All the maids were grouped together in a little crowd, guarded, as it were, by the stalwart Rouse. There was no necessity to ask the cause—it was the music in the drawing-room. Rouse, however, seemed to think that an explanation *was* required.

"It's not my fault, sir; I couldn't get them to stop in the kitchen. They seem to think that there's a spirit, sir, upstairs. The playing has been going on for half an hour and more."

"Don't let me have any nonsense. I'm ashamed of you. Are you afraid of a fiddle?"

The cook ventured on a meek remonstrance.

"It isn't the fiddle, sir; it's the fiddler."

I drove them down; Rouse, in his sheepishness, almost treading on the women's petticoats. Then I turned to Ernest.

"I, like the lady we have just been interviewing, am not partial to ghosts. With your permission, this time I will lead the way upstairs."

I led the way, Ernest following closely after. The music continued—always the same quaint air. It was pretty; but the player must have found that the absence of variety became a trifle monotonous. On this occasion, even when we reached the landing, there was no cessation. The fiddler still fiddled.

"Apparently we have managed to remain unheard. Now for your eccentric friend."

With a quick movement I opened the drawing-room door. Ernest and I entered almost side by side. For an instant, after our entrance, the playing continued. I saw that the violin was raised, I saw that the bow was being drawn across the strings. But who held the violin, and who handled the bow, there was no evidence—visual evidence—to prove. If we could trust our eyes, the room was empty. All at once, before we could say a word, or offer any sort of interposition, the playing ceased. The violin and the bow were placed upon the table—not dropped, but laid carefully down. And all was still.

II.

The next day there was a small party on the river. The party consisted of three: an old gentleman—a complacent old gentleman, who carried his complacence so far as to allow himself to be cast for the role of "gooseberry"; a young gentleman, his nephew;

and, not to put too fine a point on it, a young lady. This young lady's name was Minnie—Minnie West. There is reason to suspect that she was the cause of the party.

We started—it is probably unnecessary to observe that *I* was the complacent old gentleman—from Hurley, and we paddled up the stream—that is to say, Ernest paddled, the young lady steered, and I looked on. We kept it up some time, this paddling; but at last Ernest drew the boat into the shore. We landed—a hamper and ourselves. We lunched under the shade of the trees.

While we lunched Ernest persisted—persisted is the word—in conversing on a subject which was scarcely appropriate either to the occasion or the scene—the subject of his lost friend and his phantom violin. One does not wish to dwell on morbid subjects when one is lunching by the crystal waters; but Ernest, apparently, did not see it; and, oddly enough, what he did not see, it seemed that Miss West could not see either. When we had finished, and done justice to the fare, the young gentleman asked a question.

"Do you know why I have brought you here?"

Really the question did not need an answer. The reply was evident. The spot was charming. Sufficient shade above, mossy verdure underneath, and all around us, except upon the river side, tall bracken, which completely obscured us from the vulgar gaze. Ernest supplied an answer of his own.

"Do you remember that air which we heard played upon the violin? Do you remember that I told you it was a song of Coursault's, which he called, 'Where the Willows cast their Shade'? I told you, too, that it was written to commemorate some pleasant days which we had spent together. Those pleasant days were spent upon the river, and the pleasantest of all those pleasant days were spent where we are now."

"Ernest!"

As she called upon the young man's name the lady gave a little shudder. It must be allowed that his manner was distinctly sombre.

"It was a favourite place with him. He used to rave about it in that raving way of his. He used to say that here he would like to die and be buried. He came here often when he was alone, and it was here he wrote that song. You see it is here that the willows cast their shade."

He raised his hand with a gesture which was distinctly gruesome. Looking up I noticed, for the first time, that the trees above us were willow trees.

"I wonder why it is that the violin always plays that song?"

And there came an echo from the young lady—

"I wonder!"

As she echoed the young gentleman's interrogation she leaned back against the tree—a willow tree—and put her hand behind her to pluck the bracken. She had to stretch out some distance to do this. Suddenly she withdrew her hand with a half-stifled exclamation.

"What's the matter?" inquired the younger gentleman.

He wore quite an appearance of concern, being still in that stage in which a tight shoe upon the lady's foot would give him corns. Most transitory stage—too sweet to last!

"I—I thought I touched something."

She looked startled. She put her hand behind her rather more gingerly than she had done before. Instantly she sprang to her feet in a state of most unmistakable dismay.

"Ernest, there is someone there! I touched his hand."

She stood, trembling all over, a pretty picture of distress—in tan shoes and a white pique gown.

"What do you mean?" cried Ernest.

"You are dreaming," murmured I.

We rose together. But he was the quicker. Going behind the willow tree, he parted the bracken with his hands.

"There is, by George! What are you doing there, sir? Are you drunk? Why——" He stooped down. "Good God! He's dead!"

Suddenly, with a loud cry, he fell upon his knees.

"It's Coursault!" . . .

It was. Lying dead among the bracken— "Where the Willows cast their Shade."

We thought at first that he had been the victim of foul play. But subsequent medical examination showed that he had died of aneurism of the heart, brought on by want of nourishment—in other words, starvation—and physical exhaustion. He was nothing else but skin and bone, and it appeared that he had walked from London—it almost seemed without taking rest or food upon his way, for the identical five shillings were found in his pockets for which he had sold his violin.

The supposition was that when he had sold his violin, and played on it his last tune, he had started, possibly in some spirit of half-madness, for the identical spot which that tune commemorated, and had reached it but to die.

On the previous evening, after that final solo with which we had been favoured by the unseen musician I had placed the violin and the bow in the case, and the case upon the topmost bookshelf in my library. When I came home from that river party an accident had happened. The case had fallen from the bookshelf to the floor. In falling, the lid had opened—the violin had tumbled out. The result was that the instrument, which must have struck with surprising force against some piece of furniture, had been shivered into splinters. These we collected, and with the bow, which was also broken, we placed in Philip Coursault's coffin. The dead man and his fiddle were lowered together into the grave.

V.

THE TIPSTER

AN IMPOSSIBLE STORY

I.

"I've done it again! This is really rum!"

Mr. Gill tilted his hat towards the back of his head. Philip Major had come upon him in the Strand, standing in the middle of the pavement, staring at the fifth edition of the *Evening Glimmer*.

"That's what it is—rum! I can't help thinking, you know, that there must be something wrong."

"What's the matter?"

"Well," Mr. Gill put his hand up to his mouth: he coughed. "I've placed the first three horses for the Chichester Handicap. Here they are, large as life." Mr. Gill pointed to a paragraph in the paper. "Mary Anne, 1; The Duke, 2; and Coriolanus, 3; just as I sent 'em to my clients!"

Mr. Major laughed.

"That's all right. I thought that you professed to send three winners, for seven-and-sixpence, isn't it?"

"But you don't understand. Yesterday I done the same. I placed the first three in the Billingsgate Stakes; sent 'em to every one of my correspondents, I did, upon my Dick! Why, Mr. Major, I've been a tipster—ah, I don't know how many years—and as for placing the first three, even at a donkey race, why, I haven't come within a million mile of 'em." Mr. Gill glanced round. There was something curious in his glance. "But it isn't only horses. There's something up with me all round. Why———"

He caught Mr. Major by the arm. They were by the pit entrance to the Lyceum Theatre. A hansom went rushing by.

"There's an old gentleman with a white hat crossing Wellington Street—that cab will knock him down!"

The cab whirled round the corner. An instant after there was a sudden tumult—someone had been run over. Mr. Major stared at Mr. Gill.

"I say, Gill!"

"I've been like that for the last day or two, but this afternoon I'm worse than ever. I keep seeing things."

"Excuse me, sir." Mr. Gill stopped and addressed a passer-by. "Your wife's just going to slip down the steps which lead to the nursery landing; and as she's in a delicate situation, if I was you I'd hurry home."

The passenger, a dignified-looking gentleman about forty years of age, appeared to be, not unnaturally, surprised at being addressed in such a manner by a perfect stranger.

"Who are you?"

"My name's Gill, sir—Thompson Gill. As your wife's going to be prematurely overtaken, all owing to a piece of soap which that there careless gal of yours has left upon the stairs, I thought you'd like me to mention it."

"Gill," observed Mr. Major, as they crossed the road towards Waterloo Bridge, "you're drunk."

"Not me. I haven't had so much as a drop this day. It's something wrong with the works, that's what it is. I keep seeing visions, or something. If I'd been a drinker I should say I'd got 'em. But it isn't that, I know."

"Perhaps you're going to be a prophet after all—not three winners for seven-and-six, but the bona fide article."

"That's what I'm afraid of," sighed Mr. Gill.

When they reached the centre of the bridge Mr. Major drew Mr. Gill aside into one of the embrasures.

"Come, Gill, I'll give you a chance to exercise your prophetic gifts. Am I going to sell that picture of mine which the President and Fellows have done me the honour to sky in their exhibition at Burlington House?"

Mr. Major asked the question lightly—but there was a suspicion of earnestness beneath the lightness. Mr. Gill paused before replying. His eyes looked out over the stream.

"Yes, you are."

"Oh, I am, am I? When?"

"Next week."

"So soon as that, my Gill! Come, we're getting on. And who will be the purchaser?"

"A gal."

"A gal!" Mr. Major started. "I presume by that you mean a young lady?"

"A dark gal, with big black eyes, and black hair curling all over her head. She'll go up to the picture and she'll say, 'So this is it, is it? They've hung it as well as it deserves. So this is the man who presumes to teach me painting? He can draw, but he will never paint—never.' Then she will look at the picture again, and she'll say, 'What a fool I am!' Then she'll go to a table, and she'll ask how much the picture is. And the man will say, 'Fifty pounds!' And she'll say to herself, 'That's more than the frame is worth.' Then she'll take out a sort of pocket-book, and she'll hand over five ten-pound notes. And the man'll say, 'What name?' And she'll say 'Briggs.'"

At this point Mr. Major started again—this time most perceptibly.

"What name?"

"She'll say 'Briggs.'"

"It's a lie!"

"It's not a lie. She'll say 'Briggs.' And to herself she'll say, 'I'm not going to flatter him by letting him know I've bought it. He's fool enough already.'"

Mr. Gill paused. Mr. Major stared at him. The little man had spoken with a quiet intensity which, in its way, was most effective. All the time he had kept his eyes fixed upon the stream.

"Anything more, Mr. Gill?"

"About the picture?"

"About the picture. Can you tell me, for instance, whether the name of the lady who is destined to become, in so flattering a way, my patron, really is Briggs?"

"Wait a moment. When she goes away she'll tell the cab-driver to drive to Campden Hill Gardens." Again Mr. Major started. "When she gets home she'll have a letter addressed to" —Mr. Gill hesitated—"to Miss Davidson."

"Oh! To Miss Davidson."

Mr. Major's voice was a trifle husky.

"The handwriting on the envelope will be very fine and small. The postmark will be Oban."

Mr. Major caught Mr. Gill by the shoulder.

"Gill!—stop! That will do! Come, let's get home. Gill, I should say that you were going off your nut."

"I don't know about going off my nut exactly, but there's something wrong with the works, I do believe."

"You don't suppose that I believe a syllable of all that nonsense you've been talking?"

"It's gospel truth, every word of it."

When they had gone a few steps further Mr. Gill stopped short.

"Mr. Major, there's a man coming along the road, in a brown check coat, who's going to pay you half a sovereign which he owes you."

As a matter of fact, when they had proceeded about a hundred yards along the Waterloo Road they were approached by a man in a brown check coat, which was decidedly the worse for wear, who, at sight of them, pulled up.

"Hollo, Major! The very man I wanted to see. I think that makes us straight."

He thrust his hand into his waistcoat pocket. In the outstretched palm which he held out to Mr. Major was—half a sovereign! That gentleman stared at the man, and at the coin, in undisguised amazement.

"Hollo, Aldridge!"

"Rather unexpected, isn't it? I thought it would be—borrowed money back from me! Don't apologise, old chap! I've had a stroke of luck—so there you are!"

Mr. Major continued to stare at the coin after the man had gone.

"I say, Gill, this is very queer."

"That's what bothers me. It is uncommon queer."

II.

It was the Tuesday morning afterwards. Mr. Major was at the house in Campden Hill Gardens in the capacity of painting-master. Towards the close of the lesson he asked his pupil a question.

"Have you been to the Academy yet?"

Miss Davidson was in the enjoyment of her own fortune. It may therefore be taken for granted that she was of age. But she was more than that; she was in touch with those teachings of the age which tells us that a young woman can do without a chaperon. Her painting lessons were, as a rule, sacred to herself and her master—which, perhaps, enabled her to better concentrate her mind upon her searchings after art.

"Not yet. I suppose I ought to have gone, but I really seem to have so much else to do."

Mr. Major said nothing. Perhaps he felt that even the most earnest searcher after art might be excused from attending that Academy. Anyhow, that afternoon he himself was there. It was not his first visit by any means. He could have pointed out blindfold where all the most notorious pictures were. The position of one especial canvas he knew particularly well. It was in a far corner of the room, in a bad light, just above the line—exactly the position in which an indifferent work by an unknown man would be most likely to escape the casual visitor's eye. Mr. Major felt this very strongly as he approached that corner. The rooms were crowded—though not, on that occasion, overcrowded—but just there there was not a soul. Apparently his picture was not attracting the least attention—nothing is more unsatisfactory to a struggling artist than to be aware of that. He advanced towards the slighted work of art with an uncomfortable feeling about the pit of his stomach. Suddenly he started. He hurried forward. The frame was starred!

"By Jove!" he exclaimed out loud. "Gill was right; it's sold."

In his surprise he was unconscious of the fact that he was staring at the frame as though he were paralysed by the merits of the painting. But others saw him. More people came to stare. Then he enjoyed that rarest of all rare pleasures—the pleasure which the gentleman enjoyed in Lord Lytton's novel, *The Disowned*—the pleasure of hearing his work criticised with perfect frankness.

A gentleman made an observation to a lady who was evidently his wife. "Don't care for that kind of thing," he said.

"I think it's silly," she replied.

They moved on. A gentleman—obviously a country gentleman—stared at the picture for, perhaps, two seconds.

"What's it all about?" he inquired of a friend.

"Don't ask me. Some stuff or other."

And they moved on. Then two parsons commented, as they went by. One of them was a dictatorial sort of person. He pointed out the picture with his umbrella.

"If I wanted an example to point the remark that I was just making, there is one. I say that art in England must be at a low ebb indeed when they're obliged to admit that sort of thing."

"The colouring's not bad," ventured his companion, who did not appear to be quite so critical.

"Colouring! Pooh! Properly speaking, there is no colouring—that is, if you mean colour."

"Shows some idea of drawing."

"Drawing! After that, my good fellow, we'd better go and look at something else—say a Punch and Judy."

"Mr. Major."

As the two parsons were moving off—possibly in search of that Punch and Judy—the lucky artist, who seemed to have so hit the popular fancy, heard himself addressed by name. Turning, there was Miss Davidson. Mr. Major was momentarily confounded.

"Where is your picture, Mr. Major?"

"Here is my daub."

"Daub?" The pupil seemed surprised. The master's manner was certainly ferocious. "Why do you call it a daub?"

"I only call it what other people call it, and some fool or other has bought it!"

"Mr. Major!" Miss Davidson drew herself back with distinct frigidity. Her naturally pale face, if possible, grew paler. Mr. Major immediately perceived how grossly he had blundered.

"Forgive me, Miss Davidson. I mean that some good friend, with whom charity is esteemed a virtue, has been generous to me."

"But why should you suppose anything of the kind? Why should you suppose that a person would buy a picture he did not like, and for more than it is worth?"

"Why, Miss Davidson, ah, why?" He stood leaning on the hand-rail, his eyes on her. Her eyes she kept upon the catalogue. "It sounds ridiculous; but do you know that I am acquainted with a person who thinks himself a prophet, and he told me that this week someone would buy my picture."

"He need not be a prophet to have told you that." Lifting her eyes she looked him full in the face. "Hadn't we better be moving? Someone else may wish to look at the picture as well as we." She smiled as she said this. He flushed. "But what made you say so bitterly just now that your picture was a daub?"

"I had been the unintentional listener of the public verdict. Besides"—he flung back his head with a petulant gesture—"do I not know myself that it is a daub! Do I not know what I meant it to be, and what it is! Do I not know how far it falls short of what I dreamed!"

She was silent for a moment. Then she asked a question.

"I have more than once wanted to ask you, 'Do you think there is nothing worth living for but art?'"

"Indeed, I don't."

"I thought you didn't."

There was a dryness in her tone which stung him, especially after the glance with which his words had been pointed. He spoke coldly.

"There is only one thing better."

"Frankly, I am not quite sure what is my own mind upon the

matter. There is so much talked about that sort of thing. But really I doubt if there is anything better worth living for than art."

"For a man there is a woman."

"You mean, I suppose, that for a man there are women."

"Miss Davidson! Don't say that." He put his hand upon her arm. His face was eager and flushed. "That, if you like, is the cant of the day. There is only one woman for a man."

She laughed.

"Suppose I put the converse, and say that for a woman there are men."

"Miss Davidson! That is not true!"

She laughed again, this time a little nervously.

"Don't let us stand in the middle of the room. Pray let us keep moving on."

Just then some acquaintances came up—acquaintances of hers, but not of his. He left her with them. He wandered off into the sculpture gallery, which, so far as the general and appreciative public were concerned, he found, as usual, a howling wilderness.

"I wonder what I could do to win her love?"

This was the question which that young man addressed to himself among those lonely statues.

"I wonder if it could be won? By me? If it is won already?"

As this last thought occurred to him he actually trembled, which showed that, as a young man, he was something out of the common.

"One thing is necessary, that I should not come to her a pauper. I don't want the tale of the Lord of Burleigh told in just one more new edition. I wonder if I could do something to make money?"

Mr. Philip Major had the first-floor apartments in a house in Stamford Street. Mr. Thompson Gill had the ground-floor rooms. Thus chance, or necessity, had made the tipster and the artist acquainted. That night Mr. Major entered Mr. Gill's sitting-room, an uninvited guest.

"Well, Gill, old man, been doing anything more in the prophetic line?"

Mr. Gill, his hands in his trouser-pockets, was seated, staring into vacancy.

"Mr. Major"—he got up; with a mysterious air he approached his visitor—"I do believe there's something wrong."

"How wrong? Has the prophetic tap run dry?"

"I tell you straight, I wish it had run dry. It's quite upsetting me, that's what it's doing. What do you think of the Exmouth Stakes?"

"What about the Exmouth Stakes?"

"I placed the first three horses; that's what's about it, and I sent 'em to all my correspondents—I'm making all their fortunes. I am, straight. Why, you know, I'm a tipster; that's what I am, and I ain't ashamed to own it. But though I've been a tipster, I don't know how many years, I mention it to you in confidence that I don't know no more about horses than you do—perhaps not so much. The way I do in general's this. I take the list of probable starters, and I send one horse to one cove, and the second horse to another cove, and so on right through the whole boiling. So somehow, you see, I'm bound to strike the winner, and I don't forget to mention it! But of late I've been upsetting all my regular arrangements. Only the other day I sat down to sort out the bag of tricks as usual, but, if you'll believe me, I couldn't do it. Do you think I could send every man a different animal? Not me! I sent the same animal to all the lot of 'em; and the queerest part of it is, the beggar won!

"When I see that in the evening paper, I tell you I did feel funny. When, the next day, I began dealing them round again, I couldn't do it no more than before. I sent the first three horses to every half-a-crown subscriber, and they romped in just exactly as I'd placed 'em. That was on Friday, in the Billingsgate Stakes; on Saturday, when I saw you in the Strand, I'd just done the same in the Chichester Handicap. Yesterday was Monday, and there wasn't no racing; but to-day in the Exmouth Stakes I've placed the first three horses in the exact order that they came past the post. What do you think of that for a record? Wouldn't you say that there was something wrong with the works?"

"It does you great credit, Gill."

"It isn't so much the horses, I shouldn't mind if it was only them, but it's everything. I can't think of what has happened, but everything that's going to happen I can see quite well."

"Are you in earnest?"

"Try me and see! If there's anything you want to know about what's going to happen in the middle of next week, apply here for information. It's awful—I'm getting a regular freak of nature."

"Do you know, if what you say is correct, you could easily make your fortune—and mine?"

"I suppose I could."

"If, for instance, you were to act on your own tips."

"Just so."

"Then why don't you?"

"I'll tell you one reason why I don't—because I can see what's coming."

"But if you can, that's exactly the reason why you should."

"There's one thing coming to-morrow, and that's an end of me."

"What do you mean?"

"By this time to-morrow I'll be dead."

"You're carrying it too far, my friend."

"I am carrying it too far—I feel I am! I know I am! That's where it is! I don't only see the things I want to see, but I see the things I don't want to see; and I see that by this time to-morrow I'll be dead—ah, dead, sitting in that chair."

Mr. Gill pointed to the chair from which he had lately risen. Mr. Major eyed him. There certainly was something curious about the little man, although he spoke with a matter-of-fact straightforwardness which deprived his words of half their singularity.

"Don't be an ass, Gill! Perhaps you can tell me what, by this time to-morrow night, will have happened to me?"

"You! You'll have made your fortune."

Mr. Major laughed at this.

"Thanks awfully. Perhaps you can assist me with a tip or two?"

"That's just what I'm going to do. I'm going to give you all to-morrow's winners. You'll go down. You'll take every farthing you can beg, borrow, or steal. You'll put the whole pile on the first race at starting prices. You'll put the whole pile on again, with all your winnings, on the second race; and you'll do the same on every race; and at the end of the day you'll have won—ah, what a pot!"

"Yes, what a pot! But suppose, in this going the whole hog system of yours, once, only once, I should happen to lose? Where shall I be then?"

"You won't lose; you will win. Take a piece of paper and write down the names of the winners."

Smilingly, perching himself on the edge of the table, Mr. Major took an envelope out of his pocket. He prepared to write upon the back of it. "Now then, my Gill."

Mr. Gill took a newspaper from the table. For a moment he studied it attentively.

"It's a long programme to-morrow. There are seven events upon the card. The first is at half-past one; mind you're there. The Blenheim Plate—Ladybird will win that; write it down." Mr. Major wrote it down, still smiling. "The Windsor Stakes— King Bruce. The Maiden Plate—Sweet Violet. The Churchill Handicap—Devil's Own. The Visitors' Plate—Estrella. The Hunt Cup—Ballet Girl." Mr. Gill folded up the newspaper. "Got 'em all down? No mistakes, you know. That's six races—that'll be enough for you; you'll have made your pot by then—and what a pot it will be!" Mr. Major, as he echoed the other's words, still smiled.

"Yes, what a pot it will be!"

III.

"Yes, what a pot it will be!"

The words were still ringing in Mr. Major's ears when, on the morrow, he went down by train to that suburban racecourse. He had not carried out Mr. Gill's advice to the bitter end; he had not stolen, but he had begged and borrowed. He had applied for help in as many quarters as he could manage in the limited time at his disposal. He had told some tall tales to get it too. He had pledged his credit to the straining-point. He had in his pockets a sum of money which for him was fabulous. If he lost it he would be without a farthing in the world, almost without the hope of one.

He was quite aware that he was mad, that was the joke of it. No one knew better than he that for a man who knew nothing of horses to go punting on the turf was an act of simple insanity. Nor did he suppose that the position was improved by the fact that he was about to back the fancies of an avowed humbug who, he himself believed, was at least half imbecile. Yet he never hesitated for a moment to carry out what he knew to be the folly in his brain.

The train was crowded—by that fragrant crowd which travels to a London racecourse, even in the specials. The conversation was horsey. Tips were freely offered. Mr. Major heard the chances of the animals whose names he had written on the back of an old envelope canvassed by persons who were without doubt much better judges of a horse than he. He paid not the slightest heed. All through the din of conversation Mr. Gill's words were ringing in his ears—"What a pot it will be!"

And wherever he looked he saw, as in a waking dream, a woman's face. This young man was simply mad. The most amazing nonsense was whirling in his head. Win a fortune—he'd win her. The two ideas were surging though his head in a sort of chime. He loved the woman—with a sort of honest pride he told himself how earnestly he loved her. He'd make his pile, and tell of his love. And to make his pile he had begged, and borrowed—and lied—all on the strength of an old fool's yarning.

"Would you like a tip, sir?—for the first race, sir? I'll give you a certainty, sir, for a shilling. I'd put it on myself if I had it, sir—so help me, I would."

This was the greeting which he received as he alighted from the train from an individual who evidently thought that he was green.

When he reached the course he made straight for the ring, and for a "leviathan penciller," whom, strangely enough, he knew by sight as well as by name. No welsher for him.

"What price Ladybird for the Blenheim Plate?" He had never

made a bet in his life before, but he had a sort of dim idea that when you did bet that was the way to set about it.

"Lay you three to one."

"Put me on four hundred pounds."

Over a hundred pounds of that four hundred were his own savings, for he was beginning to keep his head above water in the artistic world; but how he got the rest of it—it was a sorry tale.

"Lay you seven to two, sir," interposed a lay-you-the-odds gentleman close by.

"I'll lay you seven to two," observed the leviathan calmly. "What name, sir? Mr. Blades, give the gentleman his ticket."

The four hundred pounds were handed over. Mr. Major received in exchange a slip of pasteboard. Someone spoke to him as he turned away, this time not a betting man; someone who had apparently been looking on.

"Jacobs has done you over that bet of yours. He has given you nothing like the proper odds. Anyone, including himself, would have given you five to one."

Mr. Major said nothing, not even to thank the speaker for the information. He took up a position to view the race. It was a fine day. Although it was probable that a crowd would come, it had not come yet. He had no difficulty in finding a favourable point of vantage from which to view the race on which he had staked more than all the money he had in the world. To show what sort of sportsman this young man was one need only mention that he had not even purchased a card. He did not know which was Ladybird, he was not acquainted with the colours she carried, he did not know who her owner was, nor her jockey—as a plain statement of fact he did not know if she was running in the race at all. He saw the start, he saw the animals rush by, he did not see but he knew that the race was over. He heard the roar of voices. He turned to a man beside him—"What's won?"

"Some"—flowery—"outsider." He turned to a friend: "What is it, Jim?"

"I don't know." There was a short pause. "There's the number. Ladybird! Who the somethinged something's Ladybird?"

Mr. Major went down to Mr. Jacobs in the ring. That dignitary greeted him with a nod.

"You were in the know, Mr. Major. Mr. Blades, give Mr. Major eighteen hundred pounds. Would you like to do anything on the next race, Mr. Major?"

Mr. Major counted over his eighteen hundred pounds. Taking out an old envelope from the inner pocket of his coat, he quietly referred to something which was written on the back of it.

"Gent's got it all written down, Jake," observed a ribald—and a rival—penciller.

Mr. Jacobs paid no heed to him.

"What price King Bruce for the Windsor Stakes?" inquired Mr. Major.

"Lay you ten to three, mister," yelled one gentleman.

"Lay you eleven to three," bawled another.

Indeed, there was quite a chorus of offers. Mr. Major was indifferent to all of them.

"What price will you give me, Jacobs?"

"King Bruce?" The leviathan regarded Mr. Major with a curious glance. "Well, Mr. Major, I'll give you eleven to three."

"Put me on eighteen hundred pounds."

There was a slight pause of astonishment

"Who is he?" Mr. Major heard someone behind him ask.

"Another Juggins!"

The response was at least as audible as the inquiry had been. There was a laugh. Even Mr. Jacobs seemed amused.

"Eighteen hundred pounds, eleven to three, King Bruce, Mr. Major. Give Mr. Major his ticket, Mr. Blades."

"Look out, Jacobs," shouted a voice, "the young gent means having you."

There was another laugh at this. Mr. Major, serenely indifferent, walked away with Mr. Jacobs' ticket in his pocket.

"Kyard, sir! Krect kyard, sir."

Someone thrust something beneath his nose. Then, for the first time, Mr. Major became conscious that he was without that convenience—especially for a novice—a programme of the day. He purchased a card. He found that for the Windsor Stakes there were five runners. King Bruce's colours were light blue. He picked them out when the horses were making ready for starting. As the animals tore past it seemed to him that the one with the light blue jockey on his back was bringing up the rear. It continued in the rear during the few moments in which the proceedings were in sight. Suddenly there arose a tumult of many voices.

"By——! He's won!"

The race was over. A man at his side, who had been following it through a pair of glasses, lowered them with a full-mouthed execration.

"Who's won?"

"King Bruce!"

Mr. Major was conscious of a little fluttering in the region of his chest, as though a pulse had all at once been set vibrating. The people were rushing off in all directions. For a moment he stood still. He studied an old envelope which he took from his pocket. Then he started for the ring. Mr. Jacobs received him effusively.

"You are in luck, Mr. Major. You must have had some private information. I shall hardly like to bet with you. How much is it, Mr. Major? Mind you let me down easy." The artist handed in his "brief." "What do you make it, Mr. Blades? Eight thousand four hundred. Is that it, Mr. Major? Why, I shouldn't have so much money in the world if it hadn't been that some other gentlemen have been paying me. I tell you something in confidence. You're the only gentleman I know who was on King Bruce. What are you going to do on the next race, Mr. Major? Back another winner?"

"What price Sweet Violet for the Maiden Plate?"

Mr. Jacobs paused. He sucked the point of his pencil. The usual chorus broke out on either side of him: "I'll lay you two to one, sir."

Mr. Jacobs spoke. "Well, Mr. Major, it's my business to lay against horses at the market odds. I'll give you seven to three, though I'm not quite sure that I am doing the proper thing, you know. How much? The lot?"

Mr. Major held out to him the handful of banknotes which he had just received.

"I don't know, Mr. Major, if you think I've brought the Bank of England out with me, because I haven't; so if I run a little short—and you do seem as though you were going to bleed me—perhaps you wouldn't mind taking my cheque; you'll find it good enough."

"I shall be delighted."

The bet was made. Sweet Violet won easily was the general verdict; though as to that Mr. Major knew nothing. He saw the number go up upon the telegraph, and that was all he knew about it. He received back his eight thousand four hundred pounds, and an open cheque to boot. The figures upon that cheque seemed to dance before his eyes. But as he handed over that cheque Mr. Jacobs' mood seemed to be by no means effusive.

"That's enough for me, Mr. Major, for to-day. I'm going to take to backing horses for a change."

Whether Mr. Jacobs meant what he said or not, at any rate, he declined to have anything more to do with Mr. Major.

"You're too clever for me!" he declared.

The artist had to seek a market elsewhere. Not that it took him long to find one—offers to deal rained on him from every side.

"Deal with me—I'm George Foote, Mr. Major."

Mr. Major knew the name—through the sporting prints—"I'll cash Mr. Jacobs' cheque; though, mind you, I shouldn't be surprised if it was a stumer! This is the shop for cheques. What's your fancy, Mr. Major?"

"What price Devil's Own for the Churchill Handicap?"

"I'll give you seven to four, and I'll go you for Mr. Jacobs' cheque."

"Why," shouted a voice in the crowd, "just now you were giving six to one."

"Very well, Mr. Major, you deal with that gentleman over there. He'll lay you six to one—in pennies. Seven to four's my price."

"I want to go for more than the cheque."

"The cheque's big enough for me. What's the size of it?

Nineteen thousand six hundred—yes, that's quite big enough for me."

Another penciller addressed himself to Mr. Major.

"How much more do you want to do?"

"Eight thousand five hundred."

"I'll do it at George Foote's price. You know me, I daresay, Tom Grainger, of Nottingham—Grainger with an 'i.'"

Directly the artist had made his bet Devil's Own seemed to be in general demand.

"Mr. Major! You here!"

As Mr. Major was thrusting Mr. Grainger's ticket into his pocket someone addressed him from behind. Turning, there was Miss Davidson. His heart seemed suddenly to cease to beat.

"You!" was all that he could gasp.

She laughed.

"I did not know that you were a racing man. Allow me to introduce you to Sir Gerald Mason." Mr. Major was conscious that a resplendent middle-aged gentleman was acting as the lady's escort.

"Are you alone?"

Mr. Major explained, stammeringly, that he was. Half unconsciously, he fell in by the lady's side. The three threaded their way among the crowd. They reached a drag.

"I daresay we can find a place for you, if it's only standing room."

Presently Mr. Major found himself, with other ladies and gentlemen, on top of a four-in-hand.

"Well, have you won?" inquired Miss Davidson, who seemed to have taken him under her wing.

"Yes." There was a choking in the artist's throat. "Nearly thirty thousand pounds."

"What!"

The artist found himself greeted with a general stare.

"Nearly thirty thousand pounds."

"To-day?"

"Yes, all of it to-day."

Sir Gerald Mason seemed to be particularly struck.

"That's a tidy little trifle," he observed.

Another gentleman came clambering on to the roof.

"I can't make it out. There's something up. Just now they were laying anything against Devil's Own. Now they want three to one on."

"I expect," said Mr. Major, "it's because of me."

"Because of you?" The new-comer stared. "Oh!"

"I've just been backing him for nearly thirty thousand pounds!"

"The deuce you have!"

"He's sure to win."

"Is he, indeed? May I ask how you know it?"

"A person with whom I am acquainted gave me yesterday the names of all to-day's winners. Devil's Own is one of them. I have them here." Mr. Major took out an old, soiled envelope. There was something written in pencil on the back of it. He held it out in front of him. There was a universal smile. The artist was aware of it. "I came out this morning with four hundred pounds. I have backed three of the horses whose names are on this envelope. I have already won nearly thirty thousand pounds. I have placed it all upon Devil's Own. Devil's Own will win. All the horses whose names are on this envelope will win. I am sure of it."

In his voice there was a ring of enthusiastic conviction. His eyes met Miss Davidson's. She smiled at him. "I hope they will, for your sake."

"Thank you. I knew you would."

He held out his hand to her. She gave him hers, blushing as she did so. The other people on the drag glanced at one another. When Miss Davidson withdrew her hand she turned to the course.

"We shall soon know if your prediction is true; they are starting."

They were starting, though they did not start just then. Racehorses are not to be induced to start by clockwork. But, at last, the flag was dropped. The runners came flying down the course.

"George!" exclaimed Sir Gerald Mason. "It's a procession!"

A horse had run off with the lead. He not only kept it, but increased it as he went. The race was finished.

"A walk over for Devil's Own," remarked the gentleman who last had clambered on to the coach. He turned to Mr. Major, "I should like, sir, to know your friend."

"How much have you won, Mr. Major?"

The inquiry came from Miss Davidson. Mr. Major glanced at his couple of pasteboards.

"I have eight thousand four hundred on with one man, and nineteen thousand six hundred with another; that's twenty-eight thousand pounds, at seven to four that's forty-nine thousand pounds."

Someone so far forgot good manners as to whistle; it was the gentleman who had clambered on to the coach. Mr. Major's glance sought Miss Davidson's. Her eyes were gleaming.

"All won? I congratulate you."

"Really?"

"With all my heart."

His cheeks were flushed. His eyes were gleaming too. Words seemed trembling on his tongue. Before he could utter them he was assailed with a question.

"What's going to win the next?"

It came in half a dozen voices. He glanced at the back of the envelope.

"Estrella will win the Visitors' Plate."

"Estrella! She'll never stay the course; and she's nowhere in the betting."

"As for being nowhere in the betting, all the better for small punters like myself," remarked the elderly Sir Gerald.

He descended to the ground; the others seemed to be all talking together. Mr. Major and Miss Davidson for the moment were unnoticed.

"What are you going to do? You're not going to do any more betting?"

"I am. I am going to put every penny upon Estrella."

"Oh, Mr. Major!"

"Miss Davidson, I know that I shall win."

"You seem very confident. But you know you cannot always have good fortune. And you are playing for high stakes, you must remember."

"I am, for the highest possible. I am playing for the greatest prize in the world."

His earnestness seemed to abash her.

"Whatever it is I hope you will win it."

"You mean it?"

She turned away.

"Of course I do."

He hesitated. He seemed about to speak. Then, with a sudden impulse, he too descended to the ground.

"Put on five pounds for me," she said to him as he went down. "I'll back your luck."

He looked up at her, his face peony red. But he was speechless. His entry into the ring was greeted with something like applause: already he was famous. In his mastering excitement he did not notice it.

"Hollo! Mr. Major," cried Mr. Grainger of Nottingham, "don't you think you're knocking 'em? Are you going for the gloves? Do you want to break the lot of us? We've all got wives and children, and we don't want to see 'em in the workhouse. What's the next article, Mr. Major?"

"What price Estrella for the Visitors' Plate?"

For a moment it seemed that there was no price. Then Mr. Grainger made a bid.

"I'll do you at evens, but not for a million, you know."

"I won't do you at any price," said Mr. Foote, who seemed unhappy. "I say with Mr. Jacobs—Mr. Major's too clever for me."

Sir Gerald Mason was standing by the artist's side.

"Evens!" he exclaimed. "Why, Estrella's quoted at forty to one."

"Oh, that was before Mr. Major was on. Mr. Major's hand-in-glove with the Old Gentleman—he's got the key of the stable."

Mr. Jacobs interposed.

"Look here, mister, I don't know who you are, but you've got twenty-eight thousand pounds of my money. Go you double or quits; evens against Estrella."

"I'll come in with you, Jacobs," cried an enterprising gentleman, whose name was Johnson—that well-known patron of "the fancy." "I'll do you the same price in any sum you choose, Mr. Major—a million if you like—I think I'm good for it!"

Mr. Major had to be content with the terms.

"I haven't done very well for you, Miss Davidson," he explained when he returned to the drag. "I've only got evens."

"It's a robbery," declared the elderly Sir Gerald; "rank robbery!"

"Rather too barefaced robbery for me." Thus Mr. Wilmot, which was the name of the gentleman who had clambered last on to the drag. "I don't think this time your friend has done you a good turn, Mr. Major. From her form Estrella hasn't the ghost of a chance. Personally, I should say the odds against her were more than forty to one."

"By Jove!" exclaimed a ruddy-faced young gentleman, with a "pane of glass" in his eye, "I hope she will win! I've a monkey on her!"

"Not to mention my five pounds," laughed Miss Davidson.

"Your money is quite safe. Estrella will win—I know it."

"Excuse me, Mr. Major," said Mr. Wilmot, "but your tone would almost suggest that you had been getting at somebody or something on a very extensive scale. You seem cock-sure."

"I am cock-sure."

"They're off!"

They were. Mr. Wilmot's glasses followed the race.

"A capital start. Bedgown's leading—Canute second. Hollo! The Squire's coming. Estrella's nowhere. The Squire's in front! What's that slipped through—Patience? Patience is coming! Come on, Patience; The Squire is racing her! Where's your Estrella, Mr. Major? She don't seem to be in this race. Patience is ahead! Bravo, Patience! By George, Canute's coming! He's in front! He's running away from 'em! Just look how he's going! It's all over—Canute for a million! Hollo! how about your Estrella, Mr. Major? What's that—what's that in blue and pink? It's—it's Estrella! Dashed if she isn't coming on; hang me if she isn't! My eyes, how she's travelling! If there's time, she'll overhaul the leader! She has! She's collared him! She's racing him! She's passed him! Gosh! she's won!"

"I've won over a hundred and fifty thousand pounds." With one accord they turned to Mr. Major. He seemed in a sort of ecstasy. He repeated the words, "I've won over a hundred and fifty thousand pounds. I knew Estrella'd win."

Mr. Wilmot looked a little white.

"It's uncommonly queer," he said.

"It is queer; I know it's queer. But I knew she'd win."

Miss Davidson spoke.

"I congratulate you, Mr. Major, with all my heart. I never knew anyone who won a hundred and fifty thousand pounds before—and in a single day!"

"I shall win more before I've finished."

"You are surely not going to tempt Fortune again?"

"No—not fortune! The man who gave me the names of the horses which I have here was inspired. It was given to him to see behind the veil. I half suspected it at the time. I see it clearly now. It is not Fortune I am tempting; I am betting upon certainties. I know that every horse he gave me is sure to win!"

The people looked at one another. They were apparently in doubt as to whether this young gentleman was altogether sane. "What has this very remarkable friend of yours given you for the Cup?"

"Ballet Girl."

"That sounds more promising. Ballet Girl's my own fancy, and the favourite. But, if you take my advice, Mr. Major, you'll keep out of the ring. Let me deal for you. If they know you're dealing it'll knock the market all to pieces; you'll get no price at all."

"What does it matter what price I get? What does it matter if I have to give ten to one if I know the horse will win?"

Mr. Wilmot shrugged his shoulders.

"Of course, if you know, there's nothing further to be said."

Mr. Major found the ring in a panic. His entry was greeted with a roar of voices.

"Mr. Major, you've about broke me," yelled Mr. Jacobs. Then

came a volley of adjectives. "I can't make things out at all. Upon my soul, I don't know that I didn't ought to appeal to the stewards."

Someone shouted in the crowd—

"Pay up, Jake, and look pleasant!"

"I'll pay up," said Mr. Jacobs; "but as for looking pleasant——"

There came more adjectives.

"What are you going to do in the Hunt Cup, Mr. Major?"

The inquiry came from neither Mr. Jacobs nor Mr. Grainger.

"What price Ballet Girl?"

It was odd, after the previous tumult, to notice the silence with which Mr. Major's words were greeted—the completer silence still which followed them. No one made a price.

"You're surely not afraid of one man? What, all the lot of you?"

"Dash me!" roared Mr. Jacobs. "No man shall say that I'm afraid of him—not if I have to go into the workhouse to-morrow. I'll tell you what I'll do, Mr. Major. I'll give you the chance to make the biggest bet that was ever made in England. You've got over a hundred and fifty thousand pounds there, and by——! most of it's mine. If you like to put the lot of it on Ballet Girl, at five to one on, I'll take you."

"Five to one on?" shouted the crowd.

"Five to one on!" vociferated Mr. Jacobs. "And that's an offer which I doubt if any other man upon this course will make you."

It was not a tempting offer, but Mr. Major took it.

"You're a very foolish man, sir," said Mr. Wilmot, who was standing at his elbow.

"Why? I know the horse will win."

"You may know, but I don't, and you've spoilt the market for other men."

The start was a long time coming. While they waited for it there was considerable excitement on the top of the drag.

"Mr. Major," said Miss Davidson, "I do hope that mysterious friend of yours is right again. It will be a dreadful thing if Ballet Girl should fail us. We are all of us on her to a man."

"And at such a price!" growled Mr. Wilmot. "Upon my word, I am ashamed of myself when I think that I ever allowed myself to be induced to back any horse at such a figure."

Mr. Major was standing by Miss Davidson. His eyes, which rested on her, were eloquent with many things. Always good-looking, just then he was even curiously handsome.

"Ballet Girl will win; I am sure of it. Then—then I shall never bet again."

"Never?"

"Never. I don't think I ever bet before. I never shall again."

"Your luck has been fabulous—really quite incredible. If I had been you I should have been content with what I'd won. To risk it all seems—seems dreadful."

"Why? You would be prepared to bet that two and two make four a thousand times in succession."

"But that is different."

"Not at all. Just as certainly as you know that two and two make four, I know that Ballet Girl will win. I shall have made my fortune. I shall have only one thing left to win. Only one!"

Someone said they were getting ready to start. All eyes were turned towards the course. Mr. Wilmot's glasses again came into play.

"Isn't that Tragedy Queen who won't stand still? Up go her heels! Now there's Chappie joining her!"

Mr. Major, under cover of the gathering excitement, half whispered to Miss Davidson—

"I shall have only one thing left to win."

"I hope you will win it, whatever it is." She faced him. "Mr. Major, I do hope Ballet Girl will win."

"I know she will."

"They're off!"

They were. Mr. Wilmot favoured them with a running commentary.

"A good start! What's that in the black and white hoops in front? Hollo! Chappie's making the pace. Tragedy Queen seems to be funking it, or is young Blades holding her in? Ballet Girl seems to be running third. White will get himself shut in if he

doesn't look out. Hollo! Chappie's ahead! Mark Antony's challenging him! They're making a ding-dong thing of it, by George!
Ballet Girl's creeping up; so's Tragedy Queen. What is that in the
black and white hoops? Isn't it Bar One? It is Bar One! Ballet Girl
is coming on. By gad, she is! Hark at the people shouting. Our
five to one chance looks rosy, Mr. Major. She's collared Chappie!
Tragedy Queen is sticking to her. It strikes me it's going to be a
race between the pair of them. Bar One's third. Isn't Ballet Girl
just flying? Bravo! Why, there must be two lengths between her
and Tragedy Queen! Hark at the people! I say, Mr. Major, the
devil must be in that friend of yours; Ballet Girl's half a dozen
lengths in front! She's having a lark with them! She's—why!—
what is that? She's down! down! My God! Why don't White pick
her up? There's something wrong! Tragedy Queen's passed her!
So's Bar One! Bar One's gaining! Bar One's in front!——!——!"
Mr. Wilmot must have forgotten the presence of ladies. And in
that hot moment it is not impossible that his forgetfulness was
overlooked. "Bar One's won!" He turned on Mr. Major. "Bar One
has won!"

There was a hubbub of many voices, a wild rush of people on
to the course, where Ballet Girl lay motionless. Her last race was
run. The flush had faded from Mr. Major's cheeks, the light from
his eyes.

"I have lost!—lost!—lost it all!" He turned to Miss Davidson.
You—you won't let it make any difference?"

"Make any difference?"

"I did it all for you. I—I did not like to come to you with
empty hands."

"Mr. Major! What do you mean?"

"Although I loved you so, I did not like to think that you were
rich and I was poor. If I had won I should have given it all to
you—it would have been for you that it was won."

The lady turned away. It almost seemed that this remarkable
young gentleman was making a declaration of affection, in public, on the roof of a drag, right before the eyes—the ears!—of a
number of amazed and bewildered strangers.

"You—you won't let it make any difference because—because I have lost."

The lady favoured him with a front view. Her cheeks were a flaming red; but, in spite of it, she was the more self-possessed of the two.

"I think, Mr. Major, that excitement has turned your brain. It is rather a singular place in which to volunteer such a statement, but I don't know if you are aware that I am engaged to be married to Mr. Philip Cumberland?"

"Engaged? To Mr. Cumberland?" It was piteous to see the young man's face. "But he's in Oban."

"I don't know how you know he is in Oban. Nor do I see why his being in Oban should make any difference to the fact of our engagement."

"But—why did you buy my picture?"

"My good sir, I have never bought any picture of yours."

"Gill said it was you."

"You seem to be favoured with some curious friends. I have not the honour of Mr. Gill's acquaintance. Had I purchased your picture, I do not see how the purchase would have warranted your peculiar behaviour. As a matter of fact, I have done nothing of the kind."

Mr. Wilmot slipped his arm through Mr. Major's.

"Come, my friend, I think you and I had better take a stroll together. You seem to have let us in for a very nice thing!"

IV.

"Gill!" Mr. Major knocked at the door again. "Gill!" There was still no answer. He turned the handle. The door was open. Mr. Major entered. The lamp was still unlighted, but he could see that Mr. Gill was seated at the table. "Gill!" Mr. Gill continued silent. Mr. Major went and touched him on the shoulder. "Gill!"

He started back. Mr. Gill was dead!

"Starvation—that's what it is."

Thus spoke the landlady, hastily summoned to the presence of the newly dead.

"Starvation!"

The young man turned his ghastly face to the woman's.

"Starvation. He's been slowly starving this ever so long. I don't believe he's tasted a morsel of meat these last two weeks. He owed me seven weeks' rent. But he was such an old lodger I didn't like to be hard on him. Now, I suppose, I shall lose it all."

"But I thought he had so many clients?"

"Not one. He used to have when first I knew him, but they turned him up—long ago! I don't believe he ever named a winner in his life. I know more than once he put me on a wrong one. Of late things have been preying on his mind. It's my belief that for nearly a week now he's been quite cracked."

Mr. Major wondered.

VI.

THE FIFTEENTH MAN

THE STORY OF A RUGBY MATCH

It was not until we were actually in the field, and were about to begin to play, that I learnt that the Brixham men had come one short. It seemed that one of their men had been playing in a match the week before—in a hard frost, if you please! and, getting pitched on to his head, had broken his skull nearly into two clean halves. That is the worst of playing in a frost; you are nearly sure to come to grief. Not to ordinary grief, either, but a regular cracker. It was hard lines on the Brixham team. Some men always are getting themselves smashed to pieces just as a big match is due! The man's name was Joyce, Frank Joyce. He played halfback for Brixham, and for the county too—so you may be sure Lance didn't care to lose him. Still, they couldn't go and drag the man out of the hospital with a hole in his head big enough to put your fist into. They had tried to get a man to take his place, but at the last moment the substitute had failed to show.

"If we can't beat them—fifteen to their fourteen!—I think we'd better go in for challenging girls' schools. Last year they beat us, but this year, as we've one man to the good, perhaps we might manage to pull it off."

That's how Mason talked to us, as if *we* wanted them to win! Although they were only fourteen men, they could play. I don't think I ever saw a team who were stronger in their forwards. Lance, their captain, kicked off; Mason, our chief, returned. Then one of their men, getting the leather, tried a run. We downed him, a scrimmage was formed, then, before we knew it, they were rushing the ball across the field. When it did show, I was on it like a flash. I passed to Mason. But he was collared almost before he had a chance to start. There was another turn at scrimmaging, and lively work it was, especially for us who had the pleasure of looking on. So, when again I got a sight of it, I didn't lose much time. I had it up, and I was off. I didn't pass; I tried a run upon my own account. I thought that I was clear away. I had passed the forwards; I thought that I had passed the field, when, suddenly, someone sprang at me, out of the fog—it was a little thick, you know—caught me round the waist, lifted me off my feet, and dropped me on my back. That spoilt it! Before I had a chance of passing they were all on top of me. And again the ball was in the scrimmage.

When I returned to my place behind I looked to see who it was had collared me. The fellow, I told myself, was one of their half-backs. Yet, when I looked at their halves, I couldn't make up my mind which of them it was.

Try how we could—although we had the best of the play—we couldn't get across their line. Although I say it, we all put in some first-rate work. We never played better in our lives. We all had run after run, the passing was as accurate as if it had been mechanical, and yet we could not do the trick. Time after time, just as we were almost in, one of their men put a stop to our little game, and spoilt us. The funny part of the business was that, either owing to the fog, or to our stupidity, we could not make up our minds which of their men it was.

At last I spotted him. Mason had been held nearly on their goal line. They were playing their usual game of driving us back in the scrimmage, when the ball broke through. I took it. I passed to Mason. I thought he was behind, when—he was collared and thrown.

"Joyce!" I cried. "Why, I thought that you weren't playing."

"What are you talking about?" asked one of their men. "Joyce isn't playing."

I stared.

"Not playing! Why, it was he who collared Mason."

"Stuff!"

I did not think the man was particularly civil. It was certainly an odd mistake which I had made. I was just behind Mason when he was collared, and I saw the face of the man who collared him. I could have sworn it was Frank Joyce!

"Who was that who downed you just now?" I asked of Mason, directly I had the chance.

"Their half-back."

Their half-back! Their halves were Tom Wilson and Granger. How could I have mistaken either of them for Joyce?

A little later Giffard was puzzled.

"One of their fellows plays a thundering good game, but, do you know, I can't make out which one of them it is."

"Do you mean the fellow who keeps collaring."

"That's the man!"

The curious part of it was that I never saw the man except when he was collaring.

"The next time," said Giffard, when, for about the sixth time, he had been on the point of scoring, "if I don't get in, I'll know the reason why. I'll kill that man."

It was all very well to talk about our killing him. It looked very much more like his killing us. Mason passed the word that if there was anything like a chance we were to drop. The chance came immediately afterwards. They muffed somehow in trying to pass. Blaine got the leather. He started to run.

"Drop," yelled Mason.

In that fog, and from where Blaine was, dropping a goal was out of the question. He tried the next best thing—he tried to drop into touch. But the attempt was a failure. The kick was a bad one—the ball was as heavy as lead, so that there was not much kick in it—and as it was coming down one of their men, appearing right on the spot, caught it, dropped a drop which was a drop, sent the ball right over our heads, and as near as a toucher over the bar.

Just then the whistle sounded.

"Do you know," declared Ingall, as we were crossing over, "I believe they're playing fifteen men."

Mason scoffed.

"Do you think, without giving us notice, they would play fifteen when they told us they were only playing fourteen?"

"Hanged if I don't count them!" persisted Ingall.

He did, and we all did. We faced round and reckoned them up. There were only fourteen, unless one was slinking out of sight somewhere in the dim recesses of the fog, which seemed scarcely probable. Still Ingall seemed dissatisfied.

"They're playing four three-quarters," whispered Giffard, when the game restarted.

So they were—Wheeler, Pendleton, Marshall, and another. Who the fourth man was I couldn't make out. He was a big, strapping fellow, I could see that; but the play was so fast that more than that I couldn't see.

"Who is the fourth man?"

"Don't know; can't see his face. It's so confoundedly foggy!"

It was foggy; but still, of course, it was not foggy enough to render a man's features indistinguishable at the distance of only a few feet. All the same, somehow or other he managed to keep his face concealed from us. While Giffard and I had been whispering they had been packing in. The ball broke out our side. I had it. I tried to run. Instantly I saw that fourth three-quarter rush at me. As he came I saw his face. I was so amazed that I stopped dead. Putting his arms about me he held me as in a vice.

"Joyce!" I cried.

Before the word was out of my mouth half a dozen of their men had hold of the ball.

"Held! held!" they screamed.

"Down!" I gasped.

And it was down, with two or three of their men on top of me. They were packing the scrimmage before I had time to get fairly on my feet again.

"That was Joyce who collared me!" I exclaimed.

"Pack in! pack in!" shouted Mason from behind.

And they did pack in with a vengeance. Giffard had the ball. They were down on him; it was hammer and tongs. But through it all we stuck to the leather. They downed us, but not before we had passed it to a friend. Out of it came Giffard, sailing along as though he had not been swallowing mud in pailfuls. I thought he was clear—but no! He stopped short, and dropped the ball!—

dropped it, as he stood there, from his two hands as though he were a baby! They asked no questions. They had it up; they were off with it, as though they meant to carry it home. They carried it, too, all the way—almost! It was in disagreeable propinquity to our goal by the time that it was held.

"Now then, Brixham, you've got it!"

That was what they cried.

"Steyning! Steyning! All together!"

That was what we answered. But though we did work all together, it was as much as we could manage.

"Where's Giffard?" bellowed Mason.

My impression was that he had remained like a sign-post rooted to the ground. I had seen him standing motionless after he had dropped the ball, and even as the Brixham men rushed past him. But just then he put in an appearance.

"I protest!" he cried.

"What about?" asked Mason.

"What do they mean by pretending they're not playing Frank Joyce when all the time they are?"

"Oh, confound Frank Joyce! Play up, do. You've done your best to give them the game already. Steady, Steyning, steady. Left, there, left. Centre, steady!"

We were steady. We were more than steady. Steadiness alone would not have saved us. We all played forward. At last, somehow, we got the ball back into something like the middle of the field. Giffard kept whispering to me all the time, even in the hottest of the rush.

"What lies, pretending that they're not playing Joyce!" Here he had a discussion with the ball, mostly on his knees. "Humbug about his being in the hospital!"

We had another chance. Out of the turmoil, Mason was flying off with a lead. It was the first clear start he had that day. When he has got that it is catch him who catch can! As he pelted off, the fog, which kept coming and going, all at once grew thicker. He had passed all their men. Of ours, I was the nearest to him. It looked all the world to a china orange that we were going to score at last, when, to my disgust, he reeled, seemed to give a sort of spring, and then fell right over on to his back! I did not understand how he had managed to do it, but I supposed that he had slipped in the mud. Before I could get within passing distance the Brixham men were on us, and the ball was down.

"I thought you'd done it that time."

I said this to him as the scrimmage was being formed. He did not answer. He stood looking about him in a hazy sort of way, as though the further proceedings had no interest for him.

"What's the matter? Are you hurt?"

He turned to me.

"Where is he?" he asked.

"Where's who?"

I couldn't make him out. There was quite a curious look upon his face.

"Joyce!"

Somehow, as he said this, I felt a trifle queer. It was his face, or his tone, or something. "Didn't you see him throw me?"

I didn't know what he meant. But before I could say so we had another little rough and tumble—one go up and the other go down. A hubbub arose. There was Ingall shouting.

"I protest! I don't think this sort of thing's fair play."

"What sort of thing?"

"You said you weren't playing Joyce."

"*Said* we weren't! We aren't."

"Why, he just took the ball out of my hands! Joyce, where are you?"

"Yes, where is he?"

Then they laughed. Mason intervened.

"Excuse me, Lance; we've no objection to your playing Joyce, but why do you say you aren't?"

"I don't think you're well. I tell you that Frank Joyce is at this moment lying in Brixham hospital."

"He just now collared me."

I confess that when Mason said that I was a trifle staggered. I had distinctly seen that he had slipped and fallen. No one had been within a dozen yards of him at the time. Those Brixham men told him so—not too civilly.

"Do you fellows mean to say," he roared, "that Frank Joyce didn't just now pick me up and throw me?"

I struck in.

"I mean to say so. You slipped and fell. My dear fellow, no one was near you at the time."

He sprang round at me.

"Well, that beats anything!"

"At the same time," I added, "it's all nonsense to talk about Joyce being in Brixham hospital, because, since half-time at any rate, he's been playing three-quarter."

"Of course he has," cried Ingall. "Didn't I see him?"

"And didn't he collar me?" asked Giffard.

The Brixham men were silent. We looked at them, and they at us.

"You fellows are dreaming," said Lance. "It strikes me that you don't know Joyce when you see him."

"That's good," I cried, "considering that he and I were five years at school together."

"Suppose you point him out then?"

"Joyce!" I shouted. "You aren't ashamed to show your face, I hope?"

"Joyce!" they replied, in mockery. "You aren't bashful, Joyce?"

He was not there. Or we couldn't find him, at any rate. We scrutinised each member of the team; it was really absurd to suppose that I could mistake any of them for Joyce. There was not the slightest likeness.

Dryall appealed to the referee.

"Are you sure nobody's sneaked off the field?"

"Stuff!" he said. "I've been following the game all the time, and know every man who's playing, and Joyce hasn't been upon the ground."

"As for his playing three-quarter, Pendleton, Marshall, and I have been playing three-quarter all the afternoon, and I don't think that either of us is very much like Joyce."

This was Tom Wilson.

"You've been playing four three-quarters since we crossed over."

"Bosh!" said Wilson.

That was good, as though I hadn't seen the four with my own eyes.

"Play!" sang out the referee. "Don't waste any more time."

We were at it again. We might be mystified. There was something about the whole affair which was certainly mysterious to me. But we did not intend to be beaten.

"They're only playing three three-quarters now," said Giffard.

So they were. That was plain enough. I wondered if the fourth man had joined the forwards. But why should they conceal the fact that they had been playing four?

One of their men tried a drop. Mason caught it, ran, was collared, passed—wide to the left—and I was off. The whole crowd was in the centre of the field. I put on the steam. Lance came at me. I dodged, he missed. Pendleton was bearing down upon me from the right. I outpaced him. I got a lead. Only Rivers, their back, was between the Brixham goal and me. He slipped just as he made his effort. I was past. It was only a dozen yards to the goal. Nothing would stop me now. I was telling myself that the only thing left was the shouting, when, right in front of me, stood—Joyce! Where he came from I have not the least idea. Out of nothing, it seemed to me. He stood there, cool as a cucumber, waiting—as it appeared—until I came within his reach. His sudden appearance baulked me. I stumbled. The ball slipped from beneath my arm. I saw him smile. Forgetting all about the ball, I made a dash at him. The instant I did so he was gone!

I felt a trifle mixed. I heard behind me the roar of voices. I knew that I had lost my chance. But, at the moment, that was not the trouble. Where had Joyce come from? Where had he gone?

"Now then, Steyning! All together, and you'll do it!"

I heard Mason's voice ring out above the hubbub.

"Brixham, Brixham!" shouted Lance. "Play up!"

"Joyce or no Joyce," I told myself, "hang me if I won't do it yet!"

I got on side. Blaine had hold of the leather. They were on him like a cartload of bricks. He passed to Giffard.

"Don't run back!" I screamed.

They drove him back. He passed to me. They were on the ball as soon as I was. They sent me spinning. Somebody got hold of it. Just as he was off I made a grab at his leg. He went down on his face. The ball broke loose. I got on to my feet. They were indulging in what looked to me very much like hacking. We sent the leather through, and Lance was off! Their fellows backed him up in style. They kept us off until he had a start. He bore off to the right. Already he had shaken off our forwards. I saw Mason charge him. I saw that he sent Mason flying. I made for him. I caught him round the waist. He passed to Pendleton. Pendleton was downed. He lost the ball. Back it came to me, and I was off!

I was away before most of them knew what had become of the leather. Again there was only Rivers between the goal and me. He soon was out of the reckoning. The mud beat him. As he was making for me down he came upon his hands and knees. I had been running wide till then. When he came to grief I centred. Should I take the leather in, or drop?

"Drop!" shouted a voice behind.

That settled me. I was within easy range of the goal. I ought to manage the kick. I dropped—at least, I tried to. It was only a try, because, just as I had my toe against the ball, and was in the very act of kicking, Joyce stood right in front of me! He stood so close that, so to speak, he stood right on the ball. It fell dead, it didn't travel an inch. As I made my fruitless effort, and was still poised upon one leg, placing his hand against my chest, he pushed me over backwards. As I fell I saw him smile—just as I had seen him smile when he had baulked me just before.

I didn't feel like smiling. I felt still less like smiling when, as I yet lay sprawling, Rivers, pouncing on the ball, dropped it back into the centre of the field. He was still standing by me when I regained my feet. He volunteered an observation.

"Lucky for us you muffed that kick."

"Where's Joyce?" I asked.

"Where's who?"

"Joyce."

He stared at me.

"I don't know what you're driving at. I think you fellows must have got Joyce on the brain."

He returned to his place in the field. I returned to mine. I had an affectionate greeting from Giffard.

"That's the second chance you've thrown away. Whatever made you muff that kick?"

"Giffard," I asked, "do you think I'm going mad?"

"I should think you've gone."

I could not—it seems ridiculous, but I could not ask if he had seen Joyce. It was so evident that he had not. And yet, if I had seen him, he must have seen him too. As he suggested—I must have gone mad!

The play was getting pretty rough, the ground was getting pretty heavy. We had churned it into a regular quagmire. Sometimes we went above the ankle in liquid mud. As for the state that we were in!

One of theirs had the ball. Half a dozen of ours had hold of him.

"Held! held!" they yelled.

"It's not held," he gasped.

They had him down, and sat on him. Then he owned that it was held.

"Let it through," cried Mason, when the leather was in scrimmage.

Before our forwards had a chance they rushed it through. We picked it up; we carried it back. They rushed it through again. The tide of battle swayed, now to this side, now to that. Still we gained. Two or three short runs bore the ball within punting distance of their goal. We more than retained the advantage. Yard by yard we drove them back. It was a match against time. We looked like winning if there was only time enough. At last it seemed as though matters had approached something very like a settlement. Pendleton had the ball. Our men were on to him. To avoid being held he punted. But he was charged before he really had a chance. The punt was muddled. It was a catch for Mason.

He made his mark—within twenty yards of their goal! There is no better drop-kick in England than Alec Mason. If from a free kick at that distance he couldn't top their bar, we might as well go home to bed.

Mason took his time. He judged the distance with his eye. Then, paying no attention to the Brixham forward, who had stood up to his mark, he dropped a good six feet on his own side of it. There was an instant's silence. Then they raised a yell; for as the ball left Mason's foot one of their men sprang at him, and, leaping upwards, caught the ball in the air. It was wonderfully done! Quick as lightning, before we had recovered from our surprise, he had dropped the ball back into the centre of the field.

"Now then, Brixham," bellowed Lance.

And they came rushing on. They came on too! We were so disconcerted by Mason's total failure that they got the drop on us. They reached the leather before our back had time to return. It was all we could do to get upon the scene of action quickly enough to prevent their having the scrimmage all to themselves. Mason's collapse had put life into them as much as, for the moment, it had taken it out of us. They carried the ball through the scrimmage as though our forwards were not there.

"Now then, Steyning, you're not going to let them beat us!"

As Mason held his peace I took his place as fugleman.

But we could not stand against them—we could not—in scrimmage or out of it. All at once they seemed to be possessed. In an instant their back play improved a hundred per cent. One of their men, in particular, played like Old Nick himself. In the excitement—and they were an exciting sixty seconds—I could not make out which one of them it was; but he made things lively. He as good as played us single-handed; he was always on the ball; he seemed to lend their forwards irresistible impetus when it was in the scrimmage. And when it was out of it, wasn't he just upon the spot. He was ubiquitous—here, there, and everywhere. And at last he was off. Exactly how it happened is more than I can say, but I saw that he had the ball. I saw him dash away with it. I made for him. He brushed me aside as though I were a fly. I was about to start in hot pursuit when someone caught me by the arm. I turned—in a trifle of a rage. There was Mason at my side.

"Never mind that fellow. Listen to me." These were funny words to come from the captain of one's team at the very crisis of the game. I both listened and looked. Something in the expression of his face quite startled me. "Do you know who it was who spoilt my kick? It was either Joyce or—Joyce's ghost."

Before I was able to ask him what it was he meant there arose a hullaballoo of shouting. I turned, just in time to see the fellow, who had run away with the leather, drop it, as sweetly as you please, just over our goal. They had won! And at that moment the whistle sounded—they had done it just on time!

The man who had done the trick turned round and faced us. He was wearing a worsted cap, such as brewers wear. Taking it off, he waved it over his head. As he did so there was not a man upon the field who did not see him clearly, who did not know who he was. He was Frank Joyce! He stood there for a moment before us all, and then was gone.

"Lance," shouted the referee, "here's a telegram for you."

Lance was standing close to Mason and to me. A telegraph boy came pelting up. Lance took the yellow envelope which the boy held out to him. He opened it.

"Why! what!" Through the mud upon his face he went white, up to the roots of his hair. He turned to us with startled eyes. "Joyce died in Brixham Hospital nearly an hour ago. The hospital people have telegraphed to say so."

VII.

THE ASSASSIN

CHAPTER I.

KENNARD passed the paper to Nash.

"Read that," he said.

Nash did as he was told; he read the advertisement to which Kennard was pointing with his finger. We give that advertisement, rendered from the original French into English:—

"An individual wishes to be rid of the insupportable burden of existence. For particular reasons this individual wishes to leave behind a certain sum of money. In exchange, therefore, for a suitable amount the advertiser will undertake to perform any deed which shall inevitably result in death.—Address, Tired, 30 bis, Rue de Pekin."

"Candid almost to a fault," was Willie Nash's comment. "Gerbert, what do you think of this?"

Having read it, M. Gerbert shrugged his shoulders.

"Well, what of it? It is nothing."

"You think it is nothing."

"It is either a hoax—in which case it is plainly nothing, or it is true—and what is it then? How many people are there, do you suppose, who are tired of their lives—look at me, for instance, look at me! You laugh!" As a matter of fact, they had exchanged glances—but the thing had not amounted to a laugh. "Very good! You English are of a different race to us French. The things which, with your coarseness, but prick you, with our delicacy cut us to the heart. My God, yes! But that has nothing to do with the advertisement." M. Gerbert waved the paper in the air. "Here is a man who announces that he is tired of his life—that is but a commonplace. He announces that he will dispose of that of which he is tired in exchange for a certain sum. There, I grant you, is a touch of the original. So many people dispose of their lives in exchange for nothing at all! But, my friends, think of the number of persons who are willing to risk, and who do risk their lives for twopence-halfpenny—who will march to certain death for a five-franc piece. This creature"—M. Gerbert rapped his knuckle against the paper—"is possibly some bravo of a fellow who says to himself, 'I will have one good hour, and then, after that—what matters all the rest!' That is so!"

"Won't your police have something to say to such an advertisement?"

"Ah, M. Nash, our police! With our police it is altogether a matter of the digestion! Good fortune!"

M. Gerbert rose. He drained his absinthe to the dregs. With a wave of the hand he walked away. Mr. Kennard drew the paper towards him.

"I've a mind to see this through." Willie Nash looked at him askance. "The advertisement, I mean—and the advertiser too."

"Are you thinking of setting him to perform a deed which shall inevitably result in death?"

"It depends upon what he calls a suitable amount. I am not a rich man. I can't afford to be unduly extravagant—even for an occasional luxury."

"Hugh!"

"William! I have something in my mind's eye which I should be willing to pay any man a fair price for doing. When he had done it I don't think he'd want to do anything more. You bet."

"Your humour sometimes lies so deep that, on this occasion, you must excuse me if I ask if you are joking."

Mr. Kennard did not directly reply. He studied the advertisement again.

"I think, by way of a preliminary, that I should like to make this gentleman's acquaintance."

"Seriously?"

"So seriously that I propose to write to him at once, making an appointment for to-morrow. If you are at my place to-morrow morning at eleven you will be able to see if he keeps it."

"If you take my advice you won't be such a fool."

"No? Are you afraid of blackmailing—or what? Go to! No one wants you. Stop away."

"I'll come; but you'll find he won't. As Gerbert suggested, I expect the thing's a hoax."

"Yes? Probably in exchange for my letter I shall receive some valuable information about a novelty in soap."

CHAPTER II.

"Didn't I say he wouldn't come?"

"It is just upon eleven. Give even an assassin a minute's grace."

"Seriously, Hugh, if the fellow does come, I would strongly recommend you to be extremely careful what you say to him. You know the French have their own point of view; it's a very different point of view from ours. If you don't look out you may be in a mess before you know it. Your joke may turn out too much like earnest."

"As I told you, it will depend, in a measure, upon what he calls a suitable amount. I can't afford to pay too much, even for murder."

"Hugh!" There was a knock at the door. "Who's that?"

"It's the assassin. Enter."

The door opened. There entered—a woman. They stared. They might not have been able to say what it was that they had expected, but they had not expected this. The woman was slightly built, of medium height. She was dressed in black. She wore a veil which was so thick that it obscured her features. But one guessed, from her carriage, that she was young. The two men stood up. She remained in the doorway with the handle of the open door still in her hand.

"Monsieur Hugh Kennard?"

Certainly, the voice was a young woman's. She spoke softly and with a little tremor, as if she caught her breath. Mr. Kennard bent his head. "I am Monsieur Kennard."

"And—this gentleman?" The woman motioned with her hand towards Willie Nash.

"This gentleman is my friend; my very good friend."

The woman seemed to hesitate. The two men said nothing. They gave her not the least encouragement. At last, apparently arriving at a resolution, coming right into the room, she shut the door.

"This, Monsieur Kennard, is your letter." She held out a letter which Mr. Kennard recognised as the one which he had written. "You said eleven. To me, the hour was a little awkward. But—I am come."

"To whom have I the pleasure of speaking?" asked Mr. Kennard, after a pause, during which he had looked at his friend, and his friend had looked at him.

"To an individual."

Stepping forward Willie Nash advanced a chair. "Permit me to offer mademoiselle a seat." He laid a stress upon the mademoiselle. She did not seem to notice it.

"Thank you. I had rather stand."

There was silence. She stood, seemingly at her ease, her hands at her side, eyeing Mr. Kennard through the thick folds of her veil.

"Mademoiselle"—he followed Mr. Nash's lead—"must forgive my observing that her description of herself as 'an individual' is a little vague."

"Monsieur understands sufficiently what that description conveys. I am the individual to whom life has become an insupportable burden."

"It is impossible!"

"How impossible?"

"It is impossible that to mademoiselle life can already have become an insupportable burden."

So far the woman's intonation had been curiously sweet, with something in it which suggested the voice of a child. Now it perceptibly changed. It became, as it were, a little caustic.

"Will monsieur have the goodness to confine himself to the

matter which is in hand? I am here at monsieur's particular request. What is it monsieur would wish that I should do?"

"I cannot conceive that mademoiselle is in earnest."

She showed signs of impatience. "How shall I convince monsieur? Does he desire from me an oath? I am ready. If, in exchange for a particular amount, monsieur will tell me what is the task he requires from me, which shall inevitably result in death, by my actions I will quickly prove that I am in earnest, at least, so far as that."

"But surely mademoiselle must perceive that she has me at a disadvantage. She knows me by name, by sight, she would even know my private affairs, yet she will not even suffer me to see her face."

"I am but an instrument. What does it matter what an instrument looks like, so long as that which it does is done efficiently?"

"Suppose, on the other hand, that, so soon as I have shared with mademoiselle my confidences, she goes from here to the police."

The woman hesitated. "What is the amount which monsieur is prepared to offer in exchange for the task which he requires?"

"What is the sum which mademoiselle has in her mind?"

"Ten thousand francs."

She drew herself upright, throwing back her head with a little defiant gesture, as if the sum she named had been a superb one. The two men started. They stared at each other. Willie Nash distinctly smiled.

"Ten thousand francs!" cried Mr. Kennard. "Is it possible that mademoiselle is willing to give her life in exchange for ten thousand francs?"

"It's not my life I give. My life is nothing—to me, or to anyone. I ask ten thousand francs in exchange for the deed which you would set me to do. In other words, I desire that my death may be worth something, though my life is of no account. What is it that monsieur requires?"

"Suppose I were to require you to kill M. le President?"

For the first time she showed signs of emotion. She started—

so unmistakably, that she had to lean for support on the back of the chair which Willie Nash had offered her.

"Kill M. le President! That—that would not be very pleasant."

"Does mademoiselle suppose that a deed, the doing of which would inevitably result in death, would be surrounded, as a matter of course, with all the elements of pleasantness?"

"Monsieur laughs at me. I desire that monsieur will not laugh. I am ready. If monsieur will give me his word that he will pay ten thousand francs in a certain quarter so soon as he learns that M. le President is—no more, I will do what he requires."

When he spoke again Mr. Kennard's tone was even unwontedly dry.

"Am I to take it that mademoiselle is in earnest?"

She hesitated. Then with both her hands she raised her veil.

"If monsieur will look at me he will see I am in earnest."

What the two men did see was that she was scarcely out of her girlhood—surely not out of her teens. She was fairer than the average French woman. Her face was broad across the cheekbones; lower down it narrowed almost to a point at the chin; her eyes were big and serious—the eyes of a child; her pretty, tempting, grave little mouth was well matched with her eyes. As she said, one had but to look at her to see that she was in earnest—with the earnestness of a child.

"Monsieur"—in her voice there came now and then a throb which was in odd consonance with the pathos of her whole appearance—"I entreat you to believe that I am in earnest; I entreat you to believe that to me life is less than nothing, that all that is left me is to die. But I would have you to understand that I am so placed that, in dying, I would wish my death to be worth more than my life to—to those who may be left behind."

Tears were in her eyes. Mr. Kennard dashed across the room to her.

"For goodness' sake, child, don't cry. Come, sit down and tell me all about it."

"Monsieur, do not touch me!"

"Touch you! Why, I'm old enough to be your father, child!"

"Monsieur, I desire you not to touch me!"

She withdrew her hand from the pocket of her dress; in it she was holding a revolver. Mr. Kennard stared at her, his whole face a vivid note of exclamation . . . "You—little firebrand!"

"I was aware that in my situation I was liable to be insulted. I can assure monsieur that I am prepared. May I again ask monsieur to confine himself to the business which is in hand."

"What do you call the business which is in hand? Do you suppose"—with sudden ferocity Mr. Kennard thrust his hands into his trousers pockets—"Is it possible that you suppose that I was seriously offering you ten thousand francs to kill the President?"

The contrast between the man's amazement and the girl's seriousness was, in its way, ludicrous.

"What, then, is the deed which you would have me do?"

"Deed I would have you do!" With both hands Mr. Kennard rumpled his hair. He turned to Willie Nash. "Nash, did you hear her? She asks me what is the deed I would have her do, as if I were the villain at the Vic and she my ruthless minion."

Although Mr. Kennard spoke to his friend in English, something in his manner seemed all at once to give the girl a glimpse at the sort of man he really was. With understanding the tears came again into her eyes.

"I perceive you have been having a jest with me. I wish you, monsieur, a good-day."

Before they could stop her she had gone. Willie Nash stared at the door which she had pulled to behind her. . . .

"Stark mad," he said.

Mr. Kennard looked from the door towards him—his face was still one vivid note of exclamation.

"There's a method in her madness. If you were to offer her ten thousand francs I believe she'd think as little of shooting me as if I were a spadger!"

Nash shrugged his shoulders; he took out his cigarette case.

"I told you that the French had their point of view and we had ours."

"Did you, indeed! William Nash, if you only had been someone else, what a clever man you might have been!" Mr. Kennard began pacing up and down, tousling his hair as he walked, first with one hand, then with the other. "The minx!—the chit!—with a voice and a face that you'd think she was an understudy for an angel, and yet to be burning with a desire to kill herself, and anybody else you like to mention—why? What for? My boy, for less than a monkey!"

Mr. Nash was lighting a cigarette.

"It is only," he observed, "after you have lived some time in France among the French that you begin to realise how much abroad you are." Mr. Kennard stood still to glare at him.

"Sententious jackdaw!" He recommenced his walking to and fro. "I say, William, how would you like to marry her?" There was the sound of someone at the door. "Hullo, is this her back again?" When the door opened, however, it was M. Gerbert who came in. Mr. Kennard went and laid his hands upon his shoulders. "Gerbert, I've been having an interview with the assassin."

Mr. Kennard was six foot four and M. Gerbert was about four foot six. The difference in their size was not only a question of height. Mr. Kennard was clumsily made, big and brawny. M. Gerbert's build was almost feminine. His hands and feet were as small as a woman's. He had long red hair, the ends of which strayed from under the brim of his big slouch hat—the size of the hat emphasised the diminutive proportions of its wearer. His face was white and eager, a typical French face of a certain class, all vivacity and nerves. Just now there was a look on it of painful tension, of something strained, as if a fever burned within. But then, M. Gerbert was apparently, in general, such a mere bundle of nerves that one drifted in the habit of taking it for granted that all his moods were evanescent. He looked up at the Englishman towering above him.

"I do not follow you."

"I say that I've been having an interview with the assassin, with the individual, you remember, who advertised that life had become an insupportable burden."

"Ah!" M. Gerbert slipped Mr. Kennard's hands from off his shoulders. "You wrote to him?"

"I wrote to him."

"Did he turn out to be the ordinary type of bravo, or merely an invertebrate animal with suicidal tendencies?"

"I don't quite know what you call the ordinary type of bravo."

"It is plain enough. I am myself an illustration. It is a fact that I am myself contemplating inserting a similar advertisement upon my own account."

"You find life an insupportable burden?"

"As for that, these many years! After one's childhood, one always wishes to make an end of it."

Mr. Kennard turned to Willie Nash to stare. Taking his cigarette from between his lips Mr. Nash addressed M. Gerbert, laughing as he spoke.

"So your glimpse of Paradise has vanished?"

"You mean Célestine—my wife? Bah! That is finished."

"It was merely an entr'acte then?"

"No, it was not an entr'acte. It was a complete tragedy of the little, sordid sort, which, at present, is the fashion."

Mr. Nash had resumed his cigarette. Mr. Kennard had poised himself against a corner of the table.

"Gerbert, the other day you were raving about your wife as if she were something higher than the angels. Do you mean to tell me, sir, that that's all over?"

"My ravings? Ah, no!" M. Gerbert had continued to wear his hat. Now, taking it off, crushing it up with his right hand, he held it out in front of him. "I shall always have my ravings, though my wife has gone."

"Gone? What the devil do you mean?"

M. Gerbert shrugged his shoulders.

"What does it matter? Perhaps she has begun to love another, or, without loving another, she has simply grown tired of me, or she finds my poverty more than she can bear."

"I suppose, young man, you have been clearing the matrimonial atmosphere, and this is the serio-comic fashion in which it pleases you to look at it."

M. Gerbert placed himself in Mr. Kennard's largest armchair.

"What sort was this fellow who found it necessary to advertise the fact that he found his life an insupportable burden?"

"The fellow was a woman."

"I might have guessed it. The curses have come home to roost. She has, doubtless, made life an insupportable burden to so many men that now it is her own turn."

"Keep it up, Gerbert, you'll be a cynic yet before you're done."

"This woman, was she old or young?"

"A girl, sir, a mere child, not out of her teens—eh, Nash? A little slip of a thing you could blow away with a breath. With the face of a saint, sir, or an angel, eyes which were the eyes of innocence, if ever yet I saw them. And yet, by George, sir, she offered for ten thousand francs to kill the President—kill him, sir! And she spoke as calmly as if she were telling you her size in gloves. Upon my soul, I believe she'd do it too!"

"Ten thousand francs—was that the sum she asked?"

"Ten thousand francs, sir. I might have understood it if she had asked ten million, but for a pittance such as that!"

"I perceive. You have yourself your price then. It is strange this woman's price is mine. Guarantee me ten thousand francs, and I will myself kill the President with my own hands."

Mr. Kennard looked at M. Gerbert for some moments in silence. Then, going to the mantelpiece, he began to fill his pipe from a tobacco-jar which stood upon a bracket.

"Gerbert," he said, "you promised to introduce me to Madame Gerbert. When are you going to keep your promise?"

"It is too late."

"Don't talk nonsense." The big man had filled his pipe. As he lighted it he puffed out clouds of smoke. "Gerbert, if you've nothing particularly on, ask me to spend this evening with you; and if you've no special objection to the fellow—such as most people seem to have—I'll bring Nash."

While M. Gerbert seemed hesitating Mr. Nash spoke.

"My dear Gerbert, Kennard is not only an Englishman, but, I assure you, he's an unusual specimen, even for an Englishman. I'll kick him if you like."

M. Gerbert raised himself out of the depths of Mr. Kennard's easy-chair.

"I see no reason why you should not come—I see no reason. M. Kennard—M. Nash—I hope to see you in my little apartment this evening about eight. For my wife, I cannot promise; I see very little of her myself. I cannot undertake that you will see anything of her at all. But, for me—to me you will be very welcome." He moved to the door. "Until this evening, my friends, about eight."

For some minutes after the Frenchman had gone neither of the Englishmen said anything. Mr. Kennard, his head thrown back, his pipe between his teeth, puffed clouds of smoke towards the ceiling. He was the first to speak.

"Not a very genial invitation—eh, William?"

"My dear Hugh, what it is to be heavy-footed. Did you happen to observe that the fellow was half beside himself with trouble?"

"I did. Because you are as blind as a bat it doesn't follow that we all are." Pause; more smoke. "Should you say that the trouble is with his wife, or with his money?"

"My experience teaches me that when a man has trouble with his money he also, as a matter of course, has trouble with his wife."

CHAPTER III.

M. and Mdme. Gerbert lived, it seemed, *au cinquième*. Mr. Kennard and Mr. Nash were conscious that, as they mounted higher, they seemed to be leaving even cleanliness behind them. The last staircase was in a state of almost dangerous dilapidation. The plaster was coming in great patches off the wall. Mr. Kennard hesitated before he knocked at the unpromising-looking door.

"If I had had any idea that things were so bad as this with him," he murmured, "hang me if I would have suggested coming. What a brute he must suppose I am."

Mr. Nash was, as he was too apt to be, sententious.

"You must never infer how a Frenchman lives, or where, from his appearance at his café."

They knocked three times, and still there was no answer. Mr.
Kennard was about to propose a retreat when M. Gerbert himself
opened the door.

"Enter, gentlemen!" They entered somewhat solemnly.
When they were in M. Gerbert stood with his back to the door.
"You see, gentlemen, this is my little apartment. I told you it was
a little apartment, did I not?" He had done so, but not how little,
nor how bare it was of furniture. The room was a mere cock-loft.
It was lighted by a tin lamp which stood upon an old wooden
table. This table, a bed in a corner, and a chair or two was practi-
cally all the furniture the place contained. It was not only the
abode of poverty, it seemed to be the abode of actual destitution.
Still standing with his back to the door, M. Gerbert took an obviously wry-mouthed pleasure in openly avowing the fact. "I heard
you knock, gentlemen, three times. Why did I not open? Because
I was ashamed. I have had the pleasure of your acquaintance now
two years. You have known me as a gentleman, as one of yourselves. You may well believe that I felt it difficult when the moment came to prove to you that, after all, I was only a beggar and
lived in a loft."

"My dear Gerbert!" stammered Mr. Kennard.

His friend was readier. "My very dear fellow, you don't suppose that you are the only man who has known what it is to be
hard up. Why, I myself have slept in a doss-house, and I've been
glad to have the fourpence to do it with."

"I understand you; I thank you, M. Nash. I am now worse off
than you were, as they say in the fairy tales, once upon a time."

"My dear Gerbert," blundered Mr. Kennard, "if you had only
hinted—if you had only told me——"

He got no further. M. Gerbert continued—after a fashion of
his own.

"If I had only told you what? You see I still have clothes—I
have a decent coat—it is true I find my shoes begin to want a little
careful touching—and I do not care to allow my shirt to become
too prominent—but so long as I could bear myself with decency,
what was there then I should have told you? You must forgive my
saying that I should have told you nothing now, if you had not,

in a measure, forced me to confession. But I seem to be lacking in hospitality. I have often been to your apartments. It is the first time you have come to mine. I beg of you to make yourselves entirely at your ease."

Mr. Kennard was already tousling his hair, as was his habit when disturbed.

"And—and Madame Gerbert?"

"My wife is gone."

"Gone, Gerbert! what do you mean?"

"She went from me this morning—that is what I mean."

"But have you no notion where she's gone to?"

"How should I have a notion? She was free to go where she chose—as free as air."

"Oughtn't you to make inquiries?"

"To serve what purpose? I know little, it is true, but what I know is more than enough. I know that she has become tired of me—of my poverty, of this." He stretched out his arms on either side of him. "She is but a young girl; a young girl soon becomes tired, it is only natural. But I am too much of an egotist. I weary you with trivialities. You must excuse me if I do not offer you to eat or to drink. I beg of you not to require from me too particular reasons for my seeming inhospitality."

Mr. Nash was seated as much at his ease as if he had been paying the most commonplace of calls. He watched M. Gerbert as though he found him unusually interesting, if only as a study. Mr. Kennard wandered about the room. Every now and then he ran his hand through his hair. He paused before a little shelf which was fixed against the wall. The only thing upon it was a photograph. He took this in his hand, and, half absent-mindedly, began to look at it. Suddenly his wits seemed to cease wool-gathering. His eyes flashed. The expression on his face betokened keen attention. He took the photograph to the table, bending over so that the lamp might show him more plainly what it was that he was looking at.

"Who's this?" He was staring as if he experienced a difficulty in crediting the evidence of his own senses. "Why—it's the assassin!"

M. Gerbert had momentarily turned away. At the sound of Mr. Kennard's voice he turned again.

"I beg your pardon?"

"It's the individual who found life an insupportable burden."

M. Gerbert went to the table. He saw what Mr. Kennard was holding.

"That is the portrait of Célestine—of my wife."

"Your wife! Your wife!" Mr. Kennard's voice rose almost to a roar. "This is the girl who came to me this morning, and who, in exchange for ten thousand francs, offered to kill the President."

M. Gerbert's eyes visibly dilated. He caught at the edge of the table as if to help him to stand.

"Are you sure?"

"Sure!" Taking his host by the shoulder, as he shouted each new insult, Mr. Kennard shook him as if he had been some naughty child. "You little mountebank! You tailor's dummy! You shell of a man!" In his excitement Mr. Kennard actually lifted his host right off his feet, and held him up before him in the air. "With your attitudinising, and the rest of your folly, you've driven that little girl, who loves you as only a woman can love a fool, to try to gain for you a wretched ten thousand francs in exchange, you little ass, for her own life."

Mr. Nash came and laid his hand upon his impulsive friend's arm.

"Steady, Hugh!"

Thus recalled to himself, and to the conventions of civilised society, Mr. Kennard replaced his host upon his feet upon the floor. M. Gerbert seemed so taken aback by the treatment he had received as to be able, for the moment, to do nothing but pant and gape. In the sudden silence a pass key was heard being inserted in the door without. It was opened. A woman came in; it was the woman who, that morning, had visited Mr. Kennard.

"Alphonse!" she exclaimed. "What is it?" She caught sight of Mr. Kennard, and knew him.

"Monsieur Hugh Kennard! Mon Dieu!"

She crouched back against the wall, as if she would shrink right through it if she could. One could see that she was trembling in every limb. Her veil was up, so that one perceived that even the muscles of her face were trembling. In the uncertain light she looked more childish even than she had done in the morning. Mr. Kennard moved forward.

"My child!" he said.

"No, no!" She put up her hands as if to ward him from her. "Alphonse! Alphonse! Do not let him touch me!"

It was pitiful to see her. It almost seemed as if it was these three men against this one little girl. In the face of her too obvious aversion Mr. Kennard all at once was tongue-tied. As usual, Mr. Nash was more self-possessed than his friend. He touched his host gently on the arm.

"Gerbert, may I beg from you the honour of an introduction to madame?"

M. Gerbert appeared to be struggling with a waking dream. As his faculties returned, with a slight gesture, he, as it were, brushed Mr. Nash aside.

"Permit me." He advanced till he stood quite close to the woman cowering against the wall. He looked at her for a moment in silence. "Ah—it is you." He turned to Mr. Kennard. "I believe, Mr. Kennard, that you are a larger man than I. On the other hand, and at the same time, it is true I am a beggar."

The big man was evidently in a state of mental confusion. He had eyes only for the girl quivering against the wall.

"My dear Gerbert, upon my soul, I beg your pardon. Won't—won't you introduce me to Madame Gerbert?"

"To Madame Gerbert?" Clasping his hands behind his back, M. Gerbert fell into a pose which, if we are to believe the painters, was a favourite one of the first Napoleon's. "It appears that you already are acquainted with Madame Gerbert."

"The acquaintance is of an informal kind."

"So I should imagine." The red-haired little man addressed himself to his girl wife. His words seemed to make her quiver as if they had been so many lashes from a whip. "So it is you. I thought that you had gone."

"Alphonse!" was all she said.

"I imagined when, this morning, you left me, that you observed that you never would set eyes on me again."

"Alphonse!"

"You told me a few things, but was it because you forgot that you omitted to tell me that, so soon as you were outside my door, you were going to pay a visit to a strange man?"

"Alphonse!"

The woman put up her hands to cover her face. Mr. Kennard grasped his friend's arm with, perhaps, unconscious vigour.

"I shall murder this little brute in a minute," he murmured.

As he whispered a response Mr. Nash disengaged his arm from his friend's too vigorous grasp.

"Did I not tell you that the French have their own point of view, and that we have ours."

M. Gerbert had continued to gaze in silence at his wife. As if moved with the courage of desperation, taking her hands from before her face, she ventured to make an attempt to offer some sort of plea in self-defence.

"Alphonse, I did it for you."

"For me?" M. Gerbert tapped his hand against his breast. "It was for me that you paid a visit to a strange man?"

"It was a little plot which I had formed to gain for you the ten thousand francs of which, you know, you are in need. I had thought to gain them for you in exchange for my life—so that my death might be worth something to you, though my life had been worth nothing at all. And, Alphonse—husband! I have only returned to tell you that I think I have gained for you the sum which you require."

"The sum which I require—my wife, at what price?"

The strangest smile flitted across the girl's face as she held out her hands and answered—

"What does it matter?"

"To you—nothing at all. To me—everything. I have my good name—I! I have my honour!" M. Gerbert crossed his arms upon his chest. "Already, because of you, my honour has been dragged in the dust. Your English friend has used me as if I were a thing of the gutter, here, in my own apartment."

Mr. Kennard interposed.

"I do assure you, my dear Gerbert, that it was a misunder-standing."

"A misunderstanding?"

Four foot six glowered up at six foot four. Before the pigmy the giant seemed to cower.

"It is a misunderstanding, M. Kennard, which can only be explained with your life or with mine."

"Alphonse!—my husband!"

The girl advanced. The man shrank back.

"Madame Gerbert, have the goodness not to defile me with your touch. To the other things which you have brought me it but remained to add dishonour. That, also, you have brought me, last of all. Since, therefore, you have lied to me, and have returned to crush me, unto eternity, with the last offering of your shame—which, unfortunately, because it is yours, a thousand times more is mine!—for me it but remains to go!"

M. Gerbert made a movement towards the door. Mr. Kennard caught him by the shoulder.

"Gerbert, don't be a fool!"

In an instant M. Gerbert was like a wild-cat in a frenzy. Leaping up at Mr. Kennard, he attacked him, literally, tooth and nail. He poured forth language which was not only unparliamentary, but also unprintable. The big man, in his turn, was so taken by surprise that he made not the slightest attempt even at defence. The first paroxysm of his fury exhausted, the little man stamped on the floor and shrieked with rage.

"If I had but a pistol!" he screamed.

His wife, who was standing a yard or two away from him, took something from the pocket of her dress.

"I have a revolver," she said.

She proved it by discovering that she had such a weapon in her hand. It was probably the same one with which, in the morning, she had kept Mr. Kennard at a distance.

Mr. Nash called out to his friend—

"Keep tight hold of him, Hugh, don't let him get near it for your life!"

Madame Gerbert turned to him with that air of simple seriousness which was so like the exaggerated seriousness of a little child.

"It is not for my husband. It is for me!"

Before they had a suspicion of her purpose she placed the barrel of the revolver against her brow and fired. It was done so quickly that, although Mr. Kennard rushed forward, while the words were still, as it were, upon her lips, he was only in time to put his arm about her body as it was falling—dead.

VIII.

THE DIAMONDS

I.—THE ONE DIAMOND.

Harold Brooke had a watchmaker's glass fitted in his eye. Through it he was intently regarding something which he held in his hand.

"One of the two finest diamonds which ever came out of Africa gone wrong! I wonder what Fungst will say?"

He moved to the window. Under the stronger light he renewed his examination of the crystal through the little microscopic lens.

"It'll be an affair of perhaps half an hour. I've known it happen in less. Tyrrel shall have it." He laughed. "Hard on Tyrrel, but harder still on me. He and I will share the loss. I wonder what Fungst will say? According to him, we had captured two of the finest diamonds Africa had ever yet produced. They were to make our fortunes. Well, Tyrrel shall have a chance of making his. I wonder how far his knowledge of this sort of thing may go?"

A few minutes afterwards a hansom dashed up in front of a quaint little shop in the neighbourhood of St. John's Square, Clerkenwell. Mr. Brooke sprang out and entered the shop. A young man was its only occupant.

"Tyrrel, I've brought you the diamond." The young man behind the counter gave a perceptible start. "I've changed my mind. You shall have it cheap."

"Cheap?"

"Dirt cheap. You shall have it for a thousand pounds."

"A thousand pounds?"

"Yes, a thousand pounds. But it must be money down. I leave

England to-night. There are reasons which compel me. I don't know when I may return. Is it a bargain? Here is the stone."

Mr. Tyrrel took it with a hand which trembled. He gave just one glance at it. His eyes gleamed.

"Will a cheque do?"

"An open cheque."

Mr. Tyrrel wrote an open cheque for a thousand pounds. He handed it to Mr. Brooke. With a mere "Thanks!" that gentleman passed from the shop, sprang into the hansom, and was driven away. Mr. Tyrrel stared after him amazed.

"I wonder what's up now?"

He picked up his purchase from where he had placed it on the counter. His hand still trembled. He went from the shop into an inner room.

"Mary, I've bought the diamond."

A note of exultation was in his voice. A young woman was leaving the room, a pile of linen in her arms. At the sound of her husband's voice she turned.

"Mr. Brooke's diamond?"

"Mr. Brooke's! What do you think I gave for it? A thousand pounds."

"A thousand pounds!"

"I think that Brooke's gone mad. He might have got ten times the sum from almost anyone. He says that he has had a sudden call abroad, and wants the cash. It's his affair, not mine. Anyhow, I've bought the diamond. I gave him what he asked for it. Here it is."

Mrs. Tyrrel laid her pile of linen on the table. She took the stone which her husband held out to her. She selected a watch-maker's glass from among several which were on the mantel-shelf. Fitting it into her eye, she examined the stone under the light of the window.

"What a beauty!" She drew it closer to her eye. "What a beautiful stone!" She turned it over and over in her hand. "What is this speck of light right in the very heart of it?"

"What speck of light?"

Mr. Tyrrel selected a glass on his own account. In his turn

he examined the stone. Hardly had he fitted the glass in its place when he gave an exclamation. He went nearer to the window.

"Give me a higher power!"

She chose another glass from those upon the shelf. She noticed that her husband's face had all at once turned pale. "What is the matter?"

He made no immediate answer. But no sooner had he begun to examine his purchase with the lens of higher power than he staggered back against the wall. He took the glass out of his eye. He looked round the room like a man who had received a sudden shock. All his animation of a moment before had disappeared.

"He's—he's ruined me! The thief! I understand it now. Why he wanted the cash, his haste, and the call abroad. What a fool I was! I had seen the stone so often, I thought I knew it so well, that I never thought of looking at it. I snapped him—I thought he'd change his mind—and he's snapped me."

His wife advanced to him.

"James, what is wrong? Isn't it the stone you thought it was?"

He laid his hand lightly on her arm.

"Hush! There's someone in the shop. See who it is."

She peeped through the curtain which screened the door.

"It's Mr. Hart."

"What does he want?" With his handkerchief Mr. Tyrrel mopped his brow. "I'll—I'll go and see."

In the shop there was a tall, portly gentleman. His overcoat, which was unbuttoned, was lined and trimmed with fur. About him there was an odour of wealth.

"How do, Tyrrel, how do? Mrs. Hart's going to be presented at the first Drawing-room—sheriff's wife, and that sort of thing, you know—and I want to give her something neat in diamonds. Thought I'd give you a turn—get them in the rough. Knew your father. He and I have had many a deal together. Got anything good just now?"

Mr. Tyrrel looked round and round the shop. He glanced behind him at the door which led into the inner room. He drew a long breath. "I—I happen to have one of the finest stones in England, Mr. Hart."

"Daresay! There are a good many of the finest stones in England about just now. And you want one of the finest prices in England for it too?"

"You are yourself something of a judge of diamonds."

"I am—something."

"Here is the stone. Examine it for yourself."

Mr. Tyrrel handed the stone to Mr. Hart. As he did so it was to be noticed that his hand still trembled. He mopped his brow as his visitor turned the stone over and over in his hands. His lips seemed parched. Mr. Hart took the stone to the door.

"Got a glass?" he asked.

Mr. Tyrrel hunted out a spy-glass. He seemed to have some difficulty in finding one. Mr. Hart fitted it into his eye.

"Not a very strong glass, this one of yours; I've seen stronger. But it's good enough to enable me to see that this is something like a diamond. What's the figure?"

Mr. Tyrrel moistened his lips. "Two thousand pounds."

"Too much!"

"It's dirt cheap, Mr. Hart. I've seen worse stones than that sold for ten thousand pounds. But I happen to be very much in want of ready cash."

"I don't deny that the stone's a good one. But it's in the rough, and it may cut up rough. And two thousand pounds is more than I care to pay for an ornament for a drawing-room, even though that drawing-room be Her Majesty's. But I'll tell you what I'll do, as I knew your father, I'll give you a cheque for fifteen hundred down upon the nail."

Again Mr. Tyrrel moistened his lips.

"I'll accept it."

A cheque changed hands almost as expeditiously as the one for a smaller amount had changed hands only a few minutes before. Mr. Hart departed with his purchase.

"I think I've scored that trick. If this diamond isn't worth fifteen hundred pounds and a bit more, why, then I'm wrong."

Mr. Hart then and there took a cab to the Bond Street headquarters of those famous jewellers, Messrs. Ruby and Golden. He was shown into the senior partner's private room.

"I want you to set this stone for me."

Mr. Ruby took very gingerly between his finger and his thumb the piece of crystal which Mr. Hart was holding out to him on the palm of his outstretched hand.

"A diamond, I see, and uncut. Rather a fine specimen." Mr. Ruby's eyes glistened. "May I ask in confidence from whom you obtained it?"

"From a friend in the trade."

Mr. Hart kept his eyes fixed upon the jeweller's face. His tone was dry.

"You don't happen to know, I suppose, if he has any more like this to dispose of?"

"Can't say that I do. What's it worth?"

"You see, Mr. Hart, the value of a diamond depends upon so many things. To us it depends in a measure on whether we have a customer who at the moment requires just such a stone."

"And you have such a customer? I see. Well, I bought it for my wife. I want you to cut it and mount it as a pin for the hair."

Mr. Ruby hesitated. He turned the jewel over and over in his hand.

"We are old friends, Mr. Hart. May I ask how much you gave for this?"

"Two thousand pounds."

It was true that Mr. Tyrrel had asked two thousand. Mr. Hart had probably forgotten that he had beaten him down to fifteen hundred.

"Two thousand pounds? You are a man of business, Mr. Hart. I daresay you have no objection to making a little profit even out of a diamond. I will be frank with you. We happen to have a valuable customer who is particularly in want of just such a stone as this. It is on that account that I venture, even in Mr. Golden's absence, to offer you for your two-thousand-pound purchase three thousand pounds; a clear profit of a thousand pounds."

"A thousand pounds!" Mr. Hart stroked his chin. "My dear sir, I'm not reduced to selling my wife's diamonds."

"Has Mrs. Hart yet seen the stone?"

"Not yet she hasn't. I bought it not half an hour ago."

"Then the thing is simplified. I will carry my offer farther. I will give you three thousand pounds for the stone, and will allow you to select, in addition, any articles from our stock to the cash value of a thousand pounds."

The corners of Mr. Hart's lips twitched. He smiled. "It's a deal."

It was. Mr. Hart left the Bond Street establishment with a cheque for three thousand pounds in his pocket, and in a red morocco case a set of very pretty diamond ornaments for a lady's hair. The stone which he had purchased from Mr. Tyrrel he left behind.

"Mr. Hart thinks himself a shrewd man," Mr. Ruby told himself when that gentleman had gone, "but he is not *quite* so shrewd as he thinks. This is the very stone the Duke is looking for. Unless I am mistaken, he will give us for it rather more than four thousand pounds."

About an hour after Mr. Golden entered Mr. Ruby's room. The senior partner rubbed his hands as the junior entered.

"I have been indulging in a little deal while you have been out—a little deal in diamonds."

The junior partner glanced sharply at the senior. In appearance Mr. Ruby was very different from Mr. Golden. Mr. Ruby was large and florid. Mr. Golden was slight and dark, with keen, bright eyes.

"I have lighted on the very stone we have been trying to find for the Duke, and I have bought it on the nail out and out."

"The deuce you have! What did you give for it?"

"Three thousand in cash and a thousand in stock."

"Let me look at it."

Mr. Golden held out his hand. Mr. Ruby produced the stone from the inner recesses of a large safe in a corner of the room. Mr. Golden took it to the window. He examined it minutely for some moments with his naked eye. Then, taking a spyglass from his waistcoat pocket, he examined it through that. Scarcely had he placed the glass in its place than he sprang round at Mr. Ruby.

"Ruby!" Strong words seemed trembling on his lips. If that were so, he exercised an effort of self-control. "You've been done!"

"Mr. Golden!"

"How many times have I asked you not to buy diamonds in my absence!"

Mr. Ruby's face was pasty-hued. "But—but it's one of the finest diamonds I've ever seen."

Mr. Golden's glance was expressive of the most supreme contempt. "Look at it through that, and tell me if you see nothing."

Mr. Ruby looked at the diamond through his partner's spy-glass. "I—I can only see that it is a very beautiful stone."

"Can't you see, right in the centre, what looks like a speck of light?"

"Now that I look into it closely, there certainly does seem to be something of the kind. But it is so slight that, even with this strong glass, it is scarcely noticeable."

"And yet, sooner or later, it will shiver that stone to splinters."

"Mr. Golden!"

"I have seen it before, and I know what it is. It is a sort of disease to which African diamonds are peculiarly liable, especially the finest stones. I wish to goodness, Ruby, that you would leave these things to me. That speck of light is a crack in the grain of the stone. It will increase in size, ramifying in all directions, until, at a certain point, the stone will shiver—blow up, in fact. The thing may happen in ten minutes. It may not happen for months. It will happen some time or other, to a certainty. Any man who really knows something of diamonds will tell you that."

Mr. Ruby had sunk back in his seat. He seemed ill at ease. "But—but can't we sell it to the Duke? It's the very stone he wants."

Mr. Golden smiled. "We can sell it to the Duke if it lasts long enough. The attempt to cut it may bring about the smash. I've known it happen before to-day."

"We'll try, at any rate—we'll try! You may be wrong, Golden; I really think you may be."

"I may be." Mr. Golden's tone was grim.

"I'll have it put into hand at once. It's a glorious stone. One of the finest stones I've ever seen. It would be a bargain to anyone at—at ten thousand pounds."

II.—THE OTHER.

"Hollo, Fungst!"

"Brooke!"

Unannounced Mr. Brooke had entered the room. He had taken Mr. Fungst unawares. Mr. Fungst stared at him amazed. He was a paunchy little man, with black, curly, well-greased hair, which he parted in the middle. Uninvited, his visitor took a chair.

"I've only just reached Paris. Left London this afternoon, and came straight on here."

"This is—this is funny. This is very funny indeed." Mr. Fungst said "dis" instead of "this," and "vunny" instead of "funny." "Is—is it anything you have come to see about?"

"Only you, my Fungst—only you."

The two friends looked at each other. Mr. Brooke's lips were parted by a smile. There was a curious look in Mr. Fungst's eyes. He seemed rather ill at ease.

"That is very funny. Do you know, I was putting a few things together to come over to London tonight to have a little talk with you."

"What was to be the purport of the talk, my Fungst?"

"It was only about a little thing. It was just a word I wished to say to you about"—Mr. Fungst glanced at the floor, then up again—"about the diamond."

"The diamond?" Mr. Brooke's smile grew more pronounced.

"Just a little talk."

"It's sold."

"Sold? What! The diamond?"

A singular change took place in Mr. Fungst's appearance. His jaw dropped. His eyes seemed to increase in size. His paunchy frame seemed to quiver under emotion.

"I found a customer this morning."

"What did you get for it? Twenty—thirty thousand pounds?"

Mr. Brooke laughed outright. "Not quite so much as that."

"Not so much? What did you get for it?"

"A thousand down."

"A—thousand—down! A—thousand—pounds! Mein Gott!" Mr. Fungst's face was a picture. He seemed divided between tears and rage. "Oh, Harold Brooke, what a fool you are!"

"Not such a fool as I look, my Fungst. The stone was a wrong un."

"A wrong un! What you call a wrong un?"

"It was afflicted with the shivers. Cracked, my boy. It is more than probable that by now it is splintered into dust."

"Oh, good 'evins! Harold Brooke, what a fool you are!" Mr. Fungst raised his two fat hands above his well-oiled head, as if he were appealing to the skies. "It is more than a week ago since I saw in my own stone, in the very heart of it, a spot like a little speck of light."

"It was only this morning that I observed the same phenomenon in mine. I knew from painful experience what it meant."

"You knew what it meant? You *thought* you knew what it meant. As a matter of fact, you knew nothing at all about it, any more than me. When I see this little spot, I say to myself, 'It is all over. You are done for. Bang goes your little pile.' I have seen stones begin like that, and pulverise within a quarter of an hour—twenty minutes. It is a mystery which no man understands, not even the man who thinks he knows the most. I was fit to tear my hair. I rushed off in a cab, determined to sell the stone at any price if I could only be in time. You know how they used to do that sort of thing at Kimberley. As I was in the cab I kept looking at my stone through my spy-glass to see how it was getting on. My heart was fit to break. All of a sudden I see something which I had never seen before. The little spot of white light had turned into a little spot of colour. It was as though a little spot of blood had got into the very centre of the stone. I say to myself, 'It is certain that if I try to sell the stone just as it is I shall get nothing for it—scarcely anything at all. About this affair there is something which I do not understand.' There is no man living who understands all the inns and outs of diamonds—no chemist, no scientist, I care not who it is. There are mysteries about diamonds which never yet have been explained. I have known some of them within the range of my own experience. So I say to myself, 'There is a mystery in this. If I sell the diamond now, a loss is certain; if I see the mystery through, the loss is problematical. I will see the mystery through.' I came back home again. I put the diamond away. I did not look at it for two whole days.

"When, after two whole days, I came to open the little box in which I had placed the diamond, I scarcely dared to open the lid. I felt that, as you say, my heart was in my boots. I felt as though my heart was made of jelly, and that it was melting all away." Mr. Fungst paused. He raised his fat forefinger. He pointed it at Mr. Brooke. "I say to myself, 'Have courage.' Then I take a little nip of brandy. That give me strength. Then I have a smoke. Then I raise the lid." Mr. Fungst raised himself on tiptoe. He seemed to increase in size. "My friend, there was the diamond. But what a diamond! It was a rose brilliant. But such a rose brilliant as the world has never seen!"

Mr. Brooke laughed a little awkwardly. "I say, Fungst, aren't you piling it on?"

"Am I piling it on? You shall see for yourself if I am piling it on." Mr. Fungst took a little leather bag out of an inner pocket of his coat. He handed it to Mr. Brooke. "Open it, and see if I am piling it on."

Mr. Brooke untied the cord which bound the neck of the bag. Within nestled a diamond—a rose brilliant, but of such a hue! "Red as a rose was" not exactly "she," but "it." Mr. Brooke feasted his eyes upon its beauties. The stone was still uncut. Its greatest beauties were therefore still unrevealed. But even in its rough state it was a masterpiece of light and colour.

"What a stone!"

Mr. Fungst stood in front of his friend. He rubbed his hands together. He sprang from foot to foot. "Do I pile it on?"

"But, I say, Fungst, this seems to me very like a miracle. I can scarcely credit that such a stone as this was only the other day a pure white diamond with something which looked very like a crack in it."

"I tell you there are mysteries in diamonds which no man understands—not any one."

"What are you going to do with it?"

"That is just the point on which I wished to speak to you. You know J. F. Flinders, the American millionaire? Billionaire he must be, rather, because they say his income is nearly a million yearly. He is in Paris. His daughter is going to be married. He is looking for a wedding present for her; something a little out of the common. I went to him. I show him this. I tell him I think I know where there is another like it. He offered me for the pair—for the pair, you understand——" Mr. Fungst leaned over. He whispered in his friend's ear.

"You don't mean it?"

"To a centime that is what he offered."

Mr. Brooke whistled. "And I sold it for a thousand pounds!"

"To whom did you sell it?"

"To a man named Tyrrel."

Mr. Brooke had risen from his seat. He began to walk about the room.

"Tyrrel of Clerkenwell?"

"The same."

"Then, after all, to-night I must go to London. It is for me to buy it back again."

"For you?" Mr. Brooke faced round. "It strikes me, Fungst, that it's for me to buy it back again."

"Very good, my friend. But it is possible that Mr. Tyrrel may know more about diamonds than you. He will want more than his thousand pounds."

Mr. Brooke bit his lip. "He knows me. He will give me credit."

"As to that we shall see."

Mr. Fungst began to cram some things into a Gladstone bag. Mr. Brooke watched him for some moments. Then he went and touched him on the shoulder.

"Look here, Fungst, what are you driving at? What do you think you're going to do?"

Mr. Fungst turned to his friend all frankness. "All I wish is that we should have the pair—just you and I."

Mr. Brooke retained his grasp upon his friend's shoulder, nor did he remove his inquisitorial glance from his friend's frank features. "Yes, just you"—with the fingers of his disengaged hand Mr. Brooke tapped himself on the chest—"and I."

III.—THE TWO.

"My friend, could you tell me just one thing?"

Ivor Dacre glanced down at the speaker. He was a little rotund fellow. He spoke with a strong foreign accent. On his features there was the impress of the German Jew, and not by any means of the highest type of German Jew. He looked oddly out of place in the midst of that gorgeous assemblage, built rather for the purlieus of Houndsditch than for the Marquis of Clonkilty's ballroom. Mr. Dacre could scarcely believe that the profusely-perspiring little man addressed himself to him, but Mr. Fungst removed all misapprehension on that score by twitching Mr. Dacre by the lapel of his coat.

He repeated his inquiry.

"My friend, could you tell me just one thing?"

"If it is in my power."

"Could you tell me which is the Duchess of Datchet."

'The Duchess of Datchet?"

Ivor Dacre smiled outright. The idea of there being any possible association between that oily Houndsditch Hebrew and the latest and brightest queen of the London season—the bride of but a month or two—struck him as too ludicrous. Mr. Dacre was possessed of that rare attribute, a sense of humour. A wicked idea entered his head.

"Are you a friend of her Grace's?"

"I am not a friend exactly, but there is a little business which I wish to do with her."

A little business! In the Marquis of Clonkilty's ballroom! With the Queen of Hearts!

Mr. Dacre's eyes wandered round the room. They passed from dancer to dancer. At last they rested upon one. As they did so he raised his hand to his moustache, possibly to conceal the smile which he could not restrain.

"You see that lady over there?"

"There are so many ladies. Upon my soul, I never see so many ladies."

"The lady in the dark green dress with the nose-glasses."

"The old girl with the moustache?"

"Precisely—the old girl with the moustache." Mr. Dacre's smile almost expanded into a grin. "That is the Duchess of Datchet."

Without a word of thanks Mr. Fungst strode off. He ploughed his way through the dancers without paying the slightest regard to the evolutions they were attempting to perform. Mr. Dacre watched him go with a degree of delight which seemed on the point of producing an inward convulsion. All at once Mr. Fungst pulled up right in front of a couple—they both were young—who seemed in blissful enjoyment of the waltz.

"She hasn't got it on, so help me!"

"Sir!"

The young gentleman whose path he had impeded addressed him with a degree of scorn which was intended to be crushing. Mr. Fungst was not at all abashed.

"I wasn't speaking to you, my friend." Then, to himself, still audibly, "Mein Gott! If she has lost it!"

Striding forward, he caught a lady by the arm. She had on a dark green dress. She wore a pair of nose-glasses. More than the suggestion of a moustache adorned her upper lip. She was beginning to be stricken in years. But that did not prevent her waltzing, with apparent enjoyment, with a gentleman who seemed at least

ten years her junior. She and her partner were still moving to the
rhythm of the music when Mr. Fungst caught her by the arm.

"Excuse me, my name is Fungst, Jacob Fungst. There is a little word I wish to speak to you just now."

The lady stopped, startled. She turned. When her glance fell
on Mr. Fungst—it had to fall some distance—she drew herself up
and shuddered as though she had come into sudden contact with
an iceberg.

"Who is this person?"

"Fungst," explained the owner of that name. "There is just
a little thing about which I wish to speak to you two words outside."

The lady addressed her cavalier, "Will you please take me
away? This person is a stranger to me."

He took her away. As Mr. Fungst continued to stare after the
retreating pair someone touched him on the shoulder. It was a
young gentleman who wore a single eyeglass. It is not impossible
that he had been commissioned by Mr. Ivor Dacre, who is the soul
of mischief.

"Don't you think you're rather blocking the way? What is it
you want?"

"I wish to say just two words to the Duchess of Datchet."

"That is not the Duchess of Datchet." The young gentleman
drew him aside. "That is the Duchess of Datchet."

As he spoke the music ceased. The dance was ended. The
gentlemen began to lead the ladies to their seats. In front of Mr.
Fungst there passed a woman who was tall and most divinely fair.
Her hair was of the colour of the rich red gold. Where its glorious
mass was thickest there gleamed a diamond. It was the diamond
and not the woman which caught the eye of Mr. Fungst.

"Mein Gott!"—he uttered what seemed to be his favourite
imprecation—"it's changed!"

Something seemed to startle him so greatly that he actually
allowed the lady to pass, and unmolested. She leaned on the arm
of a gentleman who was not only much taller than herself, but, in
his way, as handsome. There was probably no handsomer couple

in the room. And yet the lady seemed ill at ease, although the gentleman was smiling at her all the time.

"That was the Duchess of Datchet," observed Mr. Fungst's new acquaintance, who had been observing him with unconcealed amusement.

Mr. Fungst awoke as though from a stupor. Again there came that adjuration, "Mein Gott!—she's gone!"

She was. And before Mr. Fungst caught sight of her again the Duchess of Datchet's carriage had been called, and her Grace was in it, driving from the ball.

The Duchess had the carriage to herself. A gentleman had escorted her to the door. As he closed it he murmured just one word—

"Remember!"

She, leaning forward, had replied, "Do you think I can forget?"

As the vehicle passed swiftly through the night, if one might judge from the expression on her countenance, it did not seem as though she could. Once she put up her small gloved hands and veiled her face—veiled it though there was no one there to see. She took a little card from the bosom of her dress. It was the programme of the ball. It was a white card. The back was blank, or, rather, it would have been if it had not been for certain pencil marks. The pencil marks were figures. On the back of the programme was a little sum in compound addition. It was cast up. The total was stated. The sight of that total seemed to cause her Grace discomfort. "If I could only lay my hand upon the money!"

The carriage reached home. As the Duchess entered the hall a servant advanced to meet her. He addressed the lady in a confidential whisper.

"A gentleman wishes to see your Grace. He has been waiting more than an hour."

The Duchess shivered. She drew her cloak closer round her. Possibly she felt the air a trifle cold. "Has the Duke returned?"

"Not yet, your Grace."

"Show the gentleman into my sitting-room."

She did not ask the visitor's name. But when she was alone in her own apartment she veiled her face with her hands again. Only for a moment. When the door opened all traces of agitation had disappeared. There entered a young and comely man who, although he was dressed in rough-and-ready morning costume, looked as though he were a man of breeding. At sight of him the Duchess started. It almost seemed as if he were not at all the sort of person she had expected to see. She waited for the visitor to speak. This the visitor appeared to experience some little difficulty in doing.

"I must crave your Grace's forgiveness for my intrusion at this unseasonable hour, but circumstances of a peculiar nature——"

He paused. In his turn he started. His eyes were fixed upon the Duchess's head—upon the glory of her hair. He gave an exclamation of surprise.

"It's changed! Fungst was right!"

"Sir!"

The Duchess drew back. She appeared to find the stranger's demeanour slightly singular—as well she might. He continued staring at her as though he could not take his eyes away. He was, all at once, possessed with a strange excitement.

"Your Grace must forgive me if the offer I am about to make to you seems strange, as it cannot help but seem. If you knew all I am sure you would forgive me. I will give you ten thousand pounds for the diamond in your hair!"

"You will give me ten thousand pounds—for the diamond—in my hair?"

Half mechanically the lady raised her hand to her head. Her fingers lighted on the jewel which gleamed among her tresses. As they did so, and some faint comprehension of the stranger's meaning dawned upon her mind, her face became a crimson-red.

"My husband's present! Are you a madman, sir; or do you purposely insult me?"

"That diamond was mine. On its possession I had founded all my hopes of fortune. It was taken from me by means of a trick." Perhaps Mr. Brooke thought he spoke the truth. One can but hope he did. "I received for it not a twentieth part of the sum I offer you." Again he slightly erred. "But rather than it should be lost to me for ever, poor as I am, I will give you—I will give you—twelve thousand pounds."

"Twelve thousand pounds!" Her Grace's hand was lifted to her corsage. Possibly it brushed against the ball programme, with the compound addition sum upon its back, which lay within. "You will give me twelve thousand pounds?" She drew a deep breath. "But—but it's absurd! Who are you, sir, that you forget who I am?"

"What does it matter who I am? I am Harold Brooke. I am the modern equivalent of the soldier of fortune, and you have my fortune—*my* fortune—in your hair! Twelve did I say I'd give? For my fortune back again I'll give you fifteen thousand pounds!"

"Fifteen thousand pounds!" Her Grace's hands veiled her Grace's face again. "Am I going mad? Fifteen thousand pounds!" She sat down. Her agitation seemed extraordinary. She was positively trembling. "It is not to be thought of."

"I will give you twenty!"

"Twenty—twenty thousand pounds!"

There was silence. Mr. Brooke leaned forward, looking down at her. She looked up at him. With her right hand she grasped the upper portion of her corsage. This time there was no mistake about it—between her fingers she pressed that programme of the ball. Her face became cold and set. She became all at once a little older. The character of her beauty seemed to change. It was stern and hard.

"Your behaviour is that of a madman. I am scarcely less mad than you, or I should not continue to listen. How am I to know that you are not, as you very probably are, trifling with me all the time?"

"Promise me that the diamond shall be mine if I bring you the money in the morning."

"Twenty thousand pounds?"

"Twenty thousand pounds!"

"Twenty? I will give you thirty!"

The voice said "dirty." Mr. Brooke sprang round. Her Grace

stood up. A little man, almost as broad as he was tall, was standing at the open door. Entering, he closed the door behind him.

"Fungst!"

"So, Brooke," he said, "you thought to do me. But I am not done so easily, my friend."

"How did you get here?"

"That is my secret. There are more ways than one of getting into the Duke of Datchet's house, my friend."

The two men stood staring at each other. Mr. Brooke with clenched fists and a flush upon his face. Mr. Fungst with his crush-hat under his arm, his hands in his overcoat pockets, and an ungenial smile upon his lips. As for the Duchess, she stood staring at them both. The march of events seemed to have deprived her of a little of her breath. When she did speak she addressed herself to Mr. Fungst.

"May I ask, sir, what is the meaning of this intrusion, and who you are?"

"I am Jacob Fungst, that's who I am. If it was not for me he would not have had the stone at all. And when he make a fool of himself and sell it—if it was not for me he would not have known what it was that he had sold. Now, when I have found a market for the stone, he tries to do me, his friend, his very good friend indeed, out of the market I have found. That is why, when he say twenty thousand, I say thirty; and not in the morning, but cash down."

"Fungst, I advise you to be careful."

"I will be careful. Be easy in your mind, I will be careful. It is a thing of which I am very fond—carefulness."

Mr. Brooke touched his friend lightly on the shoulder. "I only seek my share of the spoil."

"Your share? Very good. Get what share you please. It is the same to me. It is your behind-the-door ways I do not like." Mr. Fungst turned to the Duchess. He stretched out his hand. "I have been running after that diamond all through the town—yes, night and day—from the pillar to the post. I trace it home to you. I learn that it was presented to you this morning to wear to-night at the Marquis of Clonkilty's ball. At the Marquis of Clonkilty's ball I see it in your hair."

Her Grace's bewilderment seemed to be increasing. "The Marquis of Clonkilty's ball! You?"

"Yes, me. I go to the door of the house. I ask for you. There was a crowd of people. They do not seem to understand. They say, 'What name?' I say, 'Fungst.' They show me up the stairs. I find myself in the middle of the ball. I say to myself, 'This is funny. Since I am here, well, I will look for the stone.' I look for the stone. I see it in your hair. The sight so surprises me, I lose my head. When I find it, I find you gone. I come after you. I come here. It takes me some time and a little diplomacy"—Mr. Fungst patted his waistcoat pocket—"to get into the house. It was more trouble, a great deal more trouble, than to get into the Marquis of Clonkilty's ball. But when I do get in I offer you for the diamond, money down, thirty thousand pounds."

Again Mr. Brooke touched his friend upon the shoulder.

"Fungst, you will have to reckon with me."

"I will reckon with you, never fear. I will tell the lady why I offer for the diamond thirty thousand pounds. It is a great price, a very great price, to offer for one diamond. It is because I have the other stone just like it, and I wish to make a pair. I will show the other stone to the lady. She will see I tell the truth." Mr. Fungst began groping in the inner pocket of his coat. He produced a little leather bag. "It is in this bag." He was holding the bag between the fingers of his right hand. Suddenly a curious expression began to creep over his features. "It is very funny." He hesitated. "It is in this bag." He began to untie the cord which bound the neck of the bag. In the midst of the operation he paused. He felt the contents of the bag with the fingers of either hand. "It is—it is very funny." His face assumed a curious leaden hue. "It is in this bag."

Mr. Brooke advanced.

"What's the matter, Fungst?"

"It—it is nothing. It—it is very funny. The stone is in this bag." He continued to untie the cord. It was all untied. With peculiar circumspection he opened the neck of the bag. He peeped within. He continued to peep within, as if to explore its depths were a work of time. He staggered backwards.

"Mein Gott! It's gone! I'm robbed!"

"Robbed!" cried Mr. Brooke. He took the bag out of Mr. Fungst's unresisting hand. There was a strange expression on his face; there was a curious glitter in his eyes. As he peeped into the bag he laughed, not pleasantly. "Not robbed, my Fungst—not robbed. The diamond's here." He turned the bag upside down upon the table. There came out a little mass of tiny sparkling crystals. They formed upon the table a small heap of glittering dust. Mr. Brooke pointed to it with his hand.

"There's your rose brilliant, Fungst."

Mr. Fungst came forward. He leaned over the table. He stared at the gleaming atoms.

"Mein Gott! It's gone off bang!"

"As you say, my Fungst, it has gone off bang. Who was right, my Fungst? Personally, I never knew a diamond which, when attacked by the shivers, sooner or later did not go off bang. I am inclined to wager that even the Duchess of Datchet's beautiful rose brilliant will go off bang."

Her Grace stared. She had been a mystified spectator of the little scene which had been enacted before her eyes. Indeed, the whole proceedings were mysterious to her.

"Rose brilliant? What do you mean?"

"The rose brilliant in your Grace's hair."

"There is no rose brilliant in my hair. There is only the diamond which my husband gave me."

"Did not his Grace present you with a rose brilliant?"

"A rose brilliant? No! He gave me a white diamond."

"Then the transformation has happened since."

"Transformation? What do you mean?"

She took the jewel out of her hair. As her glance fell upon it the fashion of her countenance changed. She scarcely seemed to believe the evidence of her own eyes.

"This—this is not my diamond."

Mr. Brooke's laughing eyes were divided between her Grace and her Grace's jewel. "I think it is."

"But—mine was white, and—this is red."

Mr. Fungst's glance was fixed upon the jewel, gloating on its beauties. "So mine was white. Then it went red. Now it has gone off bang! Oh, the lovely stone!"

Mr. Brooke laughed softly. "I am afraid that your Grace must permit me to withdraw my offer of twenty thousand pounds, or even of ten. The diamond, beautiful though it is, belongs to a rather more speculative class of goods than I quite care to dabble in."

The Duchess still held the jewel in her hand. She had never for a moment removed her glance from it. It seemed to exercise upon her gaze a sort of fascination.

"It's alive!"

"Alive?"

Mr. Brooke came nearer. Mr. Fungst craned forward. They were a curious trio. The Duchess's tones were low and eager.

"Something seems to be moving within."

"So there does." In Mr. Brooke's voice there was a sound as of laughter.

"It's changing colour." Mr. Fungst spoke almost with a gasp.

"For ever! Look out!" Mr. Brooke spoke just in time. There was a little crack. The diamond had disappeared. Three pairs of eyes were still bent upon her Grace's hand. But it was empty—the diamond had gone.

"It's gone off bang!"

"What do you mean?" exclaimed the Duchess. "What has happened?"

"When your servants sweep the room in the morning your Grace should give them instructions to be careful. A diamond which was your husband's present, and for which your Grace was offered thirty thousand pounds, lies in dust upon the floor."

With his hand Mr. Fungst scraped the perspiration from his brow. "Mein Gott! It's gone off bang!" he said.

IX.

A DOUBLE-MINDED GENTLEMAN

CHAPTER I.

"NICE people those Groomes."

Dawson had driven me over to the station, and was staying to see me off. I made this remark to him as we were standing on the platform waiting for the train.

"They are." He paused to give a vigorous puff or two at his pipe. "Nice people of the good old sort. Old Groome's a trump. He's not—well, he's not *fin de siècle*, you know, and all that humbug; for it is humbug, most of it. He puts on no side. He makes no pretension to be what he isn't. I don't say that he's either literary, musical, or artistic, although most people seem bound to at any rate pretend to be either one or the other nowadays. He's not a swell in any sense, and, what's more, he knows he isn't; but he's a homely, honest, hearty, hospitable English country gentleman, that's what old Groome is, sir. And when you come to think of it, I don't believe you'll find that a man can be anything much better."

As the train bore me onwards, in my own mind I heartily endorsed those words of Dawson's. Old Groome—as Phil Dawson rather irreverently called him—had done not a little to make my stay with Phil, in his bachelor quarters, the pleasantest visit I had ever paid anywhere to anyone. It is, perhaps, immaterial to mention that a Miss Groome—Miss Nora Groome, the second daughter—had had something to do with so desirable a consummation. But it was at least a comfort to know that she had so satisfactory a father. No, not in any sense a genius. A little stolid. A little heavy in hand, perhaps. Even curiously simple on a certain side of him;

yet, for all that, as Phil had said, a homely, honest, hearty, hospitable country gentleman. And so extremely friendly, too, to a forlorn young bachelor, who still—and very much still—had his way to make, and all the world in front of him to make it in.

Then, all the rest of the way to town, I thought of Nora.

Four or five nights after my return to my own quarters I dropped into a conversazione at the Apollo. The place was crowded. A conversazione at the Apollo Club means music. You generally hear somebody new who is worth hearing or who wishes the world to think that he or she is worth hearing. That night, however, there was not anyone particularly striking. The whole affair to me seemed dull. Perhaps that was to some extent because Gwendolen Martini—as she calls herself—fastened herself on to me like a burr, and, mentally, I was instituting unfavourable comparisons between her and someone else who was not there—which was, no doubt, unfair to Miss Martini, who is both a clever and a pretty girl. But then so many girls are pretty and clever nowadays—and nothing more.

At last I found myself in next-door neighbourhood to Stephen Bensberg. Bensberg is an extraordinary man—one of the new kind of scientific doctors, with theories, and his eyes fixed, so to speak, on the next century but one. Among other things he is a musician, a fair performer on more than one instrument, and a keen critic—one of those critics who, in a composition or an artist, are always, as it were, looking for something which others cannot see.

"Anything worth staying for?" I inquired, when I saw that he was at my elbow.

"There is. A man named Goad."

"Goad! Who's he?"

"That I have not yet made up my mind about."

Something struck me in his tone.

"What do you mean?"

"I have not yet made up my mind if he is a genius or—something else." He stopped, as if hesitating. "But he is at least worth staying for. As a pianist he is, I fancy, original."

"Is he a new importation from the Fatherland?"

Bensberg smiled.

"No, he is English, although it was I who discovered him. He occupies rooms over those of a friend of mine. One day I was with my friend. I heard someone playing overhead. I took the liberty to listen. I took the further liberty to intrude upon his privacy, and to introduce myself to the performer. It was Goad. Here he is. You will be able to judge for yourself if he is worth staying for."

"Hollo!" I cried. "There is a friend of mine. What on earth is he doing here?"

Out of the centre of the parting crowd there appeared in front of us Nora's father. He appeared to be alone. I cast as searching a glance as possible towards the part of the room from which he had come. But, so far as I could perceive, no other familiar face was with him. I should as soon have expected to see old Groome, "all by himself," at the Apollo Club as, say, at a Fleet Street bar.

I felt that Bensberg's eyes were on me—as if my surprise had communicated itself to him.

"You know him then?"

"Know him? Know whom?"

"Goad. That is Goad."

"Goad!"

Bensberg was pointing to old Groome. I supposed that he was poking fun at me; but, to my unutterable amazement, old Groome was calmly ascending the dais at the end of the room. And not only ascending the dais, but, advancing to the piano, he seated himself at the keyboard. It is no figure of speech to say that I was dumbfounded. Old Groome a pianist! Of a calibre to make his appearance before the hypercritical cognoscenti of the Apollo Club! It was old Groome, there could be no doubt of that. And yet, in his simple-mindedness, I had heard him declare, with my own ears, that he did not know one note of music from another. And I had cordially believed him—he was just that sort of man.

A hush came over the chattering throng, and old Groome began to play. We have all of us read in fiction—and out of it, for a matter of that—hysterically exaggerated accounts of wonderful musical performances. That word "wonderful" was the only word which could be properly applied to old Groome's performance then. Music? Well, it was a music—of a kind, though it was certainly the queerest music I had ever heard. The piece he played was not by any recognised composer; it was not even in the style of any recognised composer. To tell the truth, I am not sure that, in a musical sense, it was not nonsense; but, played as he played it then, it affected me in a way in which I would rather that music, or anything else, did not affect me. It made me lose my mental balance. As he played old Groome grew more and more excited, and in some strange fashion he managed to convey his own excitement to his audience. His was not the stereotyped excitement of the ordinary great pianist—of the type we know so well. That is generally confined—very much confined—to the performer at the instrument. This was communicated to the folk in front. It affected me. I fancy it affected Bensberg. And when old Groome ceased playing there ensued that silence which is more eloquent than applause, and it was only after a moment or two that a din began which was simply deafening.

Bensberg turned to me amidst the tumult.

"What do you think of it?"

"I don't know what to think."

"Did I not tell you?"

Charging into the crowd, I reached the daïs just as old Groome was coming down the steps. I held out my hand to him.

"Mr. Groome!" I cried.

He looked at me—but that was all. Not the slightest glimmer of recognition flitted across his countenance. "Sir?" he said.

"Surely, Mr. Groome, you have not forgotten me already?"

He paid not the slightest attention to my outstretched hand. He looked straight past me.

"Ah, Bensberg," he observed in the most placid tones imaginable—the placid tones I had learned to know so well—it seemed that Bensberg had followed at my heels—"what did you think of it? That was a dream I had last night—a nightmare."

"So I should imagine."

Bensberg's tones were dry. He looked from Groome to me—and from me to Groome. In my bewilderment I made a further claim for recognition from Nora's father. "Mr. Groome, what have I done that you should have so soon forgotten me?"

"Forgotten you?" He looked at me quietly, yet intently, as if I were a perfect stranger. But it was old Groome. It was impossible—out of the stories—that there could be in existence two men so much alike, though when I observed him closely I perceived that in his eyes there was a new light and fire—I had almost written a new intelligence. "I am not in the habit, sir, of forgetting anyone. Groome is not my name. I am Isaac Goad."

Bensberg interposed. He laid his hand upon my arm.

"I fancied, just now, that you might be mistaken in your recognition of Mr. Goad. Goad, let me introduce to you my friend, who is also a musician—Mr. Attree."

Old Groome—or Mr. Goad—favoured me with an old-fashioned little bow. It was old Groome to the life.

"I shall be honoured by the pleasure of your acquaintance, Mr. Attree."

Then he took my hand.

Bensberg and I went home with him to his rooms to supper. He insisted on our going—just in old Groome's hospitable way—and as, for some reason, Bensberg would not go without me, I went with him.

Throughout the remainder of that night I was in a sort of waking nightmare. If I could credit the evidence of my own senses I was in the presence of Mr. Groome. If I could credit Mr. Groome himself, I was in the presence of Mr. Goad. He played to us. I never heard such playing before. I hope never to hear the like of it again. It had such an effect upon me that, when we said "goodnight," I felt as if I had maddened myself by heavy drinking.

"Well," asked Bensberg, as we walked away, repeating the inquiry which he had put to me at the Apollo, "what do you think of him?"

I took off my hat, so that my brow might be bared to the cool night breezes.

"Think of him! Bensberg, I am beginning to think that I am going mad."

He peered into my face as he moved beside me.

"Odd that you should have mistaken him for someone else."

"You would not think it odd if you knew the person for whom I did mistake him. Two pins are not so like each other."

"Curious. Goad is not a common type. Strange that you should know his double."

On the following Saturday I ran down again to Dawson. Directly we were clear of the station I began on the subject which had been puzzling my brain.

"Do you know, Phil, the other night at the Apollo I saw a man who was the very image of Mr. Groome. Never saw such a resemblance in my life. The man was so like him that I doubt if any man living could have told which was which if they were both of them together."

"The Apollo! Do you mean the Apollo Club? What should old Groome be doing there?"

"That's the queer part of it. The man was playing."

"Playing! Do you mean performing?"

"Very much performing. He played a pianoforte solo. I never heard such playing, and I believe I've heard every pianist that ever was."

"You had better tell old Groome. It will tickle him, the idea of his playing a pianoforte solo at the Apollo Club."

I did tell him. We dined at the Groomes'. Dawson drove me straight there from the station. When Mr. Groome came out into the hall to greet us I protest that a sort of shock travelled all down my spinal column. I still had the figure of Isaac Goad clearly before me in my mind's eye. I still had, as it were, the concourse of sounds for which he had been responsible ringing in my ears. I still seemed to see him as he had stood in front of me, declining to accord me recognition. And when Mr. Groome advanced, holding out his hand in welcome, the likeness between the pianist and my host was so strangely startling that, in an impulse of momentary mental aberration, I exclaimed—

"Mr. Goad!"

Mr. Groome stared—as Mr. Goad had done, with just the same curious characteristic little smile about his lips.

"Attree! What's the matter?"

It was only when he spoke that I became conscious of the blunder I had made. The blood surged through my veins. I blushed like a schoolboy. I have seldom felt so stupid.

"Really, Mr. Groome, I beg your pardon, but, do you know, I—I was mistaking you for a ghost."

"A solid sort of ghost, I fancy. Does that feel like a ghost?" His strong, hearty grasp did not feel like a ghost's. "How are you? You will only just have time to dress before dinner."

I did only just have time. Directly I appeared in the drawing-room a move was made for the dining-room. The soup had been removed when Ethel Groome—Miss Groome—said, addressing me from the other side of the table—

"Mr. Attree, what is this Mr. Dawson tells me about your having seen someone just like papa in town?"

I do not know what Nora thought of my behaviour. All the time I had been eating my soup I could not keep myself from glancing at my host at the head of the table. It was not very many hours since I had supped with Mr. Goad. Every mouthful which Mr. Groome took reminded me more strongly of my meal with Mr. Goad. The one man reproduced, to a nicety, the other's minutest peculiarities. Miss Groome's words caused me to cease making almost unconscious mental comparisons. I fancy that I actually started.

"Most extraordinary thing, Miss Groome, it really was! Mr. Groome, were you ever at the Apollo Club?"

"Not that I am aware of. Where is it? My club's the Carlton. I haven't been in another club in London, I daresay, for twenty years. The Apollo Club? What sort of club is that? I don't think I ever heard of it."

"Do you know a man named Goad?"

"Goad! Goad! What a name!" Mr. Groome looked at me and smiled—Mr. Goad's smile. "I have no recollection of the fact. Why? Has an individual of that name claimed the pleasure of my acquaintance?"

"No, only—it was the queerest thing—at a concert at the Apollo the other night there was a man named Goad—Isaac

Goad. If you saw him, I doubt if you would know which was he and which was you."

"Was he so like papa?" asked Nora.

"Like! If you had his portrait——But there is his portrait."

I pointed to a portrait in oils of Mr. Groome which hung over the fireplace. They stared at it and then at me. Nora laughed.

"Are you joking, Mr. Attree? Do you mean that that is Mr. Goad, or that it is only like him? You know we think that it's a very good likeness of papa."

"It is an excellent likeness of Mr. Groome, but I assure you that it's an equally excellent likeness of Mr. Goad. Since I saw him I have been in a sort of waking dream. But let me tell you the story. I was, as I said, at the Apollo Club the other night. In the crowd I saw Mr. Groome—I could have sworn it was Mr. Groome. To my amazement he walked on to the platform, and, sitting down to the piano, began to play. You never heard such playing. It was more like a madman's than anything else. When he had finished I rushed forward, taking it for granted that it was Mr. Groome."

Mr. Groome interposed.

"Taking it for granted that I was a madman, I see. Much obliged for the compliment."

"I don't mean that, Mr. Groome, but let me go on. To my amazement, when I addressed him, he stared at me for all the world as you are staring at me now, Mr. Groome. I thought that I might, unconsciously, have done something to offend you. I was beginning, blunderingly, to ask what it was, when you—I mean he—stopped me by saying that his name was not Groome, but Goad—Isaac Goad. He said this in a tone of voice—you know there is something about a man's voice which is characteristic of the man, you seldom hear two voices which are alike—but he said this in a tone of voice which was so exactly like yours that, upon my word, I did not know what to think. While I was making an exhibition of myself a friend of mine came up who introduced me to Mr. Goad. Mr. Goad insisted on my friend and myself going home with him to supper. All the time that we were having supper, in every gesture, every movement, every little action, every intonation of his voice, he so reminded me of Mr. Groome that—

well, the Corsican Brothers, and Lesurques and Dubose in *The Lyons Mail* are not in it, as regards resembling each other, compared to the resemblance, Mr. Groome, which Mr. Isaac Goad has to you."

I daresay I told my story with a little excitement of manner. I think it possible that I did. I fancy that it created an impression, and that not altogether of an agreeable kind. At least, I gathered as much from the way in which Mrs. Groome spoke to me.

"Yours is a strange story, Mr. Attree. As you are possibly aware, Mr. Groome has no male relatives living, and we in the county are apt to think, not only that the Groome features have been handed down from generation to generation, but that they are, in a way, unique."

"Just so; I can easily believe it, Mrs. Groome. I certainly saw no one in the least like Mr. Groome till I had the pleasure of meeting Mr. Groome, and until I had the pleasure of meeting Mr. Goad, but that only makes the likeness between them the more remarkable."

"Is this Mr. Isaac Goad a married man?"

Mr. Groome asked the question, as it seemed to me, a little dryly.

"Not so far as I know. He occupies bachelor's chambers."

"When was this concert at the Apollo Club?"

"Let me see—it was last Wednesday night."

"How odd!" exclaimed Miss Nora. "Papa did stop in town on Wednesday night."

"In what consists the oddity?" inquired her father. "I believe that I do, occasionally, spend a night in town. But does it therefore follow that I should play the piano, like a madman, at the Apollo Club? Though I can easily believe that if I did play the piano at the Apollo Club, or, indeed, anywhere else, that I should play it like a madman. I assure you that I can give you a circumstantial and satisfactory account of every hour I spent in town, Miss Nora."

"You pique my curiosity, Mr. Attree," said Mrs. Groome. "I should like to see this Mr. Isaac Goad, though possibly, and I think probably, the resemblance would not strike me so forcibly as it appears to have struck you."

The lady's words gave me an idea.

"Mrs. Groome, your wish can easily be gratified. Mr. Goad, I believe, plays again next week, and I shall be only too happy to get you as many tickets as you desire."

My suggestion was seized with avidity, though possibly with greater avidity by the daughters than by the parents. A party was made up then and there. Dawson could not go. The assizes were coming on, and he had had the pleasure of being summoned to serve on the grand jury. But Mr. and Mrs. Groome and the two girls were all to go. I was to meet them in town. We were to dine together, and afterwards I was to escort them to the Apollo Club.

CHAPTER II.

WHEN, on the appointed day, I appeared at the hotel in time for dinner, I found the ladies awaiting my arrival. But there were no signs of Mr. Groome. I inquired into the cause of his absence.

"Has Mr. Groome not come up to town with you?"

"Oh, yes," explained Miss Groome; "but he has an engagement which will, perhaps, detain him and prevent him dining here. If it does, he will go on straight to the club. He will be sure to be in good time to hear and see this wonderful Mr. Goad. Really, Mr. Attree, we have been talking and thinking of nothing else since we saw you. I suppose that if papa asks for you they will let him in?"

I assured her that they would. In fact, when we reached the Apollo—for Mr. Groome did not turn up for dinner—I gave instructions that he should be shown into the concert-room directly he arrived. We were early, so that we were able to find comfortable seats before the rush began. Seeing Bensberg on the other side of the room, I signalled to him. When he came I introduced him to the Groomes. Taking my hint, and a vacant chair, he made himself agreeable.

The people were flocking in, but, although I kept a keen look out, still there were no signs of Mr. Groome. There were signs of their being about to commence proceedings. Mrs. Groome began to fidget.

"I cannot think what can be keeping Mr. Groome. He seemed to think it possible that he would not be back in time for dinner, but he said that, even if he were detained, he would be sure to be here in good time. I know that he has been looking forward to to-night, and he will be so disappointed if he should miss anything."

I said that I would go and see if, owing to some misunderstanding, he was wandering about downstairs. I went and saw. But, apparently, there was nothing to be seen. I inquired in the hall, but nothing had been heard of Mr. Groome. I went through all the rooms. Nowhere were there any signs of him. When I got back into the concert-room the first item on the programme had been just completed.

"How very odd!" said Mrs. Groome, when I explained to her that my seeking had been vain. "As a rule Mr. Groome is so particular in keeping an appointment. Almost finically particular now and then."

He might be now and then. But item followed item, and there was still no Mr. Groome. I had Mrs. Groome on my right, Nora on my left, and Bensberg sat on the other side of Nora.

"Ah!" all at once I heard him say, "there is Goad. I suppose we are to have him next."

At the same moment Nora began to fidget in her seat.

"Here's papa. Mamma, here's papa."

"Where, my love?" Mrs. Groome looked through her glasses in the direction in which Nora was glancing.

"There, mamma. Just on the platform. Mr. Attree, don't you see him? I think he has just come through that little door at the side."

"I see him. Whatever can have made him so late? And what can he be doing over there? Somebody must have shown him through the wrong door. Nora, can't you signal to him, so as to let him know where we are?"

Without waiting for Nora to reply Mrs. Groome stood up, and began to wave her fan in that rather aggressive manner which is peculiar to some persons when they desire to attract the attention of some other person across a theatre or a crowded room. Bensberg volunteered his services.

"If you will show me which is Mr. Groome I shall be happy to let him know your whereabouts."

"Oh, thank you," said Nora. "That is papa. Why——"

For some cause or other, in the middle of her sentence Miss Nora stopped dead.

"Good gracious!" exclaimed her mother. "What is he doing? How silly he is! Why, he's actually going on to the platform! Papa!"

"The gentleman ascending the platform is Mr. Goad."

"Mr.—who?"

"Mr. Goad, who, I believe, is now going to favour us with a pianoforte solo."

"Nonsense!" snapped Mrs. Groome with scant politeness, the more especially since, so far as she was concerned, Bensberg was only the acquaintance of a minute. "It's papa! Papa!"

I, for my part, had maintained strict silence. I had seen the person, who now had gained the platform, come into the room. My first impulse had been to exclaim that here was Mr. Groome at last. A moment's reflection, however, showed me that the individual had come through the door which led from the artists' room, and that—well, that the situation might be more complicated than I, in my first impulse, had imagined. But I was certainly unprepared for Mrs. Groome's behaviour. The newcomer, whoever he was, as I said, had gained the platform. His appearance there, considering the place, was greeted with quite a tumult of applause. Acknowledging this with the most perfunctory of nods, without loss of time, with the most modest and most unpretentious air imaginable, he seated himself at the keyboard of the instrument. The applause died away. In silence the audience waited for the performance to commence. All but Mrs. Groome, who not only continued standing up, but who continued speaking too.

"Papa! Papa!" she said, in a voice which was not only audible to every person present, but which created an unmistakable sensation. I verily believe that the individual on the platform was the only individual in the place who did not turn and stare at her. She addressed herself to her daughters: "My dears, what can be the matter with papa? He must be mad! Papa!"

Perceiving that a buzz of curiosity was beginning to travel round the room, and that people might be jumping to conclusions, which Mrs. Groome might not impossibly consider derogatory to her character, I endeavoured to explain. I spoke in a tone of voice which was intended to reach the lady's ear alone.

"Did I not tell you that the resemblance was very striking? That is Mr. Goad who is on the platform, Mrs. Groome."

The lady's tone could not have been intended to reach my ear alone; it was even unnecessarily loud.

"Mr. Goad! Mr. Attree, how can you say such a thing? Do you suppose that I don't know my own husband—the husband of nearly thirty years?"

Nora interposed. It was quite time, too.

"Mamma, do sit down. Perhaps there is some mistake; after all, it may not be papa."

Mrs. Groome sat down, I really believe unconsciously.

"May not be papa! Do you mean to tell me that you don't know your own father, girl? The man's a lunatic; he will disgrace us all. He does not know one note of music from another."

The sounds which proceeded from the platform struck the lady dumb. I noticed one or two of the committee looking in our direction, and almost began to fear that there would be a scandal. So far as appearances went, however, the individual on the platform continued to pay not the slightest attention to the lady's curious behaviour. At any rate, in the middle of her very audible remarks he commenced to play. The change which took place in the lady's countenance was really funny. As she was in the very act of speaking her mouth was open. Open it remained, with the words which were on the very tip of her tongue still unspoken. It continued open for a minute or more; she seemed to be under a spell. Then, drawing a long, gasping sort of breath, she shut her mouth. She looked about her as if she were struggling with a dream. I was conscious that Nora, on my left, was actually trembling. Bensberg I suspected of something very like a covert grin. I saw that the cheeks of the usually cool and self-possessed Mrs. Groome were a fiery red. Unless I was mistaken, tears were in her eyes. I was conscious that the position was distinctly an uncomfortable one, the discomfort of which was not lessened by the nature of the performance to which we were listening. Again, Mr. Goad favoured us with an extraordinary olla-podrida of sounds. That he was, in one sense, a master of his instrument there could be no doubt whatever. The piece he played struck me as being an actual improvisation. Transcribed in black and white, I should not have been surprised to find it something very much like nonsense; but, played as he played it then, it had an effect upon my already agitated nervous system, which, so far as I was personally concerned, I found peculiarly disconcerting. I almost began to feel, as Mrs. Groome seemed to be feeling, that these things were chancing in a dream. The effect was heightened, if I can make myself plain, by the fact that while the performance suggested frenzied excitement, the performer himself seemed to be in a state of imperturbable calm. I found it quite a relief when he finished. Mrs. Groome seemed to find it an even greater relief than I did. As the applause subsided she turned and addressed me in a manner which took away the larger portion of the little breath which Mr. Goad had left me master of.

"Mr. Attree, what is the meaning of this?"

I could not tell her. Bensberg came to my rescue with, it struck me, something of malice.

"Since Mr. Goad so curiously resembles Mr. Groome, possibly, madam, you will suffer me to introduce to you your husband's double?"

Mrs. Groome looked at Bensberg in a manner which suggested that, after all, one touch of nature does make the whole world kin, and that well-bred ladies can behave like ill-bred ones now and then.

"My husband's double? My good sir, do you suppose that I don't know my own husband? Come, girls, let us go to him."

Mrs. Groome dashed into the crowd, and we dashed after her, the Misses Groome and Bensberg and I. I should have liked to check the impetuous lady, but I felt that, in her present excited state, she was beyond my checking. She, metaphorically, collared the pianist as he stood in the centre of a little group at the foot of the platform.

"Papa!" she exclaimed, brushing the people aside as though they were so many flies. "What can you be thinking of? My dear Everard, pray come away with us at once. The girls and I have been suffering agonies; I did not think you could have been so inconsiderate, really. That you should ever have concealed from me your knowledge of the instrument was bad enough, but that you should ever have dreamed of a public performance! My dear Everard, I must beg of you to come at once."

The excited lady poured forth her grievances with a volubil-ity of which, I am persuaded, she would have been incapable—at least, in public—if she had not been excited; the pianist regarding her all the time with a degree of calmness which, under the cir-cumstances, was not without a touch of humour.

"I apprehend, madam, that you are under some misapprehen-sion."

There was a certain quaintness about the speech which was old Groome all over. So the lady seemed to think.

"Everard!—Papa!" she almost screamed. "What do you mean?"

Just then the pianist caught sight of Bensberg. He held out his hand to him. Bensberg endeavoured to explain.

"It seems, Mr. Goad, that your double is walking the earth. Allow me to have the honour of introducing you to Mrs. Groome. It appears that you so closely resemble Mr. Groome that Mrs. Groome finds it difficult to persuade herself that Mr. Groome and you are two, and not one."

"The lady is mistaken. I have not the honour of knowing Mr. Groome."

This the pianist said with Mr. Groome's old-fashioned, court-ly little bow.

"Not the honour!" gasped the lady. She was reduced to gasp-ing. "Not the honour!"

Miss Groome had enough presence of mind left to interpose.

It was time. The proceedings, so far as the rest of the programme was concerned, were at a standstill.

"Mamma, dear, let us go." Slipping her arm through her mother's, she drew her away. "Perhaps there is some strange mistake, and, after all, it is not papa."

"Not papa!" expostulated Mrs. Groome. "Do you mean to tell me that you don't know your own father, girl! Why, he is wearing your father's clothes! On his finger is the ring which I gave him on his wedding-day; in his shirt-front are the studs which were my last birthday present."

I saw the ladies into their hired brougham, but I let them drive away alone. I felt that they might desire to say things which they might prefer to say *en famille*. Still, I managed under cover to assure Miss Nora Groome that I would look in at their hotel in the morning.

When I returned to the music-room I found that Bensberg had engaged Mr. Goad to sup with him. When he asked me to make a third I readily said yes. It was a queer supper party—at least, to me it seemed queer. I perceived that even Bensberg seemed to think that there was something odd about the situation, though he never openly hinted at anything of the kind to me. But I knew him, and I noted how he never allowed his eyes to wander long from Mr. Goad, appearing unwilling to lose count even of his slightest movement. For my part, I almost felt as if I were in the presence of something supernatural. The more closely I observed Mr. Goad the more amazing became his resemblance to Mr. Groome. It seemed incredible that even the two Dromios could have been so alike; and in the face of Mrs. Groome's behaviour, what was a man to think?

Of the three of us, Mr. Goad was certainly most at his ease. I felt persuaded that Bensberg's appearance of ease was as much assumed as mine was. But about Mr. Goad's imperturbability there could be no sort of doubt whatever. That was nature itself, and it reminded me so bewilderingly of old Groome. The scene at the club seemed to have made no impression on him. Our allusions to the subject, if they had any effect upon him at all, had the effect of boring him. He appeared to think that there was nothing

in any way out of the common in an old married woman, who
had never been parted for any length of time from the partner of
her joys and sorrows, and who had only left him an hour or two,
under such circumstances mistaking, and insisting on mistaking,
a perfect stranger for her husband of thirty years.

After supper Goad and I went away together. It was a fine
night, and, as his way lay not very apart from mine, I bore him
company. As we strolled through the quiet streets he struck me as
being one of the most infrequent conversationalists I had had the
pleasure of meeting. It seemed difficult to get a word out of him
edgeways. At last I assailed him on the subject of his art. Then he
did say something.

"I suppose, Mr. Goad, that of music you have been a lifelong
student?"

"No. I have never studied it at all. Music came to me, so far as
I can remember, in a second. Of the science of music I know nothing. I cannot read a note of music on a printed page. What I play I
play because I have to play it. It comes to me I know not whence
nor how. When I must play I play. I never play unless I must."

While I pondered, somewhat taken aback at his curious confession, doubtful if he was in earnest or if he was the latest illustration of the charlatan, he suddenly stood still. Wondering why
he stopped, I turned to look at him. Something in his face and in
his bearing had on me the effect of an unexpected cold douche—
it gave me quite a start. He was staring about him in a confused,
bewildered way—just as a man who had suddenly been roused
from sleep. All at once he said, as if speaking to himself—

"I must have overslept myself." He turned to me, seemingly
with a start of surprise. "Attree!—what the deuce are you doing
here?"

"Mr. Goad!" I exclaimed.

"Goad!" He seemed to be making an effort at recollection.
"Oh, of course! That's the fellow who's so like me, and who plays
the piano like a madman. Come along, we shall be late—Mrs.
Groome and the girls will give it to us if we are."

"Mr. Goad!" I repeated, feeling as if it were I who must have
been roused from slumber.

Before I could say another word someone grasped my arm. It was Bensberg. He had had his suspicions of what was going to happen, so, unperceived, had followed us.

"My dear Attree," he said, "will you do me the pleasure of introducing me to your friend, of whom you have spoken to me so often—Mr. Groome—I believe that it is Mr. Groome?"

"My name is Groome," said he. For the moment for the life of me I could not have said if it was Mr. Groome or Mr. Goad.

"And my name is Bensberg—Dr. Conrad Bensberg. I am better acquainted with you, Mr. Groome, than you with me." He paused, eyeing the other intently, and then added, "Under the peculiar circumstances I think, as a medical man, that I had better at once be frank with you. Mr. Groome, you have had a singular hallucination."

"Hallucination!" murmured Mr.—— I will write it Groome. He did not seem to know what to make of things. Which was not strange. I did not know what to make of them either.

"Hallucination. You have just awoke from a state of cerebral unconsciousness. You have unwittingly and innocently acted the part of a double-minded gentleman. As you are possibly aware, Mr. Groome, the brain has two lobes—that is, divisions. These lobes sometimes, without their possessor knowing anything at all about it, work separately. While one works the other, so to speak, sleeps, and *vice versâ*. This is how the two lobes of your brain have treated you. Ordinarily you are—as you are—the gentleman whose acquaintance I have the honour of making, Mr. Groome. But while one lobe has been sleeping, the other lobe has insisted upon your being that very talented musician whose acquaintance I have also had the honour of making—Mr. Isaac Goad."

X.

THE ROBBERY ON THE "STORMY PETREL"

I.

THE case of the robbery on board the *Stormy Petrel* was notable for one thing if for no other—in it the Hon. Augustus Champnell received fees from three separate and, indeed, antagonistic individuals.

The Hon. Augustus had finished reading the morning papers, and was wondering—for business was slack—what the day might bring forth, when there came a tapping at the door, and there immediately entered two servants in livery, bearing between them an iron box, which they placed on a chair. One of them spoke—as if he had been an automaton.

"The Marquis of Bewlay's compliments to Mr. Champnell, and will Mr. Champnell drown the box in a cistern full of water, till the Marquis arrives."

Mr. Champnell stared.

"And when will the Marquis arrive?"

The Marquis arrived almost as soon as the servants had gone. That ancient peer came hobbling into the room, leaning on two sticks, and as soon as he saw the box on the chair he seemed more than half disposed to back out again.

"Didn't the rascals tell you to drown the box in a cistern of water?"

"The rascals did. But the Marquis of Bewlay will permit me to observe that I always require a sufficient explanation before I act on instructions which I receive from strangers."

With Mr. Champnell's assistance the Marquis took refuge in a chair.

"What's your fee?"

"My lowest fee is one hundred guineas."

"Too much."

"In the case of the Marquis of Bewlay my lowest fee will be one hundred and fifty guineas."

The Marquis glanced up at him—and leered.

"You shall have it for your impudence—the Champnells always were an impudent lot. Find out who sent what is in that box, and you shall have your hundred and fifty. Here's the key, look inside—only mind, gently does it."

Unlocking the iron box with the key the Marquis gave him, Mr. Champnell found that it contained other smaller wooden boxes, which were divided from each other by layers of cotton wool. Removing the covers of these wooden boxes he perceived that each contained what seemed to be some sort of oil can.

"Thirteen of them, aren't they?" On counting them Mr. Champnell discovered that the number was correct. "Lucky number, and pretty playthings, every one of them. All infernal machines, or I'm a hatter. They've come raining in on me by every post—if you look at them you'll see that there is a different postmark on every one of them."

"Are you certain that they are infernal machines?"

"I'll lay you ten to one in anything you like to name that they are, and leave you to prove the contrary—that's the extent of my certainty, Mr. Champnell. Only if you take my advice you'll keep them immersed in water until the thing has been shown to demonstration, either one way or the other. I have no desire to be blown to pieces, if you have."

"Have you no sort of idea where they come from?"

"Once upon a time I was fool enough to enrol myself as a member of a certain secret society. I have broken since then pretty nearly every one of its rules, which I swore to observe, and I think it quite on the cards that these things may have come from some of the society's agents. I'll tell you what I'll do; instead of a hundred and fifty guineas, I'll give you two hundred, if you prove, beyond a shadow of doubt, that they don't. I've come to you instead of going to the police, because I want the thing kept private, but at the same time I am particularly anxious to know if at last the beggars are beginning to try to do what they have threatened to do, times without number."

The Marquis's story was a long one, and not a little involved; some of Mr. Champnell's questions he declined, point blank, to answer. When he had gone, Mr. Champnell still found himself in possession of very slight data to enable him to prosecute his researches. He summed the data up in his mind, telling himself, finally, that they really amounted to nothing at all, and had almost resolved to write to the Marquis and decline the conduct of the case unless he furnished him with fuller information on certain points on which he had refused to give any information at all, when the servant came to announce that Mr. Golden, of the firm of Messrs. Ruby and Golden, was at the door and desirous of an interview.

A minute later Mr. Champnell found himself face to face with the junior partner of the famous firm of jewellers—a shrewd, sharp-looking man, who wasted no time in coming to the point.

"I have been made the victim, Mr. Champnell, of an atrocious outrage, and I come to you first, because the matter is one which requires delicate handling, and second, because the author of the outrage is a member of your own order. I may add that if you succeed in this matter we may be able to place a good deal of business in your hands—business of a kind which requires the intervention of a diplomatist rather than of a policeman."

The Hon. Augustus bowed.

"You are acquainted with Lord Hardaway?" Another bow from Mr. Champnell. "His lordship has been a customer of ours for some time, and is so largely in our debt that some months ago we felt bound to intimate that we could not allow him to add to the already large figure of his account.

"We have recently received information, through side channels, that his lordship was paying his addresses to Miss Bonnyer-Lees, the sole child and heiress of the eminent soap-boiler. And, ten days ago, we received a letter from his lordship himself, which was to the effect that he was about to start for a cruise in his yacht, the *Stormy Petrel*; that Miss Bonnyer-Lees was to accompany him, with other friends; that he had hopes of making Miss

Bonnyer-Lees his wife; and he desired us to send him, at once, for his inspection and the lady's, a selection of the finest things we had in stock; in fact, he gave us to understand that matters had reached a stage in which he was anxious to make the lady a handsome present. His lordship went on to add that if he married Miss Bonnyer-Lees our account should receive an immediate settlement; while, on the other hand, if he did not marry her, it was quite possible that we should have to whistle—the word was his lordship's own."

"Where was Lord Hardaway when he wrote this letter?"

"Staying at Miss Bonnyer-Lees' own residence in Kent. But the day after we received a telegram from him stating that they had decided to commence the cruise sooner than they had originally intended; that the day following they would be off Deal, on board the yacht, and that the goods were to be sent on board to be examined. The telegram also contained what seemed to me, under the circumstances, to be a somewhat brutal intimation to the effect that if we did not telegraph a reply to say that the goods would be sent off at once the order would be placed elsewhere."

"Did you send the goods?"

"My impulse was to telegraph a refusal. In several little matters Lord Hardaway had not used us altogether well, and it seemed to me that in this matter he was not using us altogether well either; there was no necessity, for instance, for him to threaten us with the loss of his custom. My partner, however, Mr. Ruby, would not hear of a refusal. He was naturally unwilling to lose the business which would be associated with what would, probably, be one of the weddings of the season. On one point I did stand firm. As I feared that, if he was the bearer of the goods, Mr. Ruby would quite probably allow himself to be wheedled out of them, without receiving any satisfactory promise of payment, I resolved to take the goods myself. Which I did do."

Mr. Golden paused. At this point of his narrative, which he had reached, a certain uneasiness seemed to possess him.

"It was about midday when I reached Deal. It was both blowing and raining, and what I should have called a regular gale was on. A sailor with the words 'Stormy Petrel' on his cap came to

me at the station, and, when I told him who I was, informed me
that we must go off to the yacht at once, because his lordship had
resolved to weigh anchor if I did not arrive by that train. I had
never been to Deal in my life before, and I had some idea that
the yacht might be anchored to the pier. But when I got down to
the beach I found that there was no pier, and the sailor, pointing
to what was merely a speck on the horizon, said, "There's the
Stormy Petrel." When he said that, and I saw that the yacht was
heaven knows how far from land, if I had not felt that the fellow
was covertly grinning at me, and that I should never have heard
the last of it from Ruby, I should have come straight back to town,
which would have been a wiser thing than what I actually did do.
I entrusted myself in a cranky boat to the mercy of the, literally,
foaming billows."

Again Mr. Golden paused. It might have been imagination,
but it seemed to the Hon. Augustus that, at the mere recollection
of that experience of the horrors of the ocean, Mr. Golden became
a little yellow.

"I am not ashamed, Mr. Champnell, to own that I am no sail-
or. I have felt qualms upon the Thames. What I suffered in that
cockle-shell of a boat, tossed hither and thither amidst that seeth-
ing mass of waters—I don't know if it was blowing or raining
hardest—I will not now attempt to describe. When I reached the
Stormy Petrel I was more dead than alive. Lord Hardaway received
me on deck; he was, evidently, suffering no inconvenience from
the weather. 'Hollo, Golden,' he said, 'you're looking queer.' 'If,
my lord,' I answered, 'I am looking as queer as I feel I must be
looking very queer indeed. I had no idea before I left town that
such a storm was raging.' 'Storm!' he said, 'you don't call this a
storm. It's only a capful of wind! Come below and have a peg?'
I went downstairs and I had some brandy; then I must have had
another attack of illness, because the next thing I can remember
is Lord Hardaway clapping me on the shoulder and exclaiming, 'I
say, Golden, where are those jewels of yours?'"

Once more there was a break in Mr. Golden's narrative—he
seemed to be oppressed by the weight of his recollections.

"It will give you, Mr. Champnell, an adequate idea of my

physical condition when I tell you that, until that moment, I had forgotten that I had the jewels on me, and when I add that I had taken with me from town jewels to the gross value of nearly £20,000 you will understand what that statement means. They were contained in a locked leather case which was attached to a steel belt which was locked about my waist. The keys both of the belt and of the case were in a secret pocket of my waistcoat—see here."

Unbuttoning his waistcoat, Mr. Golden disclosed a tiny pocket, which was ingeniously contrived in the lining.

"When his lordship spoke I put my hand to my waist and found that the belt and case had gone and not only so, my waistcoat was unbuttoned and the keys had vanished.

"'My lord,' I cried, as I staggered to my feet, 'I've been robbed.'

"'By Jove,' he exclaimed, 'if I didn't think so. Come along, Golden, the thief has just gone overboard with the spoil—if you don't look alive he'll get clear away.' You will understand, Mr. Champnell, that I was disorganised both in mind and body—really incapable, in fact, of collecting my thoughts. I allowed his lordship to drag me up above. It seemed to me when I got into the open air that the storm was raging worse than ever; and taking to the side of the deck, he pointed out a solitary individual who was rowing away from the ship in a little boat. 'There's the thief! I thought there was something suspicious about the way in which he came sneaking up from below. Before we knew what he was up to he had dropped into his boat and was off. If you look alive, Golden, you'll catch him yet, red-handed.' The boat in which I had come from shore was still alongside, and, before I had a chance to collect my scattered senses, his lordship had not only bundled me into it, but the boat itself was pushed off from the yacht.

"We chased that boat which contained the solitary rower, as it appeared to me, for hours. I will not dilate on what I still continued to suffer, but through all my agony I urged the rowers in pursuit. As soon as we were within hailing distance I shouted to the fellow, 'Stop!' Directly I did so, standing up in his boat, he dropped something into the sea. I distinctly saw that he dropped something, but what he was too far off for me to see. When we reached him he declared that he had merely thrown overboard some rubbish, but why he had chosen that singularly inopportune moment he did not condescend to explain. We took him in tow, he seeming not at all unwilling, and at last we reached the land. How thankful I was to do so no one but myself can have the faintest conception.

"Hardly had I set foot on *terra firma* than I became convinced that I had been duped from first to last. The fellow we had chased turned out to be an honest, simple fisherman, who had been employed to take a telegram from the post office to the yacht and who protested that he had never left his boat, and that he knew nothing of my belt or case. I believed, and I believe him. I have no doubt whatever that Lord Hardaway was himself the thief. I would have instituted a prosecution directly I returned to town only Ruby would not hear of it. Mr. Ruby is always fearful of anything in the shape of a scandal. A week has passed. We have heard nothing of his lordship or of the jewels. That, at present, is how the matter stands."

"What is it you wish me to do?"

"To see that the jewels are returned to us."

"And in default?"

"We must either have the jewels or a guarantee of payment—a sufficient guarantee!—or we prosecute. Here is a list of the jewels that are missing, with the several values attached." Mr. Golden handed the Hon. Augustus a sheet of paper. "You perceive that it is a matter which requires delicate handling."

"Quite so. Where is Lord Hardaway now?"

"No one seems to have the least idea. As you are aware, the weather has been very boisterous during the last few days, and, for all anyone seems to know, he and the *Stormy Petrel* may be at the bottom of the sea together. Altogether, for us, it is a pleasant state of things!"

"Was Miss Bonnyer-Lees on board?"

"She was not. It appears only too probable that the whole business was a deliberately planned conspiracy. As I told you at the beginning, Mr. Champnell, I have been made the victim of an atrocious outrage."

II.

When, Mr. Golden having departed, the Hon. Augustus was left alone he laughed. The story of the jeweller's sufferings appealed to his sense of humour. He studied the list of the missing jewels.

"There appears to be some pretty baubles among them, and they appear to be marked at pretty prices. If Hardaway has got clean away with the spoil they ought to provide him with a pleasant little nest egg with which to start afresh."

He turned to the mantelpiece to get a light for his pipe. Just as he struck a match his ears were saluted by a curious sound which proceeded from behind his back.

"What's that?"

With the lighted match in his hand he turned to listen. The sound continued—it seemed to increase in volume. It was as if some rusty clockwork mechanism had suddenly been set in motion.

"It seems to come from the interior of the Marquis of Bewlay's precious iron case." The case in question still remained where it had originally been placed, upon a chair. Mr. Champnell went to it and raised the lid. "By George! it does! It strikes me that it comes from inside one of these pretty wooden boxes—from inside this one, unless I am mistaken."

He removed the cover from the box in question—the noise did seem to come from inside it. No sooner had he done so than there was a sound as if a damp squib had been exploded, a quantity of what seemed like water was dashed into his face, and there drifted through the room a most unpleasant smoke. The Hon. Augustus was amazed.

"It occurs to me that the Marquis was right, and that these ingenious contrivances are infernal machines. Unless I err, one of them has justified its existence by exploding. Considering that there are twelve more of them, I seem to be in a truly comfortable situation. It is a pity Bewlay did not keep them in his possession a little longer, and allow them to explode on his own premises instead of on mine. What is this stuff on my face?" His head and face were covered with moisture. He allowed a drop to trickle into his mouth. "It tastes like sea-water. What is the meaning of this thing? I'll have a look at myself in the glass."

As he was moving towards a mirror something caught his eye which was lying on the floor.

"What the something's that?"

He might well ask—what seemed to be a circlet of scintillating light was lying almost at his feet. He picked it up, staring at it, when he had it in his hand, with growing bewilderment.

"A bracelet!—of diamonds!—As I am a sinner!—How on earth did it get here?" An idea flashed into his brain. "Can it be—it can't be—I do believe it is one of Golden's."

He examined with eager eyes the list of the missing jewels.

"It is!—Here's the thing itself!—'A bracelet of twenty-four diamonds, in a plain gold setting, with pearl fastenings. When closed the fastening is heart-shaped. Five pearls in fastening.' It is Golden's. Hollo, another of the Marquis's infernal machines seems to be evincing an inclination to go off."

The words were hardly out of his mouth when it did go off; indeed, the whole thirteen had gone off within ten minutes. They had evidently been ingeniously contrived to go off, as rapidly as possible, one after the other, so, as the schoolboys have it, to "keep the pot a-boiling." The room was full of suffocating smoke, Mr. Champnell was drenched with what seemed like sea-water, and he was in the possession of the whole of the missing jewels—they had been vomited forth by the infernal machines.

"Although this looks as if it were a fairy tale," he told himself, "I fancy it has a very simple explanation."

As, some half-hour after, he was driving down Bond Street in a cab, his attention was attracted to an individual who was advancing along the Piccadilly pavement.

"The man himself! So whatever may have become of the *Stormy Petrel*, milord himself is above water."

Stopping the cab, springing out of it, hastening towards the individual in question, Mr. Champnell accosted him—a tall, willowy man, with a dark, oval face, and big, wild, black eyes.

"I am glad to see, Hardaway, that you're not drowned, in spite of the boisterous weather which has recently prevailed in the Channel. You have probably been kept alive in order to be arrested on a warrant emanating from Scotland Yard."

"Champnell, you don't mean it?"

"Don't I? When a man steals jewels to the value of twenty thousand pounds, puts them, with about two gallons of sea-water, into thirteen infernal machines; sends those infernal machines to the address of the Marquis of Bewlay; and they are brought to me, and explode, and nearly blow me up, and the whole place besides, it is generally supposed that that man has done something which necessitates the issue of a warrant."

"My dear fellow!—it was only a joke."

"For less pointed jokes men have been sent to penal servitude."

Lord Hardaway slipped his arm through Mr. Champnell's.

"I was so devilish wild, and Golden was so devilish sick, that I couldn't help but spoof him. As for Bewlay, I owe him one for a dozen different things; I was bound to be even with him some time. There was nothing in the tins but water and Golden's jewels."

"Then it doesn't occur to you that you have been guilty of felony, and also of what a hanging judge might construe as an attempt to murder?"

"I say, Champnell, spare my blushes! I hear, dear boy, you've turned detective; you might do me a good turn, and all in the way of business. The fact is, I'm engaged to be married—the Bonnyer-Lees." Lord Hardaway winked. "It will set me on my legs."

"I thought that Miss Bonnyer-Lees was not on board the *Stormy Petrel*."

"She wasn't. That's what made me so devilish wild. She was to have gone, but when it began to blow she hoisted the white feather. I felt that I must have it out of somebody, so I had it out of Golden. But I saw her yesterday, and I made it all right, we're going to be married at once. I'm going to run straight—I swear I am! But if this tale got wind, it might spoil everything. I tell you what, old man, if, in the way of business, you'll make things square with Ruby and Golden, and with old Bewlay, I'll give you any sum in reason you like to name, say a couple of hundred guineas, cash down."

"A couple of hundred guineas, you say?" Mr. Champnell smiled; what at at the moment was not quite plain. "You don't seem conscious that it is a rather curious proposition which you are making me, especially as I happen to be already retained upon the other side, but I'll do the best for you I can."

When the Hon. Augustus reached Messrs. Ruby and Golden's establishment in Bond Street he was received by both the partners in a private room.

"Do I understand, gentlemen, if I return to you the missing jewels, exactly as they left Mr. Golden's hands, that, as they say in the advertisements, no questions will be asked?" Both partners were profuse in their protestations that he might so understand. "Then, in that case, gentlemen, here they are." He placed a leather case before them on the table. The partners stared. "If you will be so good as to examine them, at once, in my presence, you will perceive that they are intact. You quite understand, that no questions are to be asked of anyone, and, in particular, nothing is to be said to Lord Hardaway. I may mention, by the way, that Lord Hardaway is to be married, almost immediately, to Miss Bonnyer-Lees."

Mr. Ruby rubbed his hands and smiled.

"We are delighted to hear it, Mr. Champnell—delighted! You may rely on us not to breathe a word to Lord Hardaway; we quite understand that it was only a little joke of his. His lordship is so full of humour."

Mr. Golden's tone—he was examining the jewels as he spoke—was not quite so effusive.

"If you had been in my place, and had suffered what I suffered, you might not have seen the joke quite so clearly, Ruby. There is such a thing as being almost too full of humour."

Mr. Champnell went straight from Bond Street to the Marquis of Bewlay's. He found the Marquis in his smoking-room.

"You may make your mind easy on the subject of those infernal machines. Here they are." Mr. Champnell took thirteen empty tins from a bag which he was carrying. "They have all gone off, but as they were all filled with water it would seem as if somebody had been planning a practical joke at your expense. That sort of infernal machine hardly savours of a secret society."

"It certainly does not, and though you mayn't think it, Mr. Champnell, it's worth all of two hundred guineas to me to know it."

"I am very glad indeed to hear it."

And so the Hon. Augustus told himself again, when, having returned to his own quarters, he had propped up his feet against the mantel-shelf and was lighting a cigar.

"I don't think that's a bad morning's stroke of business—five hundred guineas for doing nothing at all."

XI.

THE HOUSEBOAT

CHAPTER I.

"I am sure of it!"

Inglis laid down his knife and fork. He stared round and round the small apartment in a manner which was distinctly strange. My wife caught him up. She laid down her knife and fork.

"You're sure of what?"

Inglis seemed disturbed. He appeared unwilling to give a direct answer. "Perhaps, after all, it's only a coincidence."

But Violet insisted. "What is a coincidence?"

Inglis addressed himself to me.

"The fact is, Millen, directly I came on board I thought I had seen this boat before."

"But I thought you said that you had never heard of the *Water Lily!*"

"Nor have I. The truth is that when I knew it, it wasn't the *Water Lily.*"

"I don't understand."

"They must have changed the name. Unless I am very much mistaken this—this used to be the *Sylph.*"

"The *Sylph?*"

"You don't mean to say that you have never heard of the *Sylph?*"

Inglis asked this question in a tone of voice which was peculiar.

"My dear fellow, I'm not a riverain authority. I am not acquainted with every houseboat between Richmond and Oxford. It was only at your special recommendation that I took the *Water Lily.*"

"Excuse me, Millen, I advised a houseboat. I didn't specify the *Water Lily*."

"But," asked my wife, "what was the matter with the *Sylph* that she should so mysteriously have become the *Water Lily?*"

Inglis fenced with this question in a manner which seemed to suggest a state of mental confusion.

"Of course, Millen, I know that that sort of thing would not have the slightest influence on you. It is only people of a very different sort who would allow it to have any effect on them. Then, after all, I may be wrong. And, in any case, I don't see that it matters."

"Mr. Inglis, are you suggesting that the *Sylph* was haunted?"

"Haunted!" Inglis started. "I never dropped a hint about its being haunted. So far as I remember I never heard a word of anything of the kind." Violet placed her knife and fork together on her plate. She folded her hands upon her lap.

"Mr. Inglis, there is a mystery. Will you this mystery unfold?"

"Didn't you really ever hear about the *Sylph*—two years ago?"

"Two years ago we were out of England."

"So you were. Perhaps that explains it. You understand, this mayn't be the *Sylph*. I may be wrong—though I don't think I am." Inglis glanced uncomfortably at the chair on which he was sitting. "Why, I believe this is the very chair on which I sat! I remember noticing what a queer shape it was."

It was rather an odd-shaped chair. For that matter, all the things on board were odd.

"Then have you been on board this boat before?"

"Yes." Inglis positively shuddered. "I was, once; if it is the *Sylph*, that is." He thrust his hands into his trouser pockets. He leaned back in his chair. A curious look came into his face. "It is the *Sylph*, I'll swear to it. It all comes back to me. What an extraordinary coincidence! One might almost think there was something supernatural in the thing."

His manner fairly roused me.

"I wish you would stop speaking in riddles, and tell us what you are driving at."

He became preternaturally solemn.

"Millen, I'm afraid I have made rather an ass of myself; I ought to have held my tongue. But the coincidence is such a strange one that it took me unawares, and since I have said so much I suppose I may as well say more. After dinner I will tell you all there is to tell. I don't think it's a story which Mrs. Millen would like to listen to."

Violet's face was a study.

"I don't understand you, Mr. Inglis, because you are quite well aware it is a principle of mine that what is good for a husband to hear is good for a wife. Come, don't be silly. Let us hear what the fuss is about. I daresay it's about nothing after all."

"You think so? Well, Mrs. Millen, you shall hear." He carefully wiped his moustache. He began: "Two years ago there was a houseboat on the river called the *Sylph*. It belonged to a man named Hambro. He lent it to a lady and a gentleman. She was rather a pretty woman, with a lot of fluffy, golden hair. He was a quiet unassuming-looking man, who looked as though he had something to do with horses. I made their acquaintance on the river. One evening he asked me on board to dine. I sat, as I believe, on this very chair, at this very table. Three days afterwards they disappeared."

"Well?" I asked. Inglis had paused.

"So far as I know, he has never been seen or heard of since."

"And the lady?"

"Some of us were getting up a picnic. We wanted them to come with us. We couldn't quite make out their sudden disappearance. So, two days after we had missed them, I and another man tried to rout them out. I looked through the window. I saw something lying on the floor. 'Jarvis,' I whispered, 'I believe that Mrs. Bush is lying on the floor dead drunk.' 'She can't have been drunk two days,' he said. He came to my side. 'Why, she's in her nightdress. This is very queer. Inglis, I wonder if the door is locked.' It wasn't. We opened it and went inside."

Inglis emptied his glass of wine.

"The woman we had known as Mrs. Bush lay in her night-dress, dead upon the floor. She had been stabbed to the heart. She was lying just about where Mrs. Miilen is sitting now."

"Mr. Inglis!" Violet rose suddenly.

"There is reason to believe that, from one point of view, the woman was no better than she ought to have been. That is the story."

"But"—I confess it was not at all the story I had expected it was going to be; I did not altogether like it—"who killed her?"

"That is the question. There was no direct evidence to show. No weapon was discovered. The man we had known as Bush had vanished, as it seemed, off the face of the earth. He had not left so much as a pocket-handkerchief behind him. Everything both of his and hers had gone. It turned out that nobody knew anything at all about him. They had no servant. What meals they had on board were sent in from the hotel. Hambro had advertised the *Sylph*. Bush had replied to the advertisement. He had paid the rent in advance, and Hambro had asked no questions."

"And what became of the *Sylph*?"

"She also vanished. She had become a little too notorious. One doesn't fancy living on board a houseboat on which a murder has been committed; one is at too close quarters. I suppose Hambro sold her for what he could get, and the purchaser painted her, and rechristened her the *Water Lily*."

"But are you sure this is the *Sylph*?"

"As sure as that I am sitting here. It is impossible that I could be mistaken. I still seem to see that woman lying dead just about where Mrs. Miilen is standing now."

"Mr. Inglis!"

Violet was standing up. She moved away—towards me. Inglis left soon afterwards. He did not seem to care to stop. He had scarcely eaten any dinner. In fact, that was the case with all of us. Mason had exerted herself to prepare a decent meal in her cramped little kitchen, and we had been so ungrateful as not even to reach the end of her bill of fare. When Inglis had gone she appeared in her bonnet and cloak. We supposed that, very naturally, she had taken umbrage.

"If you please, ma'am, I'm going."

"Mason! What do you mean?"

"I couldn't think of stopping in no place in which murder was committed, least of all a houseboat. Not to mention that last night I heard ghosts, if ever anyone heard them yet."

"Mason! Don't be absurd. I thought you had more sense."

"All I can say is, ma'am, that last night as I lay awake, listening to the splashing of the water, all at once I heard in here the sound of quarrelling. I couldn't make it out. I thought that you and the master was having words. Yet it didn't sound like your voices. Besides, you went on awful. Still, I didn't like to say nothing, because it might have been, and it wasn't my place to say that I had heard. But now I know that it was ghosts."

She went. She was not to be persuaded to stay any more than Inglis. She did not even stay to clear the table. I have seldom seen a woman in a greater hurry. As for wages, there was not a hint of them. Staid, elderly, self-possessed female though she was, she seemed to be in a perfect panic of fear. Nothing would satisfy her but that she should, with the greatest possible expedition, shake from her feet the dust of the *Water Lily*. When we were quit of her I looked at Violet and Violet looked at me. I laughed. I will not go so far as to say that I laughed genially; still, I laughed.

"We seem to be in for a pleasant river holiday."

"Eric, let us get outside."

We went on deck. The sun had already set. There was no moon, but there was a cloudless sky. The air was languorous and heavy. Boats were stealing over the waters. Someone in the distance was playing a banjo accompaniment while a clear girlish voice was singing "The Garden of Sleep." The other houseboats were radiant with Chinese lanterns. The *Water Lily* alone was still in shadow. We drew our deck-chairs close together. Violet's hand stole into mine.

"Eric, do you know that last night I, too, heard voices?"

"You!" I laughed again. "Violet!"

"I couldn't make it out at all. I was just going to wake you when they were still."

"You were dreaming, child. Inglis's story—confound him

and his story!—has recalled your dream to mind. I hope you don't wish to follow Mason's example, and make a bolt of it. I have paid pretty stiffly for the honour of being the *Water Lily* tenant for a month, not to mention the fact of disarranging all our plans."

Violet paused before she answered.

"No; I don't think I want, as you say, to make a bolt of it. Indeed," she nestled closer to my side, "it is rather the other way. I should like to see it through. I have sometimes thought that I should like to be with someone I can trust in a situation such as this. Perhaps we may be able to fathom the mystery—who knows?"

This tickled me. "I thought you had done with romance."

"With one sort of romance I hope I shall never have done." She pressed my hand. She looked up archly into my face. I knew it, although we were in shadow. "With another sort of romance I may be only just beginning. I have never yet had dealings with a ghost."

CHAPTER II.

At first I could not make out what it was that had roused me. Then I felt Violet's hand steal into mine. Her voice whispered in my ear, "Eric!" I turned over towards her on the pillow. "Be still. They're here." I did as she bade me. I was still. I heard no sound but the lazy rippling of the river.

"Who's here?" I asked, when, as I deemed, I had been silent long enough.

"S-sh!" I felt her finger pressed against my lips. I was still again. The silence was broken in rather a peculiar manner.

"I don't think you quite understand me."

The words were spoken in a man's voice, as it seemed to me, close behind my back. I was so startled by the unexpected presence of a third person that I made as if to spring up in bed. My wife caught me by the arm. Before I could remonstrate or shake off her grasp a woman's laughter rang through the little cabin. It was too metallic to be agreeable. And a woman's voice replied—

"I understand you well enough, don't you make any error!"

There was a momentary pause.

"You don't understand me, fool!"

The first four words were spoken with a deliberation which meant volumes, while the final epithet came with a sudden malignant ferocity which took me aback. The speaker, whoever he might be, meant mischief. I sprang up and out of bed.

"What are you doing here?" I cried.

I addressed the inquiry apparently to the vacant air. The moonlight flooded the little cabin. It showed clearly enough that it was empty. My wife sat up in bed.

"Now," she observed, "you've done it."

"Done what? Who was that speaking?"

"The voices."

"The voices! What voices? I'll voice them! Where the dickens have they gone?"

I moved towards the cabin door, with the intention of pursuing my inquiries further. Violet's voice arrested me.

"It is no use your going to look for them. They will not be found by searching. The speakers were Mr. and Mrs. Bush."

"Mr. and Mrs. Bush?"

Violet's voice dropped to an awful whisper. "The murderer and his victim."

I stared at her in the moonlight. Inglis's pleasant little story had momentarily escaped my memory. Suddenly roused from a dreamless slumber, I had not yet had time to recall such trivialities. Now it all came back in a flash.

"Violet," I exclaimed, "have you gone mad?"

"They are the voices which I heard last night. They are the voices which Mason heard. Now you have heard them. If you had kept still the mystery might have been unravelled. The crime might have been re-acted before our eyes, or at least within sound of our ears."

I sat down upon the ingenious piece of furniture which did duty as a bed. I seemed to have struck upon a novel phase in my wife's character. It was not altogether a pleasing novelty. She spoke with a degree of judicial calmness which, under all the circumstances, I did not altogether relish.

"Violet, I wish you wouldn't talk like that. It makes my blood run cold."

"Why should it? My dear Eric, I have heard you yourself say that in the presence of the seemingly mysterious our attitude should be one of passionless criticism. A mysterious crime has been committed in this very chamber." I shivered. "Surely it is our duty to avail ourselves of any opportunities which may offer, and which may enable us to probe it to the bottom."

I made no answer. I examined the doors. They were locked and bolted. There was no sign that anyone had tampered with the fastenings. I returned to bed. As I was arranging myself between the sheets Violet whispered in my ear. "Perhaps if we are perfectly quiet they may come back again."

I am not a man given to adjectives; but I felt adjectival then. I was about to explain, in language which would not have been wanting in force, that I had no desire that they should come back again, when—

"You had better give it to me."

The words were spoken in a woman's voice, as it seemed, within twelve inches of my back. The voice was not that of a lady. I should have said without hesitation, had I heard the voice under any other circumstances, that the speaker had been born within the sound of Bow Bells.

"Had I?"

It was a man's voice which put the question. There was something about the tone in which the speaker put it which reminded one of the line in the people's ballad, "It ain't exactly what 'e sez, it's the nasty way 'e sez it." The question was put in a very "nasty way" indeed.

"Yes, my boy, you had."

"Indeed?"

"Yes, you may say 'indeed,' but if you don't I tell you what I'll do—I'll spoil you."

"And what, my dear Gertie, am I to understand by the mystic threat of spoiling me?"

"I'll go straight to your wife, and I'll tell her everything."

"Oh, you will, will you?"

There was a movement of a chair. The male speaker was getting up.

"Yes, I will."

There was a slight pause. One could fancy that the speakers were facing each other. One could picture the look of impudent defiance upon the woman's countenance, the suggestion of coming storm upon that of the man. It was the man's voice which broke the silence.

"It is odd, Gertrude, that you should have chosen this evening to threaten me, because I myself had chosen this evening, I won't say to threaten, but to make a communication to you."

"Give me a match." The request came from the woman.

"With pleasure. I will give you anything, my dear Gertrude, within reason." There was another pause. In the silence I seemed to hear my wife holding her breath—as I certainly was holding mine. All at once there came a sound of scratching, a flash of light. It came so unexpectedly, and such was the extreme tension of my nerves, that, with a stifled exclamation, I half rose in bed. My wife pressed her hand against my lips. She held me down. She spoke in so attenuated a whisper that it was only because all my senses were so keenly on the alert that I heard her.

"You goose! He's only striking a match."

He might have been, but who? She took things for granted. I wanted to know. The light continued flickering to and fro, as a match does flicker. I would have given much to know who held it, or even what was its position in the room. As luck had it, my face was turned the other way. My wife seemed to understand what was passing in my mind.

"There's no one there," she whispered.

No one, I presumed, but the match. I took it for granted that was there. Though I did not venture to inquire, I felt that I might not have such perfect control over my voice as my wife appeared to have.

While the light continued to flicker there came stealing into my nostrils—I sniffed, the thing was unmistakable!—the odour of tobacco. The woman was lighting a cigarette. I knew it was the woman because presently there came this request from the man, "After you with the light, my dear."

I presume that the match was passed. Immediately the smell of tobacco redoubled. The man had lit a cigarette as well. I confess that I resented—silently, but still strongly—the idea of two strangers, whether ghosts or anybody else, smoking, uninvited, in my cabin.

The match went out. The cigarettes were lit. The man continued speaking.

"The communication, my dear Gertrude, which I intended to make to you was this. The time has come for us to part."

He paused, possibly for an answer. None came.

"I need not enlarge on the reasons which necessitate our parting. They exist."

Pause again. Then the woman.

"What are you going to give me?"

"One of the reasons which necessitate our parting—a very strong reason, as you, I am sure, will be the first to admit—is that I have nothing left to give you."

"So you say."

"Precisely. So I say and so I mean."

"Do you mean that you are going to give me nothing?"

"I mean, my dear Gertrude, that I have nothing to give you. You have left me nothing."

"Bah!"

The sound which issued from the lady's lips was expressive of the most complete contempt.

"Look here, my boy, you give me a hundred sovereigns or I'll spoil you."

Pause again. Probably the gentleman was thinking over the lady's observation.

"What benefit do you think you will do yourself by what you call 'spoiling' me?"

"Never mind about that: I'll do it. You think I don't know all about you, but I do. Perhaps I'm not so soft as you think. Your wife's got some money if you haven't. Suppose you go back and ask her for some. You've treated me badly enough. I don't see why you shouldn't go and treat her the same. She wouldn't make things warm for you if she knew a few things I could tell her—not at all! You give me a hundred sovereigns or, I tell you straight, I'll go right to your house and I'll tell her all."

"Oh, no, you won't."

"Won't I? I say I will!"

"Oh, no, you won't."

"I say I will! I've warned you, that's all. I'm not going to stop here, talking stuff to you. I'm going to bed. You can go and hang yourself for all I care."

There was a sound, an indubitable sound—the sound of a pair of shoes being thrown upon the floor. There were other sounds, equally capable of explanation: sounds which suggested—I wish the printer would put it in small type—that the lady was undressing. Undressing, too, with scant regard to ceremony. Garments were thrown off and tossed higgledy-piggledy here and there. They appeared to be thrown, with sublime indifference, upon table, chairs, and floor. I even felt something alight upon the bed. Some feminine garment, perhaps, which, although it fell by no means heavily, made me conscious, as it fell, of the most curious sensation I had in all my life—till then—experienced. It seemed that the lady, while she unrobed, continued smoking. From her next words it appeared that the gentleman, also smoking, stood and stared at her.

"Don't stand staring at me like a gawk. I'm going to turn in."

"And I'm going to turn out. Not, as you suggested, to hang myself, but to finish this cigarette upon the roof. Perhaps, when I return, you will be in a more equable frame of mind."

"Don't you flatter yourself. What I say I mean. A hundred sovereigns, or I tell your wife."

He laughed very softly, as though he was determined not to be annoyed. Then we heard his footsteps as he crossed the floor. The door opened, then closed. We heard him ascend the steps. Then, with curious distinctness, his measured tramp, tramp! as he moved to and fro upon the roof. In the cabin for a moment there was silence. Then the woman said, with a curious faltering in her voice—

"I'll do it. I don't care what he says." There was a choking in her throat. "He don't care for me a bit."

Suddenly she flung herself upon her knees beside the bed. She pillowed her head and arms upon the coverlet. I lay near the outer edge of the bed, which was a small one, by the way. As I lay I felt the pressure of her limbs. My sensations, as I did, I am unable to describe. After a momentary interval there came the sound of sobbing. I could feel the woman quivering with the strength of her emotion. Violet and I were speechless. I do not think that, for the instant, we could have spoken even had we tried. The woman's presence was so evident, her grief so real. As she wept disjointed words came from her.

"I've given everything for him! If he only cared for me! If he only did."

All at once, with a rapid movement, she sprang up. The removal of the pressure was altogether unmistakable. I was conscious of her resting her hands upon the coverlet to assist her to her feet. I felt the little jerk; then the withdrawal of the hands. She choked back her sobs when she had gained her feet. Her tone was changed.

"What a fool I am to make a fuss. He don't care for me—not that." We heard her snap her fingers in the air. "He never did. Us women are always fools—we're all the same. I'll go to bed."

Violet clutched my arm. She whispered, in that attenuated fashion she seemed to have caught the trick of—

"She's getting into bed. We must get out."

It certainly was a fact, someone was getting into bed. The bed-clothes were moved; not our bedclothes, but some phantom coverings. We heard them rustle, we were conscious of a current of air across our faces as someone caught them open. And then!—then someone stepped upon the bed.

"Let's get out!" gasped Violet.

CHAPTER III.

She moved away from me. She squeezed herself against the side of the cabin. She withdrew her limbs from between the sheets. As for me, the person who had stepped upon the bed had actually stepped upon me, and that without seeming at all conscious of my presence. Someone sat down plump upon the sheet beside me. That was enough. I took advantage of my lying on the edge of the bed to slip out upon the floor. I might possess an unsuspected capacity for undergoing strange experiences, but I drew the line at sleeping with a ghost.

The moonlight streamed across the room. As I stood, in something very like a state of nature on the floor, I could clearly see Violet cowering on the further side of the bed. I could distinguish all her features. But when I looked upon the bed itself—there was nothing there. The moon's rays fell upon the pillow. They revealed its snowy whiteness. There seemed nothing else it could reveal. It was untenanted. And yet, if one looked closely at it, it seemed to be indented, just as it might have been indented had a human head been lying there. But about one thing there could be no mistake whatever—my ears did not play me false, I heard it too distinctly—the sound made by a person who settles himself between the sheets, and then the measured respiration of one who composes himself to slumber.

I remained there silent. On her hands and knees Violet crept towards the foot of the bed. When she had gained the floor she stole on tiptoe to my side.

"I did not dare to step across her." I felt her, as she nestled to me, give me a little shiver. "I could not do it. Can you see her?"

"What a fool I am!" As Violet asked her question there came this observation from the person in the bed—whom, by the way, I could not see. There was a long-drawn sigh. "What fools all we women are! What fools!"

There was a sincerity of bitterness about the tone, which, coming as it did from an unseen speaker—one so near and yet so far—had on one a most uncomfortable effect. Violet pressed closer to my side. The woman in the bed turned over. Overhead there still continued the measured tramp, tramping of the man. We were conscious, in some subtle way, that the woman lay listening to the footsteps. They spoke more audibly to her ears even than to ours.

"Ollie! Ollie!" she repeated the name softly to herself, with a degree of tenderness which was in startling contrast to her previous bitterness.

"I wish you would come to bed."

She was silent. There was only the sound of her gentle breathing. Her bitter mood had been but transient. She was falling asleep with words of tenderness upon her lips. Above, the footsteps ceased. All was still. There was not even the murmur of the waters. The wife and I, side by side, stood looking down upon what seemed an empty bed.

"She is asleep," said Violet.

It seemed to me she was: although I could not see her, it seemed to me she was. I could hear her breathing as softly as a child. Violet continued whispering—

"How strange! Eric, what can it mean?"

I muttered a reply—

"A problem for the Psychical Research Society."

"It seems just like a dream."

"I wish it were a dream."

"S-sh! There is someone coming down the stairs."

There was—at least, if we could trust our ears, there was. Apparently the man above had had enough of solitude. We heard him move across the roof, then pause just by the steps, then descend them one by one. It seemed to us that in this step there was something stealthy, that he was endeavouring not to arouse attention, to make as little noise as possible. Half-way down he paused; at the foot he paused again.

"He's listening outside the door." It almost seemed that he was. We stood and listened too. "Let's get away from the bed."

My wife drew me with her. At the opposite end of the cabin was a sort of little alcove, which was screened by a curtain, and behind which were hung one or two of our garments which we were not actually using. Violet drew me within the shadow of this alcove, I say drew me because, offering no resistance, I allowed myself to be completely passive in her hands. The alcove was not large enough to hold us. Still the curtain acted as a partial screen.

The silence endured for some moments. Then we heard without a hand softly turning the handle of the door. While I was wondering whether, after all, I was not the victim of an attack of indigestion, or whether I was about to witness an attempt at effecting a burglarious entry into a houseboat, a strange thing happened, the strangest thing that had happened yet.

As I have already mentioned, the moon's rays flooded the cabin. This was owing to the fact that a long narrow casement, which ran round the walls near the roof of the cabin, had been left open for the sake of admitting air and ventilation; but, save for the moonbeams, the cabin was unlighted. When, however, we heard the handle being softly turned, a singular change occurred. It was like the transformation scene in a theatre. The whole place, all at once, was brilliantly illuminated. The moonbeams disappeared. Instead, a large swinging lamp was hanging from the centre of the cabin. So strong was the light which it shed around that our eyes were dazzled. It was not our lamp; we used small hand-lamps, which stood upon the table. By its glare we saw that the whole cabin was changed. For an instant we failed to clearly realise in what the change consisted. Then we understood it was a question of decoration. The contents of the cabin, for the most part, were the same, though they looked newer, and the positions of the various articles were altered; but the panels of the cabin of the *Water Lily* were painted blue and white. The panels of this cabin were coloured chocolate and gold.

"Eric, it's the *Sylph!*"

The suggestion conveyed by my wife's whispered words, even as she spoke, occurred to me. I understood where, for Inglis, had lain the difficulty of recognition. The two cabins were the same, and yet were not. It was just as though someone had endeavoured, without spending much cash, to render one as much as possible unlike the other.

In this cabin there were many things which were not ours. In fact, so far as I can see, there was nothing which was ours. Strange articles of costume were scattered about; the table was covered with a curious litter; and on the ingenious article of furniture which did duty as a bed, and which stood where our bed stood, and which, indeed, seemed to be our bed, there was someone sleeping.

As my startled eyes travelled round this amazing transformation scene, at last they reached the door. There they stayed. Mechanically I shrank back nearer to the wall. I felt my wife tighten her grasp upon my hand.

The door was open some few inches. Through the aperture thus formed there peered a man. He seemed to be listening. It was so still that one could hear the gentle breathing of the woman sleeping in the bed. Apparently satisfied, he opened the door sufficiently wide to admit of his entering the cabin. My impression was that he could not fail to perceive us, yet to all appearances he remained entirely unconscious of our neighbourhood. He was a man certainly under five feet six in height. He was slight in build, very dark, with face clean shaven; his face was long and narrow. In dress and bearing he seemed a gentleman, yet there was that about him which immediately reminded me of what Inglis had said of the man Bush—"he looked as though he had something to do with horses."

He stood for some seconds in an attitude of listening, so close to me that I had only to stretch out my hand to take him by the throat. I did not do it. I don't know what restrained me; I think, more than anything, it was the feeling that these things which were passing before me must be passing in a dream. His face was turned away. He looked intently towards the sleeping woman.

After he had had enough of listening he moved towards the bed. His step was soft and cat-like; it was absolutely noiseless. Glancing down, I perceived that he was without boots or shoes. He was in his stockinged feet. I had distinctly heard the tramp, tramping of a pair of shoes upon the cabin roof. I had heard them descend the steps. Possibly he had paused outside the door to take them off.

When he reached the bed he stood looking down upon the sleeper. He stooped over her, as if the better to catch her breathing. He whispered softly—

"Gerty!"

He paused for a moment, as if for an answer. None came. Standing up, he put his hand, as it seemed to me, into the bosom of his flannel shirt. He took out a leather sheath. From the sheath he drew a knife. It was a long, slender, glittering blade. Quite twelve inches in length, at no part was it broader than my little finger. With the empty sheath in his left hand, the knife behind his back in his right, he again leaned over the sleeper. Again he softly whispered, "Gerty!"

Again there was no answer. Again he stood upright, turning his back towards the bed, so that he looked towards us. His face was not an ugly one, though the expression was somewhat saturnine. On it, at the instant, there was a peculiar look, such a look as I could fancy upon the face of a jockey who, toward the close of a great race, settles himself in the saddle with the determination to "finish" well. The naked blade he placed upon the table, the empty sheath beside it. Then he moved towards us. My first thought was that now, at last, we were discovered; but something in the expression of his features told me that this was not so. He approached us with an indifference which was amazing. He passed so close to us that we were conscious of the slight disturbance of the air caused by his passage. There was a Gladstone bag on a chair within two feet of us. Picking it up, he bore it to the table. Opening it out, he commenced to pack it. All manner of things he placed within it, both masculine and feminine belongings, even the garments which the sleeper had taken off, and which lay scattered on the chair and on the floor, even her shoes and stockings! When the bag was filled he took a long brown ulster, which was thrown over the back of a chair. He stuffed the pockets with odds and ends. When he had completed his operations the cabin was stripped of everything except the actual furniture. He satisfied himself that this was so by overhauling every nook and corner, in the process passing and repassing Violet and me with a perfect unconcern which was more and more amazing. Being apparently at last clear in his mind upon that point, he put on the ulster and a dark cloth cap, and began to fasten the Gladstone bag.

While he was doing so, his back being turned to the bed, without the slightest warning, the woman in the bed sat up. The man's movements had been noiseless. He had made no sound which could have roused her. Possibly some sudden intuition had come to her in her sleep. However that might be, she all at once was wide awake. She stared round the apartment with wondering eyes. Her glance fell on the man, dressed as for a journey.

"Where are you going?"

The words fell from her lips as unawares. Then some sudden conception of his purpose seemed to have flown to her brain. She sprang out of bed with a bound.

"You shan't go," she screamed.

She rushed to him. He put his hand on the table. He turned to her. Something flashed in the lamplight. It was the knife. As she came he plunged it into her side right to the hilt. For an instant he held her spitted on the blade. He put his hand to her throat. He thrust her from him. With the other hand he extricated the blade. He let her fall upon the floor. She had uttered a sort of sigh as the weapon was being driven home. Beyond that she had not made a sound.

All was still. He remained for some seconds looking down at her as she lay. Then he turned away. We saw his face. It was, if possible, paler than before. A smile distorted his lips. He stood for a moment as if listening. Then he glanced round the cabin, as if to make sure that he was unobserved. His black eyes travelled over our startled features, in evident unconsciousness that we were there. Then he glanced at the blade in his hand. As he did so he perceptibly shuddered. The glittering steel was obscured with blood. As he perceived that this was so he gasped. He seemed to realise for the first time what it was that he had done. Taking an envelope from an inner pocket of his ulster he began to wipe the blood from off the blade. While doing so his wandering glance fell upon the woman lying on the floor. Some new aspect of the recumbent figure seemed to strike him with a sudden horror. He staggered backwards. I thought he would have fallen. He caught at the wall to help him stand—caught at the wall with the hand which held the blade. At that part of the cabin the wall was doubly panelled half-way to the roof. Between the outer and the inner panel there was evidently a cavity, because, when in his sudden alarm he clutched at the wall, the blade slipped from his relaxing grasp and fell between the panels. Such was his state of panic that he did not appear to perceive what had happened. And at that moment a cry rang out upon the river—possibly it was someone hailing the keeper of the lock—"Ahoy!"

The sound seemed to fill him with unreasoning terror. He rushed to the table. He closed the Gladstone with a hurried snap; he caught it up; he turned to flee. As he did so I stepped out of the alcove. I advanced right in front of him. I cannot say whether he saw me, or whether he didn't. But he seemed to see me. He started back. A look of the most awful terror came on his countenance. And at that same instant the whole scene vanished. I was standing in the cabin of the *Water Lily*. The moon was stealing through the little narrow casement. Violet was creeping to my side. She stole into my arms. I held her to me.

"Eric," she moaned.

For myself, I am not ashamed to own that, temporarily, I had lost the use of my tongue. When, in a measure, the faculty of speech returned to me—

"Was it a dream?" I whispered.

"It was a vision."

"A vision?" I shuddered. "Look!"

As I spoke she turned to look. There, in the moonbeams, we saw a woman in her nightdress, lying on the cabin floor. We saw that she had golden hair. It seemed to us that she was dead. We saw her but a moment—she was gone! It must have been imagination; we know that these things are not, but it belonged to that order of imagination which is stranger than reality.

My wife looked up at me.

"Eric, it is a vision which has been sent to us in order that we may expose in the light of day a crime which was hidden in the night."

I said nothing. I felt for a box of matches on the table. I lit a lamp. I looked round and round the cabin, holding the lamp above my head the better to assist my search. It was with a feeling of the most absurd relief that I perceived that everything was unchanged, that, so far as I could see, there was no one there but my wife and I.

"I think, Violet, if you don't mind, I'll have some whisky."

She offered no objection. She stood and watched me as I poured the stuff into a glass. I am bound to admit that the spirit did me good.

"And what," I asked, "do you make of the performance we have just now witnessed?" She was still. I took another drink. There can be no doubt that, under certain circumstances, whisky is a fluid which is not to be despised. "Have we both suddenly become insane, or do you attribute it to the cucumber we ate at lunch?"

"How strange that Mr. Inglis should have told us the story only this afternoon."

"I wish Mr. Inglis had kept the story to himself entirely."

"They were the voices which I heard last night. They were the voices Mason heard. It was all predestined. I understand it now."

"I wish that I could say the same."

"I see it all!"

She pressed her hands against her brow. Her eyes flashed fire.

"I see why it was sent to us, what it is we have to do. Eric, we have to find the knife."

I began to fear, from her frenzied manner, that her brain must in reality be softening.

"What knife?"

"The knife which he dropped between the panels. The boat has only been repainted. We know that in all essentials the *Sylph* and the *Water Lily* are one and the same. Mr. Inglis said that the weapon which did the deed was never found. No adequate search was ever made. It is waiting for us where he dropped it."

"My dear Violet, don't you think you had better have a little whisky? It will calm you."

"Have you a hammer and a chisel?"

"What do you want them for?"

"It was here that he was standing; it was here that he dropped the knife." She had taken up her position against the wall at the foot of the bed. Frankly, I did not like her manner at all. It was certainly where, in the latter portion of that nightmare, the fellow had been standing. "I will wrench this panel away." She rapped against a particular panel with her knuckles. "Behind it we shall find the knife."

"My dear Violet, this houseboat isn't mine. We cannot destroy another man's property in that wanton fashion. He will hardly accept as an adequate excuse the fact that at the time we were suffering from a severe attack of indigestion."

"This will do."

She took a large carving-knife out of the knife-basket which was on the shelf close by her. She thrust the blade between the panel and the woodwork. It could scarcely have been securely fastened. In a surprisingly short space of time she had forced it loose. Then, grasping it with both her hands, she hauled the panel bodily away.

"Eric, it is there!"

Something was there, resting on a little ledge which had checked its fall on to the floor beneath—something which was covered with paint, and dust, and cobwebs, and Violet all at once grew timid.

"You take it; I dare not touch the thing."

"It is very curious; something is there, and, by George, it is a knife!"

It was a knife—the knife which we had seen in the vision, the dream, the nightmare, call it what you will—the something which had seemed so real. There was no mistaking it, tarnished though it was—the long, slender blade which we had seen the man draw from the leather sheath. Stuck to it by what was afterwards shown to be coagulated blood was an envelope—the envelope which we had seen the fellow take from his pocket to wipe off the crimson stain. It had adhered to the blade. When the knife fell the envelope fell too.

"At least," I murmured as I stared at this grim relic, "this is a singular coincidence."

The blood upon the blade had dried. It required but little to cause the envelope to fall away. As a matter of fact, while I was still holding the weapon in my hand it fell to the floor. I picked it up. It was addressed in a woman's hand, "Francis Joynes, Esq., Fairleigh, Streatham."

I at once recognised the name as that of a well-known owner of racehorses and so-called "gentleman rider."

* * * * *

Not the least singular part of all that singular story was that the letter inside that envelope, which was afterwards opened and read by the proper authorities, was from Mr. Joynes's wife. It was a loving, tender letter, from a wife who was an invalid abroad to a husband whom she supposed was thinking of her at home.

Mr. Joynes was never arrested, and that for this sufficient reason: that when the agents of the law arrived at his residence Mr. Joynes was dead. He had committed suicide on the very night on which we saw that—call it vision—on board the *Water Lily*. I viewed the corpse against my will. I was not called in evidence. Had I been, I was prepared to swear, as was my wife, that Mr. Joynes was the man whom I had seen in a dream that night. It was shown at the inquest that he had suffered of late from horrid dreams—that he had scarcely dared to sleep. I wonder if, in that last and most awful of his dreams, he had seen my face—seen it as I saw his?

It was afterwards shown, from inquiries which were made, that Mr. Joynes and "Mr. Bush," tenant of the *Sylph*, were, beyond all doubt, one and the same person. On the singular circumstances which caused that discovery to be made I offer no comment.

XII.

THE DUKE

A FICTION OF THE FUTURE

I.

MRS. PAYNTER buttonholed a porter. "Can you tell me in which carriage the Earl of Datchet is travelling?"

"Who, mum?"

"The Earl of Datchet; or can you point him out to me?"

"No, mum, I can't. I don't know no such gentleman. By your leave, mum!"

Without her leave the porter went off with his load of luggage. The lady turned to her daughter.

"How very uncivil the servants are upon this line!" The young lady said nothing. She simply regarded her mother with an expression of placid scorn. "I wonder if this guard can tell me." A guard came hurrying along the platform. The lady laid hands of violence on him. "Guard, can you tell me which is the Earl of Datchet?"

"The Earl of Datchet, madam? Is he travelling by this train?"

"I saw in *Fashion* that the Earl of Datchet intended to travel by this morning's tidal train to Paris. Isn't this the tidal train?"

"This is the tidal train, but I don't know anything about the Earl of Datchet. Are you going by this train, madam?"

"Of course I am. But, guard"—the lady's hand stole towards her purse—"I particularly wished to travel in the same compartment as his lordship."

"I am afraid, madam, that I really don't know anything about his lordship, and if you're going you'd better get in—they're starting." The guard opened a carriage door. "Is this your luggage?" He signalled to a porter. "Look alive, attend to this luggage."

"My dear mother," observed Miss Paynter, when the heap of wraps had been bundled in, "are you coming?"

"It's most annoying——" began the lady.

The guard cut her short.

"Now, madam, if you please!"

Almost before Mrs. Paynter knew it she was settling herself in the corner of the carriage opposite her daughter. Before she had settled herself the train was off, and before the train was fairly under way she was favouring Miss Paynter with some remarks of a personal nature.

"Really, Edith, you are the most trying person I ever encountered. You know perfectly well that if I hadn't seen it in the paper I should never have dreamt of crossing to-day, and especially by this particular train, and yet you won't give me the slightest help or assistance of any kind. And now my whole labour's thrown away, and my whole purpose spoiled!"

"My dear mother, what does it matter?"

The young lady not only spoke with her lips, but also with her eyes. With her organs of vision she drew her mother's attention to the fact that they were not alone in the carriage. The elder lady grasped her daughter's meaning. But as she glanced at the stranger at the other end, she scarcely took that advantage of the hint which she was intended to take.

"And now, although you know how much I like to have a carriage to myself, and how much I object to travelling with strangers, you have allowed that insolent man—and I am thankful to think that he lost the five shillings which I quite intended to give him—to put us just where it pleased him. It's just like you!"

To this observation Miss Paynter answered nothing. She looked at her mother, and out of the corners of her eyes she peeped at the stranger. As she peeped she smiled; it was but the faintest shadow of a smile, but it was certainly a smile. The stranger was a solid-looking young man, short and broad. He had rather a vacuous expression of countenance. His cheeks, which were innocent of whiskers, were fat and red. Altogether he did not seem to be the sort of person who was likely to be hurt by a trifle, which, under the circumstances, was perhaps as well. None the less, he appeared curiously disconcerted by a remark which Mrs. Paynter all at once addressed to him.

"Excuse me, sir, but are you acquainted with the Earl of Datchet?"

"Beg pardon."

The young gentleman had his feet on the seat in front of him, his hat tilted over his eyes, and his hands in his trousers pockets, and was probably anathematising himself for not having gone at once into a smoking carriage instead of endeavouring to secure a whole compartment to himself for the solitary enjoyment, in defiance of the company's by-laws, of "a fragrant weed." But on Mrs. Paynter's addressing to him her inquiry his feet went off the cushions, his hat from over his eyes, and his hands from out of his pockets with a celerity which was comical.

"I merely inquired if you were acquainted, by sight, with the person of the Earl of Datchet."

When this question was put to him the stranger's demeanour was really singular. He half rose from his seat, and stared.

"Well, I'm blowed! That's good."

"Sir!"

Mrs. Paynter regarded him through her glasses with supercilious surprise. The stranger transferred his glance from the mother to the daughter; as it fell upon the daughter he started again.

"Beg pardon. I didn't notice. Did you ask me if I knew Datchet?"

Miss Paynter smiled; she seemed tickled by the stranger's manner.

"It was not I; it was my mother."

Mrs. Paynter did *not* smile.

"Pray, Edith, do not let us trouble this person further. I merely made a commonplace inquiry. I perceive that I made a mistake."

If the lady's manner was meant to be crushing—and it seemed that it was—the stranger remained uncrushed. He only stared the more.

"How?"

Mrs. Paynter leaned back in her corner.

"My dear Edith, *do* not let us trouble this person further."

"But I do know Datchet."

Up went the lady's glasses again. But if she meant to stare the stranger out of countenance, she simply scored another failure.

"When you say 'Datchet,' are you referring to the Earl of Datchet?"

"Dicky Datchet; yes, that's him."

"'Dicky Datchet'! Really, you appear to be upon intimate terms with his lordship. Do you happen to be aware if his lordship is travelling by this train?"

"I'll bet a guinea he isn't."

"Indeed! I understood, upon good authority, that he intended to do so."

"Not he. Dicky's at Boulogne."

"At Boulogne, is he? You seem to have a close acquaintance with his lordship's movements. May I ask if you are a friend of his?"

Mrs. Paynter was quite incapable of anything more cutting in the way of sarcastic suggestion than her manner conveyed; but, in spite of it, the stranger seemed beautifully unconscious that there was any intention of the kind.

"Well, it depends on what you call a friend."

"It depends, as you say, very much indeed upon what you call a friend."

"Of course, we were kids together."

"'Kids together!'"

"Youngsters, don't you know. I'm the Duke of Staines."

"The—— You are the——"

For the life of her, Mrs. Paynter could have got no further. The stranger supplied the rest of the sentence.

"The Duke of Staines." He turned to Miss Paynter. "Are you going to Boulogne?"

"We *were* thinking of going to Paris."

"Oh!" His countenance fell. "I wish you were going to Boulogne."

"Why?"

"Well, I'm going to Boulogne."

Miss Paynter smiled outright at this; she had more presence of mind than her mother. "The inference conveyed is very flattering."

"Is it? I don't know."

He stared at her stolidly. Mrs. Paynter found her breath again.

"Did I understand you to say—— Really, I had no idea—you must excuse me. Did I understand you to say that you were—the Duke of Staines?"

"That's me."

Mrs. Paynter regarded him askance. She could not make up her mind if he was or was not making fun of her. She was not a wise woman. She had never before come into personal contact with any member of the British aristocracy. Could such an extremely vulgar individual as this one appeared to be really be a duke? She endeavoured, to the best of her small ability, to make sure of her ground.

"You don't happen to have a card about you?"

"I always carry a pack when I'm going anywhere, but—I don't care to play."

"You don't care to what?"

"To play—unless you feel uncommonly keen."

Miss Paynter laughed.

"You misunderstand my mother. She is not asking you for a pack of cards—she doesn't, as a rule, play cards in a train—but for a visiting-card."

"Oh! I see. Exchange pasteboards and that sort of thing. Daresay I've got one somewhere."

From a pocket-book which seemed to contain a very miscellaneous collection he produced, after long searching, a visiting-card. It was a good deal soiled and the corners were dog's-eared. He commented on its defects as he handed it to Mrs. Paynter.

"There's a few figures on the back, but perhaps you'll excuse 'em. Fact is, I never seem to want a card. I've never got one, anyway."

Mrs. Paynter could not have taken that disreputable square

of pasteboard with a more dainty grace had it been the most delicate and costly thing in the world. When she saw that great name imprinted on its front—it was *just* legible, no more—she swelled, positively and visibly increased in stature. With infinite condescension from her silver card-case she took a card, stiff as buckram, and even dazzlingly white.

"Allow me to have the honour to present your Grace with *my* card."

"His Grace" looked at the card.

"Paynter? Any relation to Billy Paynter?"

"What Paynter is that?"

"Putney slogger—bantam weight—righting man, you know."

Mrs. Paynter drew herself up still more.

"My father was rector of Bodgington, in Essex. He married a Miss Abbeyfield, my dear mother, and she was a grand-niece of the late Lord Gawler. My father was related, on his mother's side, to Admiral Piper—'Percussion' Piper he was called, as of course you know, because he was so explosive; and on his father's side, as I have often heard him say——"

The lady was well launched. "His Grace," however, remorselessly cut her short. "Oh!" he said. He turned to the young lady. "Miss—Miss Paynter?"

"I certainly am my mother's daughter."

Mrs. Paynter did not seem to be at all offended at having been recently interrupted. She came sailing gaily in.

"Edith—always Edith to her friends."

"Awfully jolly name, Edith; awfully jolly."

Edith drew herself a little closer into her corner.

"It is very good of you to say so."

If Miss Paynter's manner, all at once, was a little glacial, Mrs. Paynter's continued to be beautifully beaming.

"I cannot tell you how delighted I am at so unexpectedly encountering your Grace, and under such agreeable circumstances. It is such an honour, and such a pleasure. And you are going to Boulogne? Does your Grace purpose staying long at Boulogne?"

"Don't know. Awful bore, the whole thing. Fact is, I'm going to keep an eye on the old woman."

His Grace winked—distinctly; but the lady was puzzled.

"On whom?"

"My wife."

He winked again. The lady was taken aback; but she recovered.

"Of course. I ought not to have forgotten that your Grace is married. So absurd of me. How is the dear Duchess?"

"Eh? Who? Oh, Polly! She's going it, I hear."

"Polly is—the dear Duchess?"

"Was Polly Perkins, the Pearl of the Peris, you know; used to be all the go at the halls. Her great song, you know, was 'He tallowed his nose with a candle.' Ever hear it? She *could* sing it! She sings it sometimes now, but she's got so jolly uppish that sometimes she will and sometimes she won't."

Mrs. Paynter looked slightly startled, as well she might be. The Duke of Staines was a young gentleman who was well calculated to startle her. Elderly ladies, respectable elderly ladies, read about such things in the papers, and delight in them. But as they never actually encounter the principal actors in the "scandals," they have not a favourable opportunity of judging what sort of characters those principal actors must really be. To Mrs. Paynter the Duke of Staines was the Duke of Staines—with an accent on "the." That a "Polly," whose "great song" was "He tallowed his nose with a candle," could be the Duchess of Staines—she couldn't realise the thing at all. However, she was a lady whose mental processes, under certain conditions, and in a certain sense, travelled quickly.

"And is the dear Duchess"—she was still "the dear Duchess"— "at Boulogne?"

"Yes—hang it! And Dicky Datchet's with her, too."

"Dicky Datchet! Do you mean the Earl of Datchet?"

"That's him."

"Dear me! How sad! I never thought that the Earl of Datchet was that kind of man."

"What kind of man?"

"I always thought that the Earl of Datchet was a nobleman of the strictest propriety—as one of our first nobility ought to be, for the sake of the public example. It is expected of him."

"What, Dicky Datchet! Well, I'm blowed; that's good!" His Grace stared at the lady as though she were some strange animal. "I'll punch his head for him if he don't take care. I can fight if I can't do anything else. I'm not going to have him messing about with my wife, and I'll let him know it."

His Grace was most affable, and quite confidential. He told them the most amazing stories about himself and the Duchess and the Earl of Datchet, and other persons of similar rank and refinement, connected with the "halls" and otherwise. He was a most astonishing young man. He shocked Miss Paynter into speechlessness. Mrs. Paynter would not for worlds have owned that she was shocked.

When they were on the boat she made to her daughter this— under the circumstances—singular remark: "Edith, it is quite evident that his Grace is greatly struck with you."

"That wretched little cad! Mother, how could you let him go on talking? If I had been a man I should have knocked him down."

"There is no doubt that he is a character, as a Duke of Staines can well afford to be. Edith, when I heard that the Earl of Datchet was going to travel by that train I made up my mind that we would travel with him. I have more belief in the power of such beauty as yours than even you have. You have money, good birth; one never knows what may happen. Instead of an earl, chance has thrown a duke into your way. Edith, if you ever become the Duchess of Staines, my wildest dreams, at which you have so often laughed, will be more than realised."

"Aren't you forgetting that there happens to be a Duchess?"

"She is a person of the worst character, my dear. I remember the story now quite well—a most disreputable story. She entrapped him. This Earl of Datchet, who is plainly also a person of the loosest morals—I am deeply thankful that he wasn't in the train!—is evidently philandering about with her. Under such circumstances, of course——" The lady pursed her lips.

"Mother, for shame!"

"Edith, don't be a fool!"

"And you compare such a person as the Duke of Staines with Douglas?"

"Edith, haven't I forbidden you to mention that man's name?"

"Douglas is at least a gentleman."

"He is a penniless adventurer. Hush! here comes his Grace."

The Duke came. He addressed Miss Paynter.

"Have a liquor?"

"I beg your pardon?"

"Have a liquor—just a moistener? Gin and seltzer's not bad swill if you've got a knack of getting a little bit turned over, though I should think on a day like this anyone could look a basin in the face. What do *you* think?"

The young lady did not know what to think. This duke was such an extraordinary duke. The great middle class is aware that there are members of the British aristocracy who are deficient in brains, manners, morals, and even education. But, as a matter of fact, even in these democratic days individuals of that class seldom come into actual contact even with a baron, and when, by some wondrous accident, they stumble on a duke, they expect that duke to be a duke. If to all outward seeming he appears to be a cross between a billiard marker and a stable hand, they are apt to be surprised.

When they reached Boulogne, his Grace of Staines was so good as to offer the ladies the honour of his escort to their hotel. As, however, they were leaving the boat together someone stopped the peer.

"Hollo, Teddy! What are you doing here?"

The speaker was a gorgeously attired gentleman, who wore, as decorations, a single eyeglass and a pair of spotless "lavender kids." He was accompanied by a little lady, who was remarkable for an enormous quantity of golden hair, and a pair of large blue eyes which would have been filled with the light of innocence if their effect had not been marred by a superabundance of "complexion." His Grace of Staines surveyed this pair with a glance which was not a glance of affection.

"So it's you, is it? I ain't been long in finding you."

"You might have been a bit longer, Teddy, if you'd dropped us a line to let us know that you were coming."

"—— your eyes!" The pillar of the British Constitution used language which was not exactly ducal. "You'd better mind your p's and q's, my lad, or I'll give you what for, and no mistake." The lady interposed. She took the eyeglassed gentleman by the arm.

"Come away, Dick, and for gracious sake don't let's have a row out here." The Duke seemed struck by the lady's words.

"Come away with him, is it? That's good. You'll come with me, my girl, or by——"

Mrs. Paynter and her daughter drove away before the conversation became *too* personal. They did without his Grace's escort, that great nobleman appearing to be "spoiling" for a fight upon the quay, all the passengers and all the loungers looking on.

"Mamma," observed Miss Paynter, as the vehicle began to rattle over the Boulogne cobbles, "I am not going to stay here. I am going straight to Paris."

"Nonsense!" The elder lady was slightly flushed. "Don't be absurd!" It was difficult to argue the question then and there.

"At any rate, mamma, you will please to understand that nothing will induce me to have any intercourse with that wretched man."

The mother said nothing—prudently.

"I don't believe that he is the Duke of Staines."

"As to that, nothing will be easier than to make inquiries. He would not be able to carry on that fraud long. Besides, I remember now quite well hearing that the present duke was an eccentric character."

"An eccentric character! You call that animal an eccentric character! Why, my dear mother, the man's a blackguard—an utter blackguard, neither more nor less."

The words were strong, but the mother deemed it wiser to let them go unchecked, lest, peradventure, they should be followed by even stronger.

Some hours later Mrs. Paynter paid a visit to Miss Paynter in the young lady's own apartment at the hotel.

"Edith, there can be no doubt that he is the Duke of Staines."

"It would make no difference to me if he were ten thousand times the Duke of Staines."

"Don't talk nonsense, my love! The Duke of Staines *is* the Duke of Staines!"

"If *that* is the Duke of Staines, he certainly is—with a vengeance."

"His income is nearer three than two hundred thousand pounds; and when he came of age he received nearly two millions in ready money."

"Mamma!" The magnitude of the figures seemed momentarily to impress the maiden. "But you may be quite sure that the ready money is long since spent, and the income mortgaged up to the hilt."

"You are entirely mistaken. Major Bagshawe, who is staying at the hotel, knows all about him. There can be no doubt that the Duke's manners are—peculiar."

"Peculiar!"

"Well, aren't they peculiar? But it seems that his tastes are low rather than expensive. Major Bagshawe says that, financially, his position is even better now than when he came into his estate."

"Mamma, what are you driving at?"

"My dear, it is common talk that if he chose to apply for a divorce to-morrow, he would have ample grounds to go upon. If he married again—and he, of course, would marry"—Mrs. Paynter paused—"the Duchess of Staines would occupy, if she chose, one of the proudest positions in England—a position which even royalty would be glad to fill. She would have everything which the heart of a woman could desire. She would have the world at her feet."

II.

"You're awfully down upon a fellow. I ain't used to it, you know."

"No?"

It was after dinner. Miss Paynter and the Duke of Staines were alone together on the verandah of the Hotel des Bains. The Duke was smoking. He puffed at his cigar. He wore an air of injury.

"No, I ain't, and so I tell you straight."

"I am sorry."

"Yes, a blooming lot of that, I make no doubt."

"Might I ask where you acquired that conversational style of which you are so fond? It isn't only that you are habitually addicted to the use of slang; it is such peculiar slang. It always reminds me of—shall I say a 'busman?"

The Duke puffed in silence for a moment.

"Do you know that I've never stood from any girl in England the half, nor yet the quarter, of what I've stood from you?"

"And do you know that I have never had to endure from any man in England, not to speak of any gentleman, one thousandth part of what I have had to endure from you. Singular, isn't it? And you're a duke!"

"Well, I'm blow'd! You are a oner!"

"Am I, indeed? What is a oner?"

"Look here; what is it you want? I'll give you anything you like. I've got something in my pocket now."

From some mysterious inner pocket he took a flat leather case. He opened it. It contained a necklace of diamonds.

"What do you think of that? Shiners, ain't they? I gave five thousand pounds for that little lot."

She took the case into her hands. Her countenance betrayed no symptoms of surprise.

"Did you? I have seen necklaces which seemed to me to be quite as good as this, which cost much less. I am afraid they overcharged you."

"Not they! I may be a fool about some things—I don't need

you to tell me that!—but I'm all there when there's any money on. I'm not one to give one-and-twenty shillings for what's only worth a pound—not much, I ain't. Well, ain't you going to say even thank you?"

Closing the case, the lady returned it to the gentleman.

"Thank you—for the sight."

"What do you mean? It's for you; I got it on purpose for you—it's a little present."

"My dear young man—although you are a duke—pray don't be absurd. Do you see that light out at sea? I think it must be a steamer. I've been watching it for some seconds."

"What's the good of humbugging? Damn the steamer! You know very well I'm gone on you—fair gone! You know very well that the more you play off the more you drive me on. But I ain't going to stand it any longer, so I tell you straight."

She was quiet for some seconds. Then she said, very quietly, still looking across the sea—

"What do you mean?"

"You know very well what I mean. You know I love you."

"You—love me?" Then she turned to him. A smile played about her lips. "And the Duchess?"

"Oh, the Duchess! what has it to do with her?"

"Your ideas are original. Good-bye."

She turned right round. Passing through the open window, she entered the sitting-room. He followed her.

"Don't put me off like that—don't. Upon my word, I don't believe you know who I am—I'm the Duke of Staines."

When he followed her she turned again and smiled.

"It's easy enough for you to laugh, but for all that I don't be-lieve that you know what it means to be the Duke of Staines."

"Although you are, doesn't it strike you that it is just within the range of possibility that you are insulting me?"

"That's all nonsense! It isn't as though I was some low cad."

"I see. You think that makes a difference?"

"Of course it does. Edith——"

He was interrupted by a tapping at the door. A waiter en-tered. He had a letter on a salver. Miss Paynter took it. It was an English letter, addressed to her in a masculine hand, and marked "Immediate." As her glance fell upon the handwriting she flushed.

"Edith," resumed the Duke, when the waiter had disappeared. The lady cut him short.

"You continue to insult me!" The lady's manner all at once had changed. All traces of a smile had disappeared. Her eyes flashed fire. "Be so good as to let me pass, and this time do not follow me!"

"What is the good of all this humbug? What is your little game?"

"Let me pass!"

She moved forward. He put his arm about her waist. But only for an instant. Almost as soon as he had put it there he took it away again. The young lady swept past him through the window and out on to the verandah.

Possibly one of the reasons which had induced his Grace of Staines to so speedily remove his too intrusive arm was the fact that Mrs. Paynter had entered the room. The lady came in very quietly. Miss Paynter's back had been turned to the door, so that, although the mother's entrance had been sufficiently obvious to the gentleman, it had been unnoticed by her daughter. When the younger lady had gone the elder lady and the Duke remained face to face.

The ball of conversation was opened by the lady.

"Is it possible that your Grace was offering insult to my child?"

His Grace had his hands in his trousers pockets. He seemed huffed, and jerked his elbow towards the leather case which lay upon the table.

"I don't know what you call insult. I was offering her that."

"And pray what may that be?"

"It's a present I got for her. I didn't mean it for an insult. It cost me a cool five thousand, I do know that."

"Five thousand? Pounds? Your Grace!" The lady took the case into her hands. She opened it. "Diamonds! And you have given them to Edith! What prodigal generosity!"

"I don't know about given 'em, because she wouldn't take 'em."

"She wouldn't take them?"

"Jiggered if she would! She treated them as though they were bits of glass, and I was a barber's clerk."

The lady reflected.

"Possibly she misconstrued the motives which actuated you in offering her so costly a gift."

"I don't see how she could, because I told her I offered it because I loved her."

"Because you—loved her! Your Grace! I presume you mean in a platonic sense."

Outside the window was Miss Paynter. When she first left the room she had passed to the end of the verandah, the precious letter, marked "Immediate," held tightly in her hand. She opened it, and read it in the dim light out there. It was short, and pithy, and sweet:—

"My Darling,—I have been offered a berth worth eight hundred a year—such a stroke of luck! It isn't much, but there'll be more to follow; and it's enough for a start. I vote we make a match of it at once—you said you would. I'm coming over by Friday's boat; mind you meet it at the quay.—Douglas."

That was all the letter.

"Friday's boat? That's to-morrow. Douglas!"

There was a great tenderness in her voice as she emphasised the name. With the letter pressed against her bosom she strolled back along the balcony. The sound of voices reached her. She had approached the open window of her mother's private sitting-room. The Duke was speaking.

"I don't know about platonic sense; I ain't good at that kind of thing. I know I'm fair gone on her."

There was a pause. Then her mother spoke.

"I can only hope that I misunderstand your Grace."

"I don't know why you should. I tell you I love the girl."

"Your Grace! And the Duchess?"

"Oh, blow the Duchess! If it comes to that, I'll marry the girl."

"Does your Grace, then, propose to commit bigamy?"

"Bigamy? Not me! I'll get a divorce."

Another pause. Miss Paynter, without, could fancy her mother's smile of bland maternal love.

"Of course, if you were free, that would be another matter. And, if a little bird tells the truth, you should have no difficulty in obtaining your freedom."

"Then a little bird just lies! Polly's as deep as they make 'em; she's not to be caught with chaff; she knows what it means to be Duchess of Staines—trust her! She don't mean to get lost for nothing! Carry on to any amount she will; but just so far, and not a small bit farther. I've had detectives on her track for the last six months, watching her night and day, but they tell me it's no good up to now."

Still another pause. The young lady without could hear the Duke pacing up and down the room. "But I'll corner her at last; see if I don't. Then I'll marry Edith—if she'll have me. Upon my word, I ain't so sure that she will—I never saw such a oner. She treats me as though I was a dirty bagman. I'll give her anything— anything! I'll make her the greatest lady in England! I'll settle on her twenty thousand pounds a year! Twenty thousand! I'll settle on her anything she likes!"

While the distinguished nobleman within gave free rein to his chivalrous sentiments, the young lady without pressed the precious letter closer to her bosom. Her mother spoke—softly, almost purringly.

"You see, your Grace places me in rather a difficult position. Having declared your affection for my daughter, it is necessary that I should protect her by every means in my power. Would your Grace object to giving me some sort of memorandum which would embody, in some form, the sentiments which you have just now uttered, and which do you so much honour?"

"I mean business, I tell you straight. Come along to my room, and I'll give you a written promise of marriage right off the reel, hanged if I won't!"

Mrs. Paynter "went along" with him. Miss Paynter heard the door shut after them. As she heard it she knew that she stood within measurable distance of being one of the greatest women in England—a woman who, if she chose, might rule society. She knew, too, that, physically and intellectually, she was just the woman to play the part of social queen—that she would be a ruler who would have no rivals. She knew that she had but to stretch out her hand for all the gifts of all the gods to fall into her open palm; yet she only pressed that letter closer to her breast.

Several sitting-rooms opened out on to that verandah. The French windows of the room adjoining were thrown right back. As she stood there, thinking of all that grand future to which she possessed the "open sesame," she was conscious that into that adjoining room had come two persons, a man and a woman.

The man spoke. "Is everything ready?"

The woman answered, "Everything."

"The train leaves at ten minutes to two. We can catch the five minutes to nine in Paris, and we shall be in Nice by a few minutes past six on Saturday afternoon."

"Dicky, you will be true to me?"

"Isn't it rather late in the day to ask me such a question? Don't you know I will?"

"But swear you will!"

"I swear it for the hundredth time!"

"You will marry me afterwards?"

"I will, upon my honour."

The woman's voice was low and earnest, even painfully in earnest. The man's tone was light and flippant. The woman drew a long deep breath. Miss Paynter heard her, as she stood without, pressing the letter closer and closer to her breast.

"When I think of how I nearly jumped out of my skin for joy when I became the Duchess of Staines, it seems impossible that after all it should have come to this."

"Exchange is no robbery—you're going to be a countess for a change. Don't you think it sounds well enough—Countess of Datchet?"

"It's all very well for you to laugh, but you don't know what it means to me. You think what he thought. Because I was a music-hall singer—a seriocomic—the Pearl of the Peris—he thought that I was anybody's money. But I wasn't, and so he found—and so you'll find! Dicky, if you don't marry me directly you can, I'll murder you—I swear I will!"

"There's not time enough for tragedy, Polly. Put it off until we're in the train."

"Do you think those—those brutes will follow us?"

"If you mean the detectives, I take it for granted that one, if not two of them, will be our fellow-travellers to the sunny South. They will enjoy the trip at Teddy's expense."

There was silence. The woman was pacing to and fro. When she spoke again it was in tones of the intensest bitterness.

"If I were to tell you what I've stood from that man, you wouldn't wonder at what I'm doing now. He's treated me worse than a dog from the moment he married me, and I was such a fool that I thought that if I was once the Duchess of Staines everything would be all right. He made no settlement on me. As for money, I haven't had it. He told me that if I sent any of my bills to him he'd thrash me within an inch of my life. And he'd do it too, especially if he had been drinking. He's never introduced me to a respect-able woman. He had detectives to watch me——"

"I know, Polly. I've heard some of it before, and I'll hear the rest when we're in the train."

"Look here, Dick Datchet, I've been an honest woman up till now, and although I'm going to run away with you, I mean to be an honest woman still. You put it down in black and white, that you promise to marry me the very first moment you can."

"What would be the good of that? Such a promise wouldn't be valid. I can't promise to marry a woman who's married al-ready. Besides, don't you love me enough to trust me? Come here, Polly."

Although she could not actually see that it was so, Miss Paynter knew that the Earl of Datchet had taken the Duchess of Staines into his arms.

"Don't you love me?"

"Yes." There was the sound of a kiss. "You know that I do."

"Then you may trust me to see you through it all." The woman drew another long deep breath, but she said nothing.

"Hadn't you better go and get ready?"

"No," said Miss Paynter, as she passed through the window. "I wouldn't if I were you."

The Earl of Datchet was leaning against the table. The Duchess's waist was encircled by his arm. They stared at the intruder in not unjustifiable surprise. Miss Paynter addressed herself to the Duchess.

"I wouldn't go and get ready if I were you."

"What do you mean?" the Duchess replied.

"Why, my dear child, because in real knowledge of this wicked world I believe you're nothing but a child; you're only biting off your nose to spite your face. You're jumping out of the frying-pan into the fire. This gentleman has not the slightest *real* intention of marriage—have you?"

This frankly-put inquiry seemed somewhat to startle the Earl.

"Really, I—I have not the pleasure."

"Of knowing me? But I know you very well, both by sight and reputation. I assure you, my dear Duchess, that you would be a very foolish woman to trust yourself in the least degree to him."

The Earl of Datchet roused himself to the best of his ability.

"May I ask, Miss Paynter—I believe you are Miss Paynter—what business this is of yours?"

"It is the business of every honest woman—to use the Duchess's very proper phrase—to save other honest women from being ruined and tricked by gentlemen; don't you think it is?" There were voices without. "Here is the Duke—just when he is wanted." That distinguished nobleman appeared outside the window. Mrs. Paynter was with him. "Your Grace, prepare to be shocked—to receive a crushing blow. You have been deceived—betrayed—by a friend. Your own friend proposed to elope with your wife by the train which leaves at ten minutes to two for Paris, only I appeared upon the scene in the very nick of time."

The Duke lumbered into the room.

"What the devil——" he began, then he stopped.

He glared at the Earl. The Earl beamed at him.

"Edith," said Mrs. Paynter, going to her daughter, who had her arm about the Duchess, "what is the meaning of your peculiar behaviour?"

"Come into the other room! Come, Duchess, into the other room."

When they were in the other room, Mrs. Paynter repeated her inquiry.

"Now, Edith, perhaps you will explain."

"I don't know that there is anything to explain, unless—Duchess, what do you think? I'm going to be married."

The mother gasped.

"You are going to be married, Edith! When?"

"Perhaps next week."

"To—to whom?"

"To Douglas!"

Printed in the USA
CPSIA information can be obtained
at www.ICGtesting.com
LVHW011057260923
759254LV00011B/597